THE GUARDED HEART

BLAIR LEBLANC

Copyright © 2019 by Blair LeBlanc

All rights reserved.

No part of this book may be reproduced in any form or by any electronic or mechanical means, including information storage and retrieval systems, without written permission from the author, except for the use of brief quotations in a book review.

Cover design by Okay Creations

Photography by Joseph Sinclair

ISBN: 9781080818983

Chapter One

Cassian

SHE'S MY NEXT JOB?

My eyes landed on a purple-haired hottie that made my latest conquest seem drab. Her heart-shaped face and round cheeks revealed her youth. The shy, bubble-gum-pink smile hinted at vulnerability. Her heavy gaze brimmed with innocence.

She looked like a handful.

"Pop star?" I spoke into the phone.

God, I hated them. High-maintenance assholes with egos the size of Texas. They didn't tip, gave me less respect than their rat-sized dogs, and expected me to overlook their rampant drug abuse. I'd walked out on more than one coked-out loser in Chateau Marmont. It didn't matter how well celebrities paid. If someone under my care overdosed, who was at fault? The dickhead celebrity or me?

Most would blame me.

My career would end the day my name popped up in a Google search next to an obituary. I'd spent too long building a rapport with security firms and bodyguard agencies to have it all ruined by some blowhard.

Fuck celebrities.

"Guess again," Richard wheezed through the speaker.

"B-lister?"

"She's a politician's daughter," Richard said. "Twelve-hour shifts. You'll work with Quentin."

"Ugh."

"What's wrong with Q?" His violent cough bit off his last words. "Excuse me. Stupid post-nasal drip."

Richard needed to stop smoking. "Quentin is too young."

"He's your age when *you* started."

I frowned at the comparison. "With half the maturity."

An impressive bench press number didn't equal a good bodyguard. Quentin was a combat veteran, and like many who'd been through intense warfare, he was high-strung.

People who excelled in stressful environments didn't always make good bodyguards. He'd proven that by getting us fired from the last job. He roughed up a client's ex-boyfriend in front of paparazzi, resulting in a sea of nasty tabloid articles that made the starlet go ballistic. I was the other bodyguard attached to the job. She canned us both.

"At least he's personable," Richard said, delicately. "No offense, but you're not the warm and fuzzy type."

"I know that. Hell, it's a point of pride."

"Right," he snorted. "How's that going for you?"

"Not bad." I wrenched open my fridge, grabbed a carton of milk, and sniffed the opening. It reeked. I tossed it aside. "Tell me more about the job."

"You'll live in a mother-in-law unit beside the house. Separate rooms, and you won't see Q when you're off the clock." Richard paused, coughing. "The contract is for a few months. Low risk. Easy money."

"She looks feisty."

"Who cares? It's work."

True that. I trusted Richard. He hooked me up with my first job—protecting an actress who wore a twelve-million-dollar dress to the Cannes festival. He was an instructor at the executive protection specialist school in Virginia. He left teaching to start a security agency. Called the moment I graduated to give me the gig.

I switched the cell to my other ear as I paced the living room. "What else do you have?"

"Hold on." The sounds of shuffling paper filtered through the speaker. "A budding pop artist needs a bodyguard to accompany her on a world tour."

"Next."

"A princess of the Saudi royal family and her entourage are coming to San Francisco for a shopping trip."

"No thanks."

"Their offer is really competitive, Cassian. Sure you want to pass?"

Saudis paid well, but they were *extremely* high-maintenance. I'd been on more than one job where I had to explain to an irate hotel manager why the prince's room was in shambles. He was cooking with open flames in the suite. Nearly burned down the goddamn building.

A groan echoed from my bedroom. My head whipped in that direction before I whispered into the speaker. "Can I call you back? I have company."

"Oh, a girlfriend?"

He knew me better than that. "A lay."

"Someday, you'll have to settle down." Richard sighed. "Even if you regret it forever."

"Not a chance. Bye."

I ended the call and slid the phone over the kitchen counter. Richard was a nice guy. Never missed a birthday. Always found reasons to invite me over. He didn't like that I lived alone and spent my free time at the shooting range or the gym.

My life was as empty as the walls of this apartment.

I didn't care.

I had zero inclination toward relationships.

Friendly banter with Richard was fine, but personal attachments were not. They were extra bricks weighing my backpack. I spent a lot of time on my own. Some days I didn't speak a word to a single human being, except for the teeth-pulling exchanges with women I wanted to fuck. They were depressingly easy to seduce in spite of my cardboard charisma, because Walnut Creek was filled with desperate women.

My flings were nothing more than receptacles. I needed to get off—so did they. Scratching an itch was all it ever was, but every so often a girl became clingy and then I'd have the uncomfortable task of cutting them loose. I was better off alone.

Speaking of conquests, the one in my bed needed to leave.

I returned to my bedroom. A king-sized mattress sat over a steel frame next to a nightstand. A blonde mane peeked from my comforter. I needed her gone, so I wrenched the blinds until sunlight bleached the room. A ray hit her closed eyes.

She moaned.

I grasped the crumpled jeans on the floor and threw them on the mattress.

"I have to go soon," I growled at the stirring lump. "You have ten minutes."

In the other room, my cell beeped with a reminder to be at Swanson's Jewelry at eight. I snatched a bulletproof vest and yanked it over me. My hands fumbled as I buttoned my shirt—damn these hands. Hundreds of hours dry firing and years of physical therapy, but I'd never be the same. I tugged at the crisp whiteness over my scarred monstrosities, hoping my next client wouldn't ask questions.

"Cassian, come back," she moaned. "What time is it?"

"I have to work."

A pout formed on her lips, and I racked my brains for her name. Honest to God, I couldn't remember.

The blonde stood, yawning. She plucked her jeans and shoved her legs through. "Do you have coffee?" she asked.

"Nope." I didn't do stimulants or any drug for that matter. "Sorry."

My nameless lay shot me an irritated glance, but I couldn't summon the effort to care. I pulled on slacks and slung a holster over my shoulders. I secured my Glock in the holster. Two small knives went into my buckle. I stuffed a bag I kept in my car's glove box with another pistol, along with a flashlight, a spare cell, and more knives.

She must've noticed the weapons. Her eyes widened. "Are you a *cop*?"

I needed to be more selective with my hookups. "Used to be."

"Why are you wearing a gun?"

"We did the twenty questions thing last night. I have a

job to get to, and I'm sure you have a pissed off husband to deal with."

"I'm not married, you *prick*." She flashed her ringless finger before flipping me the bird.

"Must've confused you with someone else."

Her flushing face said I was going from bad to worse.

I cleared my throat. "The way out is there."

"Jackass."

She dressed with lightning speed and stormed from the room, heels dangling from her fingers. The door slammed, leaving blissful silence in her wake.

I put on a black jacket and laced my boots. A suit and tie was my standard uniform. First impressions were vital. An untucked shirt, cheap shoes, or even a lousy haircut could mean losing a job.

My phone trilled.

I answered. "Cassian."

"Hey, it's Richard again. I need an answer on the senator job. The guy's pushy."

"What's the girl's name? I might have time for a background check." Vetting clients before taking jobs was essential. Too many drug dealers wanted my services for their illicit actions. She didn't look like a meth distributor, but still.

"Rain, and you don't have time for a check."

"Sounds like a hippie, not a senator's daughter." I adjusted my tie in front of a mirror. "Which senator?"

"She's Montgomery's kid. Heard of him?"

Dormant flames licked my heart, chasing my indifference into a cold, dark corner. Until five years ago, just the name *Senator Montgomery* was enough to make me fly into a rage.

Now I burned. "Montgomery doesn't have a daughter."

"He does now. She's a lovechild."

"His bastard."

"Lovechild. *I'm* a lovechild. Don't be a dick."

"He has a daughter?"

"Jesus, the brains on this one. Yes, *Cass*, yes. He has a daughter. She sued him for paternity rights two years ago. The jerk—I mean—client refused to acknowledge she was his. So she sued him, did the DNA test, and bingo."

"Intriguing."

How close was the senator to his daughter?

I slid my finger across my phone's screen, studying her rosebud lips with a different interest than moments ago.

I usually went for jaded women, not doe-eyed jailbait —if Walnut Creek had anything in spades, it was bored housewives married to tech moguls and doctors who spent way too much time at work. But lately my hookups failed to give me a good time. Maybe I'd banged too many women in the same scenarios.

Young and sweet sounded pretty damned good, and Rain oozed joy. Her glow warmed me through the photograph as though the sun hit my face. How did anyone put out that kind of happiness? I searched for the answer in the picture, but that smile looked mischievous.

"I can't tell if you're serious, but yeah. Anyway, he got her to drop the suit by committing to pay for her college tuition if she lives with him for three years."

"Touching." I headed for the door. "Let me guess. She's blowing it on coke and Dom Pérignon."

"Will you stop being a judgmental ass?"

"Fine," I snapped. "I'll do the job."

Anxiety bled into his voice. "I talked you up to these people. Don't make me regret this."

"Don't worry. I'll behave." I ended the call.

Clients were off-limits, but this was *Montgomery's* daughter. I'd protect *and* tame her. He'd see me claim those bitable lips if he didn't throw me out of his house.

Banging his daughter wouldn't make us even, but it'd feel good.

My mouth pulled into its first real smile in days.

Hell, this was an opportunity.

A *golden* one.

∼

Fog choked the streets as I strolled into a ritzy neighborhood. Rain lived with her shitty father in Presidio Heights. San Francisco's obscenely rich lived here. Five-million-dollar houses crammed side-by-side. Victorian homes dominated the blocks before they gave way to a stretch of McMansions.

Montgomery's house didn't match anything on the block, and I wouldn't be surprised if neighbors filed cease and desist orders about this monstrosity of modern architecture. It towered above its neighbors like a gigantic LEGO block, a huge rectangle with boxed windows. A Tesla was parked in the driveway—Montgomery had terrible taste—and next to it sat a silver Prius—way more reasonable. Must've been the wife's.

I approached the wrought iron gate and buzzed the house. The lock clicked after I hissed my name into the speaker. Deep green lawn spread to hedges of rose bushes and across the courtyard to butt against the house's walls. I avoided the tended grass and kept to the rock path, climbing steps to the porch where the security guard demanded my ID.

I fished it out and flashed it at him. "Here you go."

"This way, please."

My shoes glided over white reclaimed wood as the doors yawned open. The inside was decorated with shades of cream, eggshell-white, and frost-blue, accented with abstract art that popped with vivid reds and blues. I liked everything, hating myself for it.

The guard led me into a room with a shag rug under a marble coffee table surrounded by two chairs and a sofa.

Photos of the wife and kids hung everywhere—like props on display. As I strolled in and studied their happy faces, rage pulsed in my chest. Purple Hair was missing from every family photo. *Black sheep.*

Was I dealing with crippling drug addiction or a spoiled brat? My money was on the latter.

"Can I get you anything?" an aide asked. "Coffee? Tea?"

I tore my gaze from the family portraits and faced him. "No, thanks."

Slowly, the knob turned, and a paunchy seventy-something man with a shock of white hair emerged. Barefoot, he crossed the room in cargo shorts and a light polo.

Flames leaped inside me, but I suffocated them. I was here for his daughter, not him.

"Ah, Mr. Grant," he said in a ripened voice. "So glad you could make it on short notice."

He offered me a veiny hand.

I shook it, forcing a grin. "Nice to meet you, Senator."

"Please sit."

He gestured toward the steel blue wingback chairs facing each other. My nerves buzzed with adrenaline as I sank into the cushions.

Montgomery sat, expelling a painful sigh. "Bad back. All the chiropractors in the world can't fix me."

I hoped it hurt like hell. "Sorry to hear that."

He adjusted himself, wincing. "Your colleague highly

recommended you. One of the guards said they'd worked with you on a job—Brent?"

"Brian," I corrected. "Yes, that's right. A journalist hired us for about a week in Afghanistan. I'll have to thank him for the recommendation."

"Look, I'll level with you. I've already been through two of you. My daughter is *complicated*." He grimaced as though that sounded worse than he meant. "She's not used to all the scrutiny. I'm at my wits' end and hope you can bring her to heel."

"That won't be an issue."

"Rain's very headstrong," he warned. "Petulant. Reckless. I need a man with a firm hand. Someone who won't be ruled by a young woman's whims."

"All due respect, Senator, but I can handle a nineteen-year-old girl."

"You say that now." He chuckled, his gaze softening as though he felt sorry for me. "She gives her bodyguards the slip and takes off. Attends protests, leaves without telling anyone, and sneaks to her friends' houses. I'm trying to avoid an underage drinking scandal."

"She needs protection from herself as well as others."

"*Yes*. That's precisely what I mean. I've installed a tracking app on her phone that you'll have access to. You'll have to monitor her social media accounts." Montgomery gave the door a worried glance. "You might have to be —*rough*."

"Rough?"

"You might have to drag her around. I don't want her wandering into any seedy parts of the city."

Get physical with your daughter? "Not a problem, Senator. I've been in similar situations before. You can count on me."

I smiled, hoping he couldn't read any misgivings in my eyes.

Montgomery leaned forward and squeezed my shoulder. "That's what I like to hear. Want to meet her?"

"Please."

Senator Montgomery lurched to his feet and headed for the door. He squared his shoulders before opening it, speaking in a tight voice. "Come in."

I stood, hiding my excitement from this moron. He trusted me with his daughter, giving me license to manhandle her when he should've kicked me out.

This would be fun.

A willowy girl sauntered through the door, wearing a floral dress that cinched at her waist and fell in a semi-transparent skirt, grazing the floor. A brown headband pushed her light purple tresses back, framing her beautiful face. She'd aged since the photograph, or maybe the hot pink lips and winged eyeliner added a few years.

A dreamy smile spread across her face. She looked relaxed, confident, and most of all, *happy*.

How was anyone that happy?

The hair was striking, but what made my throat close was her bright-eyed optimism that filled the room. She radiated warmth. I'd never met anyone who did that with a smile. As I held her gaze, heat baked my skin. I didn't know why, but I could not hurt her. My plan lay at my feet, shattered.

She bounced to greet me, flip-flops smacking the floor.

"Cassian, this is my daughter." Montgomery palmed her shoulder. "Rain, your new bodyguard."

She offered her hand first, beaming. "Nice to meet you, Cassian."

Her voice wasn't the girlish, breathy sigh of a nineteen-year-old, but the rich growl of a woman.

"Likewise."

I shook her hand. She glanced at my scars, probably alerted by the unusual texture gliding against her soft skin, but she quickly recovered. Gold ringed her moss-green eyes, which bored into mine. She wasn't intimidated. If anything, her smile grew.

It stripped me bare. I paused to regroup, corralling my thoughts into order.

Montgomery checked his watch. "Right. I've got to go. I'll let you get acquainted."

"Bye," she said.

Rain slid her hand from mine, watching her father, who barely gave her a backward glance as he left. She still glowed when the door closed behind him, leaving us alone.

"Cassian," she said, whispering my name in her husky voice. "Is that short for something?"

"No. What do I call you?"

"Rain."

"Such a melancholy name for a girl with purple hair."

"Mom's a hippie." Rain lifted a creamy shoulder in a shrug. "She was into the nature baby names, unlike my father."

"I see."

Rain swept the long dress to the side as she took the wingback chair her dad had vacated, crossing her legs. "Please sit down."

I preferred standing. Towering over her gave some measure of control, because I'd been dead wrong about my protectee. She didn't carry herself like a sulky brat. I liked her, and that bothered me.

She patted the chair beside her.

I sat, knees angled toward the girl. "What do you want to know?"

"Everything."

Happiness radiated from her, and I leaned closer to bask in it. "I'm thirty. I've been a bodyguard for seven years. Before that, I was a cop in Walnut Creek. I grew up in San Leandro, and then studied at San Jose State."

Rain's chin rested on her palm. "That's not much to go on, Cassian."

"What else do you want to know?"

"Why are you working for my father?"

Because her father was a bastard, but she was delectable. Gaps in the dress showed off inches of smooth thighs I imagined wrapping my waist.

Why the hell did I want her?

My heart hammered as I met her shockingly warm pools. A reckless ball of lust fought my instinct to shelter her. "The job seems well within my capabilities. Low risk. Good pay."

Rain's smile was encouraging. "What do you like to do on days off?"

Fuck around. Shooting range. Work out. "I practice my skills and exercise."

"That's what you do to stay sharp. What do you *like* to do?"

Discomfort rattled my insides. Personal questions bugged me because my answers revealed so much damage. "Work out and practice."

"What's your passion?"

It used to be surfing. "You're digging pretty deep. I'm not sure I have one."

She changed tack. "Do you like jazz?"

"Not really."

"Rock?" she offered.

"Some."

"Heavy metal, progressive, or alternative?"

I sighed through my nose. "*Classic* rock."

Humor glinted through her gaze. "So you wouldn't be wild about open mic nights at the jazz club."

I'd be excited about my face between your legs. Jesus Christ, *why*? "It's not my business to care where the protectee goes unless it's a security risk."

"Do you carry a gun?"

"Several." I showed her the one on my waist. "There's another in my shoulder harness."

Along with an arsenal in my car, but I didn't have to tell her that.

"And you wear a vest, too?"

"Always." I yanked my collar, showing her the body armor. "I never leave for a job without it."

"Isn't it overkill, though? No one wants me *dead*."

"That you know of. I've been around longer. People are capable of horrible things."

"I believe you." She played with a purple strand, dragging it across her chest. "But I think most people are decent."

Oh, to be that naive. "I beg to differ."

"If they got to know me, they wouldn't want to hurt me."

"If you're holding out on universal popularity, you're going to be very disappointed."

"You don't like me?"

That landed like a gut punch. "That's not what I meant. Psychos can't be reasoned with. They don't need a reason to hate you." She was silly if she thought she was safe walking the streets. "Don't believe me? Take a stroll through the Tenderloin."

"Cassian, I don't take stupid risks. I'm just questioning the need for twenty-four-hour surveillance on *me*. You seem like a fantastic bodyguard, but I hate being followed everywhere I go. I'm nineteen. Do you remember what it's like to be my age?"

That was a decade ago. My freshman year at San Jose State was a whirlwind of girls, bad sex, and classes I didn't remember. "You're not missing much."

"Well, that's not for you to decide."

"Yeah, it is. Your schedule is subject to my discretion. If I don't think an event is safe, you aren't going. Period."

Rain didn't take that well. She blanched as her diplomatic approach crashed around her ears. "I don't know what my father told you, but I'm in charge of my security."

"No, sweetheart. *I* am." I zipped my spine, towering over her even as I sat. Time to let her know who was boss because protecting a woman this young meant establishing boundaries *now*. She couldn't defy me without swift punishment. "Your dad is my client, not you. He's the one I need to keep happy, not you."

She flinched at my rough delivery. "Oh, I don't know. I dismissed the last two bodyguards. What makes you think I can't do the same to you?"

Heat spiraled in my chest as I inched into her space,

my body mammoth-like over hers. "I'm not going anywhere."

"All I need is to ask my dad—"

"Your dad left me in charge," I boomed, cutting her off. "So don't think you'll get anywhere with the daddy card."

"I don't appreciate being talked to like that."

Rich people got bent out of shape for every little thing. I'd never get five out of five stars on a customer service survey, but come-the-fuck on. "Well, you're not getting an apology, so I suggest you get over it."

"You are unbelievable," she gasped. "Who talks like that to their client?"

"Once again, you're not my client. You're my protectee. I've tamed girls like you before, and I'll do it again."

Pink patches burned on Rain's cheeks. "You have the biggest chip on your shoulder I've ever seen."

"And I've never met a more delusional woman. Refusing protection in your position is insanity. You're gambling with your life because you want anonymity. Guess what? That's gone forever." Anger rippled from my voice, wiping the smile from her face. "There are people out there—sick people who cannot be reasoned with—who'd run a blade between your ribs. You'd never see it coming. I would, but if you turn down security you'll be *dead*."

Rain shrank into her seat, flinching when she met my

gaze. Her eyes glazed over with tears. "Why are you like this?" she demanded, flushing a deep magenta. "You're so...harsh."

I'd frightened her. *Good.* "You have so much life ahead of you. Don't throw it away."

She stood, and I followed suit. She glanced at the door. I blocked the way out. Her chest pulsed as I impeded her exit.

Poor girl would have to get used to never getting her way.

"Listen up, Rain." I tapped her chin, and her watery gaze slid to mine. "I'm not going *anywhere*. I'm not kind or gentle. I'll throw you over my shoulder if need be."

"And I'll cause a scene that'll give the press something to talk about for weeks. How long do you think you'll last after that?"

"Make my job hard, and I will send security recommendations to your father that you'll *hate*. Like pulling you out of college and canceling trips to D.C."

"You can't stop me from visiting my dad!"

She stepped forward, but I gently pushed her back. "I can, and I will if you give me trouble."

"What is wrong with you?" Rain said in a tone that could frost glaciers. "Never mind. You don't have to tell me. I knew the answer the moment I walked into the room. It's all over your face. You are utterly *joyless*."

"I don't need joy." She recoiled from my words as

though I'd struck her. "And I don't need you to be happy with me."

The life at stake was all that mattered. I'd failed once.

Never again.

Never fucking again.

Chapter Two

Rain

I was a stain.

An ugly blemish on my father's legacy that refused to be scrubbed away. I was the scarlet letter etched on his forehead. I couldn't be erased, much like the spill on the countertop.

A brown ring marked the kitchen island where I spilled the tea. Cursing, I grabbed a dishtowel and scrubbed, but the stain glared from the beautiful, creamy white marble. Poetic as hell, considering what I'd done to my father's career. His Wikipedia page listed my name under Personal Life, and when my father couldn't clean the stubborn spot from his record, he caved, finally acknowledging me as his daughter. His supporters hated that he'd cheated on his wife with my mother, but they lauded him for doing the right thing and taking me under his wing.

Seventeen years too late, but whatever.

A kitchen timer ticked the seconds counting down to zero as I paced the flawless mansion, which still didn't feel like home, even after two years. San Francisco's damp chill took getting used to, but the real problem was me. I didn't belong here. Maybe I didn't belong *anywhere.*

Dad's frequent trips to D.C. with his wife, who wanted nothing to do with me, meant a lot of solitude. My social life wilted the longer I stayed in this house. I could've visited Mom, but I left her house for a reason. Weeks of loneliness killed my soul, and I took out my frustration on the bodyguard.

I'd called him *joyless.*

What was wrong with me?

I needed to make it right, which was why I rolled out of bed to bake scones. Nothing said *I'm sorry* better than fresh pastries. I hated hurting people and loathed losing control even more. A gut feeling told me my bodyguard was already wounded. Something caused those scars.

Cassian.

I loved his name. Saying it out loud felt like whispering a spell or reciting a prayer. He was a mess of contradictions. Protective but detached. Damaged yet powerful. Beautiful and rough. *So* damned rough.

More muscle flexed in his finger than in my entire body. He was all harsh edges and straight lines. Hollowed cheeks led to a prominent jaw. Full lips emphasized his cupid's bow, which was his only soft feature. Exceptionally handsome, but *not* easy on the eyes. Nothing about Cassian was easy. Looking at him was like staring into a bold flame. You wanted to blink and turn away from the heat.

What made him so hard?

What gave him those horrific scars?

Why was he such a brute?

The kitchen timer shrieked as my scones finished baking, and I yanked them from the oven. I scraped the golden wedges from the parchment paper and slid them onto a plate, trying to picture Cassian's reaction.

Hopefully, he'd forgive me. We got off on the wrong foot, but that didn't mean we couldn't be friendly. My mom always said you attracted more flies with honey than vinegar.

So I grabbed the plate and headed to the garden-side doors.

Cassian lived in the mother-in-law flat across the backyard. He stood on the hardwood porch, his large frame wrapped in a suit. At a distance, he intimidated me. His ferocity blazed across the lawn. As I grasped the doorknob, my nerves failed. Approaching him on his turf scared the hell out of me.

Cassian's laser-like attention swung toward me. I couldn't back out now.

You have to do this.

I opened the door and strolled under a gray sky. San Francisco's damp mornings took getting used to. Two years under a cloudy sky had stolen my sun-kissed glow. The chill stung my bare legs as I slipped into flip-flops and kicked through grass. My heart begged me to turn around, but I wasn't a coward. I owned up to my mistakes.

He held up a hand in greeting and shook the sleeve over his wrist. The discolored scars twisting his flesh unnerved me, but the real horror was in his stormy-blue gaze. His eyes were dark waves under a troubled sky. A restless disquiet seemed to grip his soul.

"Morning. Did you—ah—sleep okay?"

"You didn't." An arrogant smirk broke his melancholy. "Did our conversation last night upset you?"

His voice throbbed inside me like bass, and the taunt did nothing to alleviate my nerves.

"I'm here to make it right."

His amusement grew as he took me in, pastries and all.

Jesus. What's his deal? "May I come in?"

His smile spread. "After you."

I swept inside. Dad spared no expense in making this mother-in-law livable. Dove-gray walls and cream flooring matched the color palette of the house. Cassian led me into a bright kitchen with teal cabinets. Quentin, the other bodyguard, sat at the square table. I met him yesterday, but our conversation was a lot less memorable. The younger man wore his sandy hair in a gentle wave that rolled over his head. He was good-looking in the traditional sense—rakish smile, a straight nose, hunter eyes—but his gaze didn't fill me with liquid heat.

Quentin perked up, eyes zeroing in on the food. "Hey. What's that?"

"Scones." I slid them over the table. "Just came out of the oven. Help yourselves."

Shock registered over Quentin's face, but Cassian merely raised an eyebrow.

"Thanks." Quentin flashed a boyish grin. He grabbed one and ripped off a chunk, spraying the table with flakes.

Cassian glanced at him. "All yours. I don't do carbs."

Of course he didn't eat scones. He was built like a linebacker. Probably survived on a diet of meat and little else. That made me feel worse for going through the trouble.

"Don't be an ass." Quentin's irritation with Cassian melted when he faced me. "They're fantastic. Thank you."

"You're welcome." I ignored Cassian, who watched me with fiendish delight. "Could I get a moment alone with Cassian? It won't take long."

"No problem." Quentin stood, squeezing my shoulder. "Later."

He grabbed a plate from the cupboard and took another scone. Cassian's lips thinned as Quentin whistled a merry tune before disappearing into his room, but when his gaze returned to me, the smirk reappeared. He said nothing as I stood, fists balled at my sides.

Just say it.

My nerves frayed the longer I was in his presence.

Cassian crossed his arms. "Are you going to say something or just stare at me?"

My heart lodged in my throat. "I'm nervous. You're kind of intense."

"Why are you here?"

"To apologize," I blurted. "Things got out of hand yesterday."

He invaded my personal space with one massive stride. "And?"

"And I'm sorry." Adrenaline surged in my veins as I met his gaze. He was gorgeous, though older than me by a decade, and it caught me off guard. "You were right. I appreciate that you—you're trying to protect me. Even if you're a little over the top."

"Nothing I said was over the top."

"I was mostly talking about your delivery. Anyway, I'm sorry."

Cassian's eyebrows lifted. "Apology accepted."

Relief quashed my embarrassment but did nothing to dampen my nerves from his closeness. "Um, I was going to take the metro to see my mother."

"If you're visiting her, it'll be in a car. Your days of riding public transportation are over."

That sank inside me like a boulder. "I don't get a say?"

"I'm in charge," he said in that unaffected tone I hated. "If I say *jump*, you say *how high*. If I tell you to get on the floor, hide, or run, you will *obey*. Without question."

"I have to go alone."

"Not happening. You don't go anywhere without Quentin or me."

He didn't understand, but I argued anyway. "I'm more than capable of taking a subway."

"Did I imagine the last five minutes, or did you completely lose your mind? You cannot disregard my security suggestions whenever it's convenient for you." His eyes flashed. "What part of you can't go anywhere alone don't you understand?"

I understood that perfectly, but showing up to my mother's house with a bodyguard might ruin everything. I balled my fists, more and more irritated by the second.

"Come with me if you have to, but don't tell my father. Anything you might see or overhear is none of his business."

"I'm a bodyguard, not a narc. I don't care about your drama." Cassian fired a text into his phone. "Just be honest with me."

Honesty with my bodyguards? Impossible. No one

knew about my mom's issues, and I wanted to keep it that way.

"Did I tell you about my raging coke addiction?"

Cassian snorted. "You're not on drugs."

"You don't *know* that."

"Yeah, I do. I've got you pegged."

"Well, don't tell me. I've had my fill of brutal honesty."

Cassian fixed me with a stare that licked heat everywhere. "Maybe I wasn't planning on being harsh."

"It's hard to imagine you any other way."

A text chimed his phone. He read it and thumbed a reply. "Did you still want to see your mother?"

Startled by the change in topic, I gaped at him. "Yes."

"I'll text the driver."

～

I STEWED as we drove to the East Bay. The ride was awkward. Cassian sat in the front seat while I rode in the back. After a few failed starts at a conversation, I gave up. Cassian didn't want to chat. He wasn't interested in what I had to say. All he cared about was getting from point A to point B until his shift ended.

When we rolled onto Monument Boulevard, I tossed thoughts of him aside and squirmed at the urban decay outside my window. Mom lived in a dump. Shame nagged my thoughts as we rolled into her neighborhood. My blood wasn't too rich. I just had to live with the facts. I'd escaped, but my mother hadn't.

I'd left her there.

While I lived in a mansion, she rotted in a neighborhood packed with gangbangers. Break-ins were a weekly occurrence. Around the time I moved out, someone pistol-whipped the local gas station clerk. I worried about Mom all the time.

Not only did she live in a rough area, but she had the worst taste in men. I'd been around long enough to witness seven of Mom's so-called "true loves." She discovered someone new every couple of years. Every time, she'd "never felt this way," and before the anniversary made its first or second lap, her heart was broken.

Her latest was a burnout named Travis who wasn't violent, thank God, but terrible with money. And controlling. He hated me—emotionally abusive prick—but I wouldn't let him stop me from visiting her. Luckily, her boyfriend wasn't home. I'd called ahead to check.

Mom's salmon-pink triplex popped into view.

I tapped Cassian's shoulder. "That one."

He grunted a command for the driver to stop. We parked beside a broken down Ford packed to the windows with junk. Cassian stepped from the car.

The sun bleached the streets with heat. Cassian's hair shone as he walked around the vehicle. I admired how he appraised the area and his head jerked toward the woman walking her dog before I saw them. Her brow furrowed as she passed my bodyguard. People didn't dress like him in this part of town. Hell, most of California went to work in board shorts and flip-flops.

He opened the door. I got out.

The black Lexus shone like a gem among rows of dead lawns. Cassian wore a button-up rolled to his elbows and charcoal slacks. A sprinkling of fine, dark hair covered his arms. He was so manly—so different from the baby-faced boys on campus. Perspiration dotted his neck.

Cassian's indigo eyes became aqua in the sunlight. "I have to clear the house before you enter."

"That's crazy. She's my mother."

His voice darkened. "Are you arguing with me?"

I gritted my teeth. "No."

"*Good.*"

A ripple of anger ran through me. Then a shadow moved across the curtains. They parted, revealing a man's bearded face. Travis. My mother's fucking boyfriend.

Shit, shit, *shit*.

"What's the matter?" Cassian must've sensed my alarm—he was a freaking bloodhound.

It was too late to leave. Travis had already seen me.

"Oh, no. He's seen you and the car." I didn't have time to answer the questions burning in his eyes. I locked my hand around his other wrist. "You *have* to follow my lead. No time to explain."

"What do you mean?"

Cassian glared at Travis, who backed from the window. "Marie," Travis shouted, perfectly audible outside the house. "Your daughter is here. She's with some meathead."

Lazy fucker couldn't be bothered to answer the door.

"Please, just go with it," I begged, close to tears. "I'll do anything you want."

The door swung open.

"Rain!" My mom's happy greeting rang out. "Who's that strapping young man?"

"Mom, this is Cassian," I shouted before he chimed in. "He's my boyfriend."

Chapter Three

Cassian

Boyfriend?

I was the anti-boyfriend.

Rain and I went together like sriracha and beer. We made no sense. I'd break Rain's spirit a thousand ways before she broke up with me.

I knew all this, and I said nothing.

Rain distracted me by sliding her fingers to my bicep. She leaned into me and pressed her mouth to my cheek. Her lips grazed my skin, and blood rushed to my groin. My cock saluted her curves as she molded against my body. I forgot about the consequences because I craved her like oxygen. Everything disappeared when her heart-shaped face tipped toward mine and beamed. An unspoken plea burned from her.

I corralled enough brain cells to reject her. "No."

"Please, Cassian," she whispered in a honeyed tone. "I wouldn't ask unless it was important."

Every lesson learned in Bodyguard Ethics 101 screamed to shut her down, but a louder voice begged me to wait, that Rain was wound tighter than a steel spring, and desperation leaked from her pores. I'd kicked out countless women from my apartment, but I guess I was a sucker for Rain's doe eyes because I caved.

Something was wrong. She needed me.

Fuck.

I gave her mom a sheepish smile. "Hello."

"Hi, Cassian. I'm Marie." Once her petite frame slid into view, Rain's taste in fashion made more sense. Marie wore a long, banana-yellow dress with a white and black floral print. It drowned her legs. The conservative cut struck me as strange because she wasn't that old, and the heat must've been unforgiving. Her ebony mane was twisted into a French braid streaked with gray. She stepped outside, arms outstretched. Faint bruises dotted her skin. "Come here!"

Marie engulfed me in a fierce hug, her bony limbs digging into me. Hugging wasn't my thing, but I patted her shoulders.

She pulled back, beaming. "Wow," she said when she felt my muscles. "He's handsome! And so strong."

"Thanks."

Her mother didn't seem to give a shit I was older than her daughter. Her expression said that Christmas had come early. "You never said you had a boyfriend!"

"Surprise!" Rain giggled as they embraced. "We just met."

Happiness radiated off the pair. They were twin suns, and looking at them made me ache. Rain returned to my side, clinging to my arm. Purple hair spilled over her creamy tank top that rode an inch above her skintight jeans.

She was a fantasy, not a girlfriend.

Marie grinned. "Nice to meet you, Cassian."

"Likewise."

I disengaged from Rain and opened the door. Marie smiled at the gesture, her gaze lingering on my hands. I judged people by how they reacted to them. Over the years, I recognized patterns. Everyone gave my scars a double take. Most responded with fear and disgust. Others pretended my disfigurement was invisible. A few would ask me what happened.

Marie didn't make a fuss. Her ebony braid swung as she stepped inside a carpeted living room packed with boxes and furniture. A glass kitchen table stood over linoleum at the far end of the room. Wall-to-wall mirrors provided the illusion of a bigger space, but it was tiny.

Protocol dictated that I sweep the entire home before allowing my protectee to enter, but that was fucked the moment Rain called me boyfriend, and like a moron I hadn't refuted it. She'd broken my rules left and right, and I'd let her because she'd looked at me with puppy-dog eyes.

Not acceptable.

Rain dragged me to the couch, but I resisted her pull. "Babe, don't you want to show me around?"

Marie bustled in the kitchen, banging cupboards. "Go on, Rain. I'll get everybody drinks."

"Yeah," Rain muttered, cottoning on. "Okay."

"Pick your poison, Cassian," Marie shouted. "Beer, wine, whiskey?"

"Water, thanks."

Under the guise of a tour, I cleared the house. We stopped in an area filled with exercise equipment. A square window allowed a patch of sunlight through, illuminating a rainfall of dust. There was nothing in here to reminisce over. Hopefully, Marie assumed Rain and I were making out.

What the hell was wrong with me?

Rain released my hand as soon as the door shut. Her brows pinched, and her voice dropped lower than I'd ever heard it. "I'm so, so sorry."

"Don't waste time apologizing."

"Travis wasn't supposed to be here. She said he wouldn't be." Rain paced, wringing her hands. "He's not a good man."

My stomach clenched. I should've known. Faded yellow circles all over Marie's arms. Either she had a drug habit, or someone had hurt her.

"That explains the bruises. Why didn't you tell me?"

"What?" Rain sounded and looked appalled. "He doesn't hit her. Those marks are from micro-needling. My mom's a skincare nut."

Bullshit. "Is that what she tells you?"

Rain closed the distance between us, heat coming off her in waves. Hatred for Travis rippled within her, but she resented me for speaking the truth.

"Travis isn't violent," she growled, as though the mere suggestion was an insult to her. "He's a parasite. He has no clue about my dad or that I'm living in a mansion. He thinks I'm in student housing, up to my waist in debt."

"Why?"

"Because he'd hound me for money." Rain's voice wound down to a whisper. "I'd say no to him, but I can't refuse her."

I rubbed my forehead, hating myself. This wasn't part of the goddamned job. "Christ, Rain. It's called growing a backbone."

"I know."

"Your mom won't buy this."

"It doesn't matter," Rain blurted. "I promised her not to spill the beans about Dad."

She forgot one crucial detail. "I'm thirty. You're nineteen. Nobody in their right mind will believe we're a couple."

Rain shrugged, eyes swimming with tears. "He will."

"What about your mother?"

"Who cares?" she hissed. "Mom won't sell me out to Travis. She doesn't want him interfering in my life."

Yes, she fucking would.

I'd seen this situation play out thousands of times. Douche bag boyfriend abuses Mom and makes her cut off the daughter. Daughter grows desperate. Abuser sucks the soul out of everyone involved until someone dies, or Mom finally leaves him.

I didn't blame Rain. She was a hopeful, selfless, sweet girl who hadn't experienced enough of life. She was a bowl of bright treats left on the sidewalk. She was a magnet for predators. Travis would sink his hooks into her.

Over my dead body.

"Just act like a boyfriend." Rain slipped her hand in mine, and it was disturbingly comfortable. "Let's go back before they get suspicious."

"They already are."

Was I doing this?

Apparently.

I allowed Rain to steer me into the living room crammed with junk. I'd never seen so many copies of *Vogue* magazine in one place. Despite her kind disposition, Marie had a hoarding problem. Rain yanked me onto a floral-patterned loveseat. The cushions squeaked as I sat, her thigh flush against mine. I wrapped my arm around her tiny shoulders and pulled until her hair grazed my chin. I wanted to press my lips where her neck met her shoulder.

We'd never been this close. I kissed the top of her head, a chaste gesture that turned Rain's skin tomato-red.

Did she have a crush on me?

Rain's face still burned. "Cass?"

"*Cassian*." I leaned in, my mouth grazing her cheek. "You're on your own. And you owe me."

Marie swept into sight, a bright flower somehow surviving in a landfill. She balanced our drinks, sliding my water over a California-shaped coaster. A tablecloth almost hid the coffee table's battered surface. Marie sank into the cross-hatch sofa opposite ours and grinned.

"You're so sweet together." She shifted, frowning. "Travis? Come join us."

"Coming," a reedy voice called from the kitchen.

Travis graced us with his presence after he dug a Miller Lite from the fridge. He was tall and thin, wearing oversized khakis he cinched around his ass with a belt. A black beard partially obscured his pointed chin. His short hair and its receding growth reminded me of Buzz Aldrin.

Tattoos of gang symbols covered his arms, mingling with tribal imagery he probably picked from a waiting room catalog. Not handsome by any stretch of the imagination. He radiated a bad boy aura that might've appealed to some women.

Travis snapped the can. Foam spilled over his fingers, which he wiped on his Oakland A's shirt. He dropped onto the couch with a sulky sigh. He took me in, his menacing features darkening.

"Travis, this is Cassian." Marie grasped his arm and leaned into his shoulder. "Rain's boyfriend."

I nodded at him. "Hey."

"Never heard that name before." He sneered. "What is it, French?"

"No idea. You'd have to ask my dad."

"Well, it's great to meet you." He shook my hand and choked on his drink, pulling my hand toward him and staring at it. "Damn, bro. What happened to you?"

That sealed it. He was a dick.

I glared. "I fell down some stairs."

Travis gaped. He slid the beer over the coffee table, glanced at Marie's pained expression, and laughed. Mirth shined from his malevolent gaze as he turned his attention back to me.

"Funny guy," he drawled. "How old are you, though?"

"Thirty." I jumped in before Rain lied.

A frown marred Marie's sunny mood. She didn't

expect me to be a decade older. It troubled her, and it should have. That didn't bother me. What poisoned my gut was Travis' response.

"*Nice*," he said, extending the vowel. "Good for you."

Marie might've been blind, but I caught the leer he flashed in Rain's direction. I wanted to slap the shit-eating grin off his face. Disgust made my stomach roil as the asshole dug into a bowl of Cheetos.

"What line of work you in, Cass?"

Now *he* was calling me that? "I'm a bodyguard."

Travis eyed my waistline. "Dude, are you strapped?"

You better not be checking out my bulge.

My jaw clenched. "Yes."

"That's metal as fuck." He offered me a fist bump, which I reluctantly returned. "I thought getting a concealed carry permit was hard in California."

It is. "Not if you have the right background."

"I see." He straightened, more and more captivated. "What kinds of clients do you get?"

"All sorts."

"You're a man of few words. Comes in handy when dealing with this one." He took Rain's knee. She jerked it from him, hiding the movement by crossing her legs.

A white-hot fury blinded my vision. She was mine—or pretending to be, anyway—what was he thinking?

Don't you dare touch her. The demand hung on the tip of my tongue.

He laughed, looking me up and down. "You don't seem like her type."

And you are?

It sounded condescending, coming from him. "Opposites attract, I guess."

"They must," he drawled. "I figured she'd go for a rainbow-haired wuss wearing a pussy hat, not the Rock. Wow, Rain. You did something smart for once."

A ripple of anger ran through me, joining the frenzy that swelled whenever he peeked at Rain. Was he insulting her in front of me? Her boyfriend? Was I supposed to sit there and take it? Rain and Marie might've expected nothing more, but I sure as hell wouldn't tolerate it.

I leaned forward so that the shithead wouldn't mistake my wrath for a joke. "Don't insult my girlfriend. Rain is mine. If anyone needs to put her in her place, I will. Not you."

Either he'd back down, or fight. I hoped he'd throw a punch. It'd give me an excuse to kick his ass.

Travis gaped, the tips of his ears burning red. "Think you can come into my house and tell me what to do?"

"I can when it concerns me or mine."

Rain touched my thigh, the sensation barely registering through my hatred. When I didn't respond, she dug in. "It's fine. Travis was joking."

Travis guzzled his beer, ignoring the pleading looks

Marie threw his way. The aluminum sides of the can buckled. "I respect a guy who sticks up for his woman. Apologies for stepping on your toes, brother."

You're not my brother.

I grunted an acknowledgment that I'd heard his piss-poor apology. Rain owed me so fucking big. I couldn't remember the last time I'd been on a meet-the-parents date, and this one was spiraling into a disaster.

"So, Cassian," Marie asked in a high-pitched voice, "where are you from?"

I launched into a cobbled version of what I'd told Rain when we first met. "San Leandro. Lived there until I moved to Walnut Creek."

"No shit?" Travis nudged Marie. "We should have you over for dinner sometime. Right, hon?"

Fuuuuck.

Still upset, Marie attempted a smile. "Of course."

Travis' brow furrowed. "Oh, come on. He's the best thing to happen to this girl. She could be dating some loser, but she's with a real man." He leaned forward and slapped my shoulder.

I wanted to burn where he'd touched, and break his arm. He liked me. That disgusted me more than anything.

Gradually, the tension diffused as I answered Travis' stupid questions. He quizzed me on everything from my kill count—*zero*—to demanding how many celebs I'd slept with—*also zero*. I hoped I'd bore him, but the bastard seemed entertained. It was excruciating, talking to this brainless moron. My patience ran thin. I wouldn't last without exploding. His admiration for his girlfriend's daughter made my skin crawl.

After another one of these exchanges, he beckoned me. "Between us. What do you see in her?"

I glanced at Rain, who sat at the table with Marie. A tense grin twitched on Rain's face. Her hand slid across the glass and seized her mother's clenched fist. I saw lightness, beauty, and hope that'd never die.

Travis wasn't interested in those qualities. He wanted to hear about her tits and ass. I'd humor him.

For now. "I see what every red-blooded man does."

Travis grinned, mouthing, *hell yeah.*

God, he was revolting.

"Cassian." Rain's husky voice broke. "We should leave."

Thank fuck. "Okay."

Travis looked disappointed. "Do you have to?"

I stood, darkly amused by Travis' dismay. "We have a dinner reservation in the city."

Something happened between Rain and her mother. A flushed Marie pleaded with Rain soundlessly, but Rain ignored her. She bit her lip, her tearful gaze begging me. Even the dimwit noticed the tension.

He shot a look at Marie, whose radiance dimmed to a

dull luster. "What's the matter with you? You've been weird all day."

"Bye, Mom," Rain deadpanned, facing me. "Let's go."

I approached Marie. "Lovely to meet you."

Her eyes were like crystal orbs fractured with pain. "Yes, you too."

I shook hands with Travis, who sighed in silent commiseration. *Women, what can you do?*

"Later," he said. "Let us know about supper."

Go to hell.

I found Rain outside, standing on the dead lawn. Sunlight washed her in vivid colors, but melancholy radiated from her. She crossed her mother's property and walked the street, heading into a bike trail surrounded by a chain-link fence. I tracked her down the empty path overgrown with yellow grass.

"Thank you." She stopped, clutching the metal links. "You didn't have to defend me. That was kind."

"Kindness had nothing to do with it. He's a prick."

A smile wiped most of her sadness aside. "Yes, he is. I can't stand him."

"Same. Why doesn't she dump him?"

"I don't know." A tear spilled over her lid and streaked her cheek. "She says she's in love."

That rammed a knife in my chest.

Oh, Rain. "You can't fix her."

"I thought if I—if I kept showing her how awful he was

she'd leave him," she growled, lips shaking. "I'm not giving up. I will force her to see sense."

"You can't. Nobody can." I didn't carry tissues, so I loosed my tie and slid the silk over her skin. "Your mom has to make that decision."

Rain startled from my touch, fixing me with an expression I knew too well from wading through Walnut Creek's dating pool. "What's the point of being a Montgomery if I can't even help my mother?"

"No idea."

"I have to do something. Travis is—"

"—bad news," I finished for her. "I don't want you anywhere near him."

Her mouth opened and closed. "What?"

"I'm serious. You can't visit her if he is there."

"You are not keeping me from my mom." Her deep voice cracked with despair. "Cassian, no."

"It's not her I'm worried about, sweetheart."

"Cassian, please."

"Travis is a disaster."

"You think I don't know that?" Rain stormed from the fence as though she could escape me if she power-walked fast enough. "He has a record, and Mom is with him. You have no idea how concerned I am. It's a nightmare."

"It's too much for anyone to deal with, especially a nineteen-year-old."

She whirled around. "Don't talk to me like I'm a child."

I took her wrists, leaning in close. "I did what you wanted. Now you'll do something for me—stay the hell away from your mother's boyfriend."

"Cassian, please! He wouldn't hurt me. He's just a creep."

"With gang tattoos over his arms."

She ripped from my grasp. "Talking to you is so frustrating. You are emotionless. It's like arguing with a wall."

"I disagree."

She snorted. "Thank you, Cassian. You've shown me what I never want to become."

I followed her as she stomped to the car.

Drama queen.

∼

It was Quentin's shift. Thank God.

By the time we got home, Rain had returned to her pleasant self, but my blood raged with fire. Meeting her family troubled me. I couldn't keep Rain from her mom forever, and I didn't want to involve Montgomery. That was a step too far into someone's personal life.

Quentin hit my shoulder as he sauntered from the house. He wore a pair of jeans and a button-down shirt, his hair slicked with gel. He looked fit for a night out on the town.

My suspicion grew as Rain's smile widened. "Ready to go? There's a folk band playing at the Chapel."

"Oh, sweet." Quentin beamed. "Can't wait."

Quentin enjoyed folk music as much as I jammed to Taylor-fucking-Swift, but that didn't stop him from lying through his teeth. Rain fumbled with her purse as he approached, her face burning when she dropped it. They stooped to grab the bag at the same time, and their hands touched.

"Thanks," she said, pink rising to her cheeks. "The band's like Fleet Foxes if you know them."

"I love them."

Bullshit, I wanted to yell. Yesterday, he was headbanging to Finnish death metal.

Was he *flirting* with her?

I crashed my fist into the mother-in-law's door and stepped into the living room. Their conversation filtered through the window that Quentin kept open despite the chilly mornings.

"Really?" She sounded impressed. "What else do you listen to?"

"Lorde, Lana Del Rey, Gorillaz—"

"Me too!" she exclaimed. "Gorillaz is coming to San Francisco soon. I have tickets. Would you like to come?"

Was she asking him out on a date?

"Yeah, I'm down."

A vein pulsed in my neck as I stared at the wall and imagined strangling Quentin.

"It's pathetic, but I bought them hoping I'd find someone to take. Since my friends have ditched me."

"Don't take it personally. Everyone's a jerk at nineteen."

"Even me?"

"Hell no. You're awesome."

Stop hitting on her, you asshole.

"Thanks," she gushed. "I love that you listen to Lorde."

Sweet Jesus, Rain. He doesn't. He just wants to get in your pants.

"Yeah," Quentin chuckled. "I don't really fit the demographics of her fan base."

A softness crept into her voice. "You're all right, Q."

Quentin's aw-shucks laughter stoked the flames of my rage. Did he think he had a chance with Rain?

"Thanks, doll," he purred. "Let's go."

He did. The bastard wanted her.

Their conversation faded as they walked away. I listened to the silence as my anger filled the room. I swept his dirty mug into the sink, shattering it.

If anybody was going to be fucking Rain, it'd be me.

Chapter Four

Rain

My father burst into my room without giving common courtesy a single fuck—the man never knocked. I could've been on the phone, watching porn, or doing something no father wants to see. That didn't stop him from barging into my space uninvited. You'd think after raising boys, he'd know better, but he treated me like a former addict who shot up heroin.

I'd never so much as touched a cigarette.

"Hey, Dad." The staccato word bounced off my tongue. I wondered if it'd ever feel comfortable. "Make yourself at home."

My father strolled to the reclaimed wood desk which

held all my knickknacks and dragged a chair up beside the bed. "We have an unlocked door policy in this house."

"Does that mean I can walk into the bathroom while you're using it?"

He sat with a world-weary sigh. "No."

"Then why do you do it? This is my private area. You shouldn't just barge in."

According to Dad, tattoos and dyed hair turned people into Justin Bieber. Two years should've convinced him I wasn't a budding felon.

"Where do you get the idea I'm up to no good? From my dull schedule? The hours I spend in the library researching tenant law to fight my mom's ridiculous landlord? Maybe my habit of drinking soy milk tea worries you."

"It's not that I don't trust you. Karen's harder to convince."

Really, Dad? Throwing the wife under the bus? "Tell her I didn't ask to be born."

"I'm not great at this." Dad sank into his palms and rubbed his face. He peeked from his fingers as though hoping an advisor, campaign manager, or personal assistant would swoop in and soothe my wounded feelings. "I'm doing my best to please you both. She doesn't like that you're in the house all day."

No shit.

Karen wasn't keen on my presence, given I wouldn't

exist if Dad hadn't cheated on her with my mom. I never planned on ruining his marriage, but that's precisely what I'd done. Like a wrecking ball, I'd smashed into their home. She despised me, and I couldn't blame her, so I did my utmost to stay away.

"Karen can order my bodyguards to back off, and perhaps I'd leave more often."

"No," he snapped.

Some days, I regretted my decision to live with Dad, but it was that or sue him. A portrait of him in his twenties sat on my desk. We had the same thick, straight slash of eyebrows, and shared a small mouth. His lean body, broad shoulders, and attached earlobes mirrored mine. I clung to these similarities, especially when he looked at me like that. "When will you get rid of the purple hair?"

"I cover my tattoos," I whispered. "Everything you loathed is gone from my wardrobe. Now you want to take my hair?"

"Rain, you asked to be part of this family."

A needle pierced my heart. "Ouch."

"You know I—I'm delighted to have you as a daughter."

He had more enthusiasm over a three-point lead. "You never wanted me here."

"No," he sighed. "No, that's not true."

As a positive person, I struggled to see the bright side. "You can't stand the sight of me. It's like I'm contaminated."

"I'm having a rough time adjusting. That doesn't mean I don't care."

He cared, all right. Keeping the peace with his wife. About his constituents—what the voters would think.

It was always about them.

I was the free-loving hippie he railed against at his campaign rallies. A lavender-haired child did nothing to help his career, but he couldn't sever me from his life without looking like an utter ass, so he nitpicked my appearance. Ripped jeans made me look homeless. Purple hair was for jobless losers. What kind of irresponsible mother let me get tattoos? When I brushed off his complaints, he flat out demanded change.

I shouldn't be here. "Living with you was a mistake."

"Don't say that! I've put too much effort into this for you to leave now."

I swallowed a fist-sized lump. "This isn't working."

"Certain sacrifices are expected of you, Rain."

"I'm not altering my identity!"

"Don't be difficult."

"Difficult?" I burst. "*You're* the one demanding changes. I won't bleach my hair to blend in for your family in photo ops."

He groaned.

When I found my dad, I couldn't take my eyes off him. The other half of my DNA—the one missing all my childhood—suddenly appeared. My fatherless existence drove my desperation for a connection. Then I met the man.

And I was nothing like him.

Curt Montgomery identified with the opposite of the political spectrum. He enjoyed watching himself on television and critiquing his own speeches. His hobbies involved wine tasting, an activity that bored me to tears considering I couldn't drink, fine dining, weekends in Cabo, and winters in Tahoe. Too many awkward dinners with his forty-year-old children, who hated me for being born, turned me off a relationship with anyone else. They all believed I was a money-grubbing asshole or that my mother pulled the strings.

I just wanted a father.

"Rain, can you come downstairs? Your guard made a security recommendation, but you should hear it from him."

"Cassian." Sweet one moment, ruthless the next. "Let's get this over with."

I followed Dad down the impressive hall to the narrow staircase kissing the wall. My bare feet slapped the wood as he led me into his study toward a man at odds with the light colors and soft edges.

Cassian faced a family portrait. I'd never known a guard to ignore my father's presence. They snapped to attention whenever Dad walked into the room, but not

Cassian. He tore his gaze from my half-siblings, smoothing his frown into determined calm.

"Good morning, Rain." My bodyguard's stony features twitched, and he moved forward as though reanimated. "Quentin and I have something important to discuss."

Quentin waved from a wingback chair, looking unhappy. Cassian's steel-blue eyes zeroed on me, a smirk carving a dimple into his cheek. Invisible flames erupted around me, banking higher with every step he took closer. He scared me, but it was a thrill to go toe-to-toe with him.

My insides needled apprehension. "What is it?"

My anxiety peaked as he stood like a Greek statue, bearing over me.

"We can't let you attend the show. I'm removing it from your schedule."

"What?" The breath whooshed from my lungs as I looked from him to Quentin, whose grimace confirmed the bad news. "But I've had the tickets forever."

"The venue won't allow Quentin to conceal carry," Cassian said smoothly. "He can't be unarmed in a crowded space packed with drunk people. It's a terrible idea."

"Oh, come on!" This had to be a punishment for the whole fake-boyfriend thing. "What are the chances anyone will recognize me?" When he didn't budge, I turned to Quentin. "You could stand beside me. Heck, I'll exchange my floor ticket for a seat."

"They're sold out, but it doesn't matter." Cassian

demanded my full attention. "General admission won't work."

"I bought them months ago. I've been looking forward to this for ages." Rage spiraled in my chest. I was sick and tired of running everything by a man as distant as the moon.

I whirled to Dad, who reached for the door handle. "Dad, tell him it's fine. It's a Gorillaz concert, for God's sake."

He chewed his lip, hating that I'd caught him before he slipped outside. "Sorry, but I'm siding with Cassian. I have to go. I'll see you next Saturday."

Dad left. The door shut, the sound ringing inside me. His presence in D.C. wasn't needed until Monday, but he was always early. He never stayed home a minute longer than necessary, and it made me grind my teeth. My ire flashed when Cassian headed for the exit. "Where do you think you're going? I'm not done with you."

Cassian stopped, even though he could've pushed me aside. "You don't dictate how I spend my free time, and I refuse to waste it with a petulant teenager."

Anger burned the backs of my eyes. Since when had I been anything but accommodating to his ridiculous demands? "What is your problem?"

"You." His glare shot to Quentin. "And you."

Cassian stepped away and loosened his tie, as though being around me made him hot.

"Dude, that's uncalled for." Quentin pushed out of the wingback chair, his voice rising. "Nothing would've happened. I'd never put her in danger."

"Shut the hell up," Cassian growled. "You're out of line and have forgotten your purpose. She's your protectee. Not your buddy."

"She asked me!"

"Then you should've said no." Cassian seized Quentin's collar and shoved. Quentin's back slammed into the wall.

So quick to violence.

My heart pounded like a drum.

Quentin didn't raise his hands. His only defense was his dry, unaffected tone. "You're way too paranoid. She's right. Most of the attendees will be too high to point out California on a map, let alone recognize a senator's daughter."

"You don't know that." Cassian fumed as Quentin readjusted his shirt. "You act like a fucking rookie. Get it together."

"I'm not the one getting pissy." Quentin grinned at Cassian's angry face. "Nobody knows she's going to the concert. She could wear a hoodie. They'll assume we're on a date."

The word made Cassian rigid. "No. My decision is final."

Unconcerned, Quentin rolled his eyes and approached

me, a sympathetic frown replacing his annoyance. "There'll be other concerts, Rain."

My spirits sank. The highlight of my summer ruined, all because my pearl-clutching bodyguard couldn't stand to give me an ounce of freedom.

Quentin pulled me close, engulfing me in a bear hug. "I was looking forward to it all week."

"I know," I said. "Me too."

Quentin's arms tightened, and his aftershave stung my nose. His broad smile filled me with warmth, a candle compared to the inferno when Cassian held my hand. Nice, handsome Quentin was the safe option, whereas Cassian was a self-destruct button.

"Why don't you grab her ass while you're at it?" Cassian snarled behind Quentin.

Quentin disengaged, and I admired the way he refused to rise to Cassian's bait. "I'll wait outside, Rain."

When he disappeared, Cassian closed the distance between us. He seeped into me like steam from a bath. I craved his touch. "Q is just a friend."

"He wants to get laid." His calm rippled with disguised wrath. "Can't you tell?"

A thrill ran down my spine, but it didn't curl my toes or boil my blood. "Is this more paranoia, or the truth?"

"He wants you so badly he's willing to sit through two hours of the worst music."

"You're such a jerk."

His menacing, platinum gaze slanted as he pushed me against the wall. "Only stating the facts, darling."

"Why—why do you care about Q and me?"

Cassian seized me, his voice diamond-hard. "You won't be Quentin's next conquest."

You'll be mine.

∼

Did he ever relax?

Slowly, I got used to Quentin. But Cassian?

Yeah, right. What a nightmare.

He wasn't a companion, more like a hulk whose sinister presence scared the locals. People skirted us on sidewalks. He had no clue how to look unthreatening.

I pitied him. His existence must've been miserable. He spent his free time alone, as far as I could tell. When he wasn't jogging the hills, he exercised in the gym or drove to the shooting range every damned day. Unlike Quentin, he never invited friends over.

Cassian survived, but he didn't live.

Pretending he was mine at my mother's was nice. I replayed his cheek sliding against mine, and the gentle brushing of his lips.

It felt safe—so right.

Did he love with the same intensity he approached everything else? No idea, but he wasn't completely unfeeling. He worked so hard to be detached but he'd wiped my tears. He comforted me.

The man seemed incapable of dropping his guard, but he'd broken his rules once. Why couldn't he do it again? The closest explanation was jealousy.

If my safety concerned him, fine. But my personal life? Why butt in?

I stretched out on my beach blanket, sunlight kissing my bare legs and stomach. My tiny, white bathing suit was too risqué for paparazzi, but who cared? Body shame didn't exist in this city. A naked parade graced the event calendar of the official San Francisco website. Donning a teeny bikini wasn't a scandal.

Seducing my bodyguard was.

I didn't want to manipulate Cassian. Satisfying my curiosity was my priority. What better way than sunbathing?

Dolores Park was a bowl-shaped, grassy hill where hipsters, children, and potheads joined to enjoy the sun. The southern tip reeked of marijuana, and families dominated the north. A bell from an ice cream cart rang as a vendor shouted about his wares. Couples sprawled on the lawn. Shirtless men tanned side-by-side as they gabbed about their tech jobs. I blended in.

Cassian didn't. He stood behind me, several feet up the slope. People threw my well-dressed bodyguard curious looks. San Francisco was known for its quirks, but slacks in eighty-degree weather was weird.

He was probably boiling.

It was fun, imagining his misery. I played with keeping him there for hours, but guilt crept in. He might get a sunburn. Or heat stroke. Selling those Gorillaz tickets destroyed me, but retaliating at Cassian like this felt cheap. Rule-breaking was far more entertaining.

I rolled on the grass and dug a bottle from the cooler. I stood with the blanket held to my bikini top. Light rippled through the plastic bottle and bounced off.

I approached Cassian. Sweat beaded on his neck, and his nostrils flared, but his stony expression registered zero discomfort.

No surprises there.

"Thirsty?" I offered him the bottle.

"In more ways than one."

Cassian's eyes dragged up and down my body, scorching a path from my tits to my toes. He took the water and guzzled, winking at me.

Well, that wasn't subtle. I never pegged him as shy, but *wow*. "You could wear shorts."

"Are you dying to see the rest of me?"

Coming from most men, that would've been cringeworthy, but Cassian's grit made every downright filthy comment sound decadent. And I was curious. Mostly about his chest and legs. Were they as hard as the body armor? Was he soft anywhere?

"Let's continue this conversation in the shade." Guilt throbbed in me for the wicked, red weal near his collar. "You're burned."

His scars flashed through my mind, and a stone fell in my stomach. I forgot—shit—"I'm sorry."

"What about?" A puzzled frown creased his forehead beading with moisture.

"Your hands."

"Oh." A bitter smile tugged his lips. "You thought I'd hear the word burned and burst into tears?"

He hadn't told me what caused the scars, but I'd guessed it was fire. The way they blurred his skin painted a grotesque picture of blackening flesh.

I shuddered. "I'm trying to be sensitive."

"Fuck's sake, Rain. Do I look like a wimp?"

"No, but you're someone I'd rather not hurt."

Cassian's eyes softened, and he almost smiled. "You don't have to concern yourself with that. I'm the help."

"I want us to get along, Cassian."

He didn't glance away for a long time. "Well, I'm fine. I've been in worse conditions. Try Dubai in July with a bulletproof vest drenched in sweat."

"Tell me about Dubai."

"It's weird. Lots of restrictions. The place is very westernized, but they segregate the sexes."

I gathered my things and moved to a shaded patch, watching Cassian sigh when he crossed into the shadows.

"Please sit."

"Why?"

I needed a reason? "You're not bad company, and nobody will murder me with you around."

"What's with the flattery?"

"It's called 'killing with kindness.' Do you know what that is? It's the opposite of mean—"

"Hush. I'll sit. Whatever shuts you up."

My heart soared when he dropped to my blanket. His jacket slipped down his shoulders, the cotton underneath translucent with his perspiration. He removed the coat. It fell to the ground. I took it. Pure male pheromones mingled with cedar wafted from the wool. I imagined that smell clinging to my sheets.

Heat dipped in my belly as I folded it. Cassian ripped the first buttons loose, tempting a breeze over his shining neck. He tugged the shirt from his pants, and it slid up his muscular torso. He rolled the sleeves as high as they'd go, revealing rippling, corded muscle.

All right, he was sexy.

Cassian tickled the horny bone of the general female population. He was sculpted, perfectly built, and tall. With the holster strapped to him, he looked like a superhero wet dream.

Women walking the hill noticed him, smiling at the

broody man who wouldn't glance in their direction. Cassian's eyes never strayed far from me. It was his job.

I passed him another bottle, and he poured it over his head. The water turned the rest of the fabric transparent, and while the armor covered his chest, I pretended I could see broad slabs of muscle.

"Why did you cancel the concert?"

Cassian ran fingers through his hair. "It was unsafe."

"Tell me the real reason."

"Safety."

I sat upright, tired of talking to him from the ground. I bunched my mane and slid it over one shoulder. "You won't be Quentin's next conquest," I echoed what he'd said. "What did you mean by that?"

"I intend to protect you, even from yourself."

"Q's a danger to me?"

"I don't trust him. He cares more about fucking you than protecting you."

My cheeks burned hotter than the sun. What did he gain from being so damned rough all the time? "You don't mince words."

"Nope."

"Whatever." I sighed, frustrated with the conversation. "I like him. He's a blast, and he makes me laugh."

"What else does he do?"

An undercurrent of bitterness ran under his growl. Mentioning the other guard forced him to scowl.

Was he jealous?

I hid my smile. "Q and I text. Sometimes we talk."

Cassian didn't like that. His thick eyebrows narrowed, and then he leaned closer, legs bumping mine. "About what?"

He was so *hostile*.

"Stuff."

"Elaborate."

"I don't know. We have a lot in common, and he's fun to chat with."

Cassian made a sound through his nose. "Why's a girl like you calling her bodyguard? Don't you have friends?"

I did. "Ever since I've lived at my dad's, I'm isolated. My friends don't understand. They're wrapped up in their high school drama, and I'm moving on from that. Maybe we'll hang out in a few years."

"I doubt that," he said. "Your world will change, while theirs is static. You'll never be anonymous again. You can't drink at a rave or a club without a reporter writing about it. What you do and say will be used against your father. A journalist will approach anyone who's dated you with a blank check."

"What do you mean?"

"Come on, Rain," he groaned. "They'll ask your friends for stories that'd humiliate your dad or alienate his base. Alcohol and drugs. Kinky sex."

I hadn't thought of that. "I guess I should delete my furry porn, then."

"Yes."

Good God. Did he think I was *serious*? "I'm not into that."

"No shit." Cassian's posture relaxed. He raked his sweaty hair and yanked on his button-up shirt.

"Tell me something personal."

"Why?"

"You never do anything but grunt, and it's getting old." I glanced at the hand splayed over his knees. "What caused the scars?"

His lips thinned. "Seriously?"

"I'm not asking because I'm nosy."

"Yeah, right."

"It's obvious you're hiding a lot of pain. Maybe you'd feel better if you talked."

"Hiding a lot of pain," he echoed, laughing. "I'm good, thanks."

"Oh, Cassian. Mocking me is obviously a defense mechanism."

"You need a hobby besides analyzing me."

We were together twelve hours a day. Did he think I'd ignore him the whole time? "You hide your hands. You hate when anyone notices your wounds. What happened?"

"People who claim I have no boundaries should meet

you." Cassian glowered. "When I was young, there was a fire. The rest is private."

"But I think—"

"You want to get along? Don't pry about my goddamned scars."

Fine.

I slumped onto the blanket, skin tingling from his stare. "Do you have a girlfriend?"

"I don't do girlfriends."

Not surprising. Cassian struck me as a hit it and quit it guy, but I definitely wanted more.

"Well, I want a boyfriend, and I'm realizing I can't date without you or Q lurking nearby. Most guys won't be crazy about that."

"Probably not." Cassian was nothing but honest.

Aside from a few clumsy attempts in high school, I was inexperienced. I'd never felt comfortable bringing a guy home. Mom's boyfriends left so much to be desired. They had all but killed my romantic spirit. Time away from that toxic climate had allowed it to spring back to life.

"I can't accept that. I want too many things."

"Like?"

"Passion. Intimacy."

He grinned. "You'll only get one of those from a guy your age."

"You don't know that."

"Oh, I do," he countered, tapping his chest. "Speaking

as a former boy. We don't last long."

"You're bragging about premature ejaculation?"

"I'm saying it happens to every boy before he becomes a man." Cassian hovered over me, his shirt hanging.

I imagined Cassian covering me, burying his face in my neck. He couldn't seriously mean himself—that I should—that *we* should be together. I wasn't sure, but his reaction when I mentioned Quentin piqued my interest. Pleasure wrapped my body and squeezed when he acted like a jealous prick.

"You're right. Maybe I should ask Q if he's game."

Cassian's brows rose further. "Over my dead body."

He was jealous. Elation fluttered my heart as I bumped his thigh. "*You* could've gone to the show with me."

"I meant what I told you. It wasn't safe."

"Nothing is. I'll have death threats for years. Am I supposed to give up everything?"

Cassian's lips thinned, his displeasure with me growing. "No."

"I guess I'll tell Dad you restricted access to my mother."

His frown darkened. "Go ahead. It's my judgment against yours."

"You'll be overruled. You underestimate the effect of a daughter's tears on her father. I'll win, and you'll have to play my boyfriend again."

"Stop acting like a teenager."

"I am one," I growled. "Boyfriend or concert?"

"I'm calling your bluff." Cassian snatched his jacket. "We've been here long enough. Let's go."

"Make me."

He wheeled around. "Excuse me?"

"I'd like to see you grab me while I'm wearing this. Wouldn't look great for your boss."

A smirk carved out his dimples. "No, it wouldn't."

He grasped my biceps and rolled, yanking me across him. Another jerk brought us within kissing distance. Our noses touched, and I pulled back, but he refused to slacken his grip.

My skin burned from the tips of my ears to my neck. His chest rose against mine, slow and steady.

Would he kiss me?

I couldn't move, even if he released me.

His fingers sank into my arm. "Damn. Your pulse is racing. Would that have anything to do with me?"

Of course.

Cassian stole my breath, making speech impossible.

His grin revealed that the answer dangled in front of him. He slid down my arms to grasp my hands, which he moved over his damp shirt and up his neck. I held his hot skin, my palms sliding over him as my heart convulsed like a terrified bird. He was messy and covered in sweat, but when our eyes met, a liquid heat stroked between my clenched thighs.

"Go on. Kiss me."

Kiss him?

I swallowed hard, unable to articulate a sentence. I'd never kissed a man, period. Plenty of boys, sure, but Cassian was on another level. He intimidated the hell out of me.

"I—I can't."

Even if I had the nerve, people were everywhere. Though nobody had given us a second glance.

"Would you rather I did it for you?" Cassian's touch disappeared, and I trembled as his smile broadened. "Imagine the headlines. Wayward Daughter Straddles Bodyguard. Senator's Lovechild Frolics with the Help."

"What are you doing?"

"Teaching."

I was a broken record. "What?"

"Teaching you, sweetheart. I don't care about your father's reputation, or what'll happen if they photograph us. Want to know why you can't be with Quentin?" Cassian's head turned, his lips touching my ear. "Because you're already mine. When you're ready to admit it, come to me."

A fiery whip wrapped my heart. "*Cassian.*"

He brushed my thigh, licking warmth between my legs. "That's my name. My door's open. Anytime. Day or night."

Chapter Five

Rain

I couldn't get Cassian out of my head. Since the park, he'd invaded my mind and much like the real thing, he wouldn't leave. Avoiding him was hopeless. Even if I stayed in my room and closed the blinds, his words echoed in an endless loop.

My door's open. Anytime. Day or night.

I picked a random program and let it run through the episodes, barely taking it in. Binging shows didn't distract me from being propositioned by my bodyguard. My father could ruin his career with a phone call, but that didn't stop Cassian.

Jesus, he was bold.

We were nothing alike.

Cassian's darkness battled my light, and yet I found myself drawn to him. He didn't say much, but when he did his remarks struck my core. Stone surrounded his heart. Mine wasn't so guarded.

After two days, I was stir-crazy. I opened the kitchen side doors and prayed it was Quentin's shift. My feet mowed through sprinkled grass. My Chucks glistened by the time I reached the mother-in-law unit. Quentin and Cassian relied on security cameras instead of standing outside for hours on end.

I rapped the wood.

Heavy footsteps groaned the floorboards. He unlatched the lock and cracked the door. A sharp jaw line and bowed lips peeked through, the frame widening to reveal his stunning face.

Dread bottomed out in my stomach.

Cassian.

He wore a V-neck shirt that wrapped his muscled torso. The royal blue matched his eyes. He joined me, his running shoes sliding over the porch as I held my breath and waited for my pulse to calm.

"What is it?"

Reading him was *impossible.* "Is it Q's turn?"

"It's mine." He took a giant step forward, invading my space. "You look flustered."

"You're very close."

"Who's watching?" Cassian's knuckles grazed my chin.

"Quentin's gone for the day."

Flames leaped to my cheeks. "Why does that matter?"

"Do I need to say it? I thought I was blunt at the park." His grin widened at the memory, even though my insides squeezed. "I want you."

Nothing had prepared me for the way those words burrowed and took root, nestling in the place that ached for affection.

I had to be smart. Cassian was fucking with me.

"You're lying," I accused him. "At my mom's house, you claimed we made no sense."

"As a *couple*, not as two consenting adults. You said you wanted intimacy and passion. I can give you both if you let me." Cassian's voice lowered to a silky caress. "You'll have a good time. I promise."

I didn't doubt him. "You're a huge hypocrite for what you told Q."

"Yeah," he deadpanned. "So?"

I couldn't believe him. "You've got balls, but you're also the reason I can't visit my mother, and why I missed Gorillaz. I won't sleep with someone I don't like."

Plus, I'm a goddamned virgin.

"How do I win you over, Rain?"

I smiled, meeting his steely gaze. "You can start with a compliment."

"Is your self-esteem that fragile?"

"No, it's not. I just think you should."

"Why?"

Cassian frustrated me to no end. "Because that's how you win people over."

"No, sweetheart. That's what men do to get in a woman's pants. I don't dish out half-assed sentiments to get sex. It's pathetic and demeaning."

Jesus. Fine. "Then do something nice for me."

"I'd be happy to cook you breakfast after getting to know you all night."

God, he was hopeless.

"Are you afraid to be anything but a lewd ass?"

Cassian closed the distance between us, his laughter dying. "At least I'm honest about what I want."

I backed away, confused by the glow in my chest.

Cassian's warmth vanished like a blown-out candle. "Did you have plans to go somewhere?"

I hugged myself as his chill seeped into my bones. "Um—yes. Fisherman's Wharf."

"That's far."

"You look like you can handle it."

Cassian shot me a glare at odds with his behavior of a moment before.

Back to being rude.

"Let's go," he muttered grumpily.

Fisherman's Wharf was a long way, but I loved walking. Most days, I chose a direction and strolled for hours. San Francisco's dozens of microclimates and subcultures never got boring, and a lifetime of living in the East Bay meant I rarely went into the city. I wanted to explore the place with someone.

Conversation with Cassian was like yanking teeth with rusted pliers. He responded in one-word replies, proving he was only interested in fucking me. Imagining my first time in Cassian's capable hands made my mouth go dry and my lips burn, but we didn't have a connection. Without that, I'd regret every kiss.

When we reached the tourist-chocked Fisherman's Wharf, it was noon. White sails drifted over sparkling blue like swans. The sun burned higher, its rays punishing as we explored the docks. My feet ached as I rested on the wooden railing. A brackish smell saturated the soaked piers, where the sea lions lounged on filthy planks, barking up a storm.

"Aren't they sweet?"

"Not the word I'd use," Cassian deadpanned, breaking his silence. "Stinking, bloated sacks of screaming flesh."

"They can't help what they are."

"You see the good in everything, don't you?"

"I try," I said. "Life's too short to be a cynic."

Sweat ringed his forehead. He unbuttoned his shirt, revealing an inch of his smooth chest. "You're the only person I know who likes the wharf."

"It's a tourist trap, for sure, but there are highlights. Sea lions. Ghirardelli. Cable cars. People-watching."

"That's what I do all day."

"What for?"

"It's part of my job, sweetheart. If I couldn't read people, I'd be a shit bodyguard." He gestured at a woman in a tight bodycon dress. "She's a prostitute. Probably on her way to her next john."

"Say it a little louder, Cassian."

He pointed at a couple engaged in a tense conversation. "She's cheating on him. He's clueless."

"Oh, come on. You can do better. Even I could've guessed that."

"Okay, fine." Cassian studied the man and woman, grinning. "He telecommutes for a tech startup because he's wearing a custom Patagonia vest with the company's logo. His relationship status is a guess based on his demeanor. See the crossed arms? He's pissed, but his shoes are pointing toward her."

I followed his gaze, fascinated. "What does that mean?"

"Means he's in love with her."

"You can tell whether someone's in love by their shoe position?" I gaped at them, wondering if he was bullshitting. "Why didn't someone mention this in high school?"

"It doesn't work like that. There are *many* tells—"

"—Yeah, yeah, yeah. Get back to her."

Cassian wheeled to the woman. "She's in that outfit because she wants to be noticed, but she's turned to the side. She doesn't want him to touch her. Dressed like she's down to fuck, but it's more of a power play."

"Okay, but how do you know she's cheating?"

"The hickey on her shoulder," he muttered. "She's probably breaking up with him right now."

"Pretty strange place to do that."

"They just left a corporate event." He gestured at the man again. "Look at his plastic bag. It's the same tech logo, but bros don't hang out on Embarcadero, so it has to be related to his job."

The girl stormed off, and the guy chased after her.

"Wow, Cassian. I'm impressed. Even if you're full of shit, that was entertaining." I chuckled, facing him. "Do you ever turn your gift for introspection on yourself? Everyone gives you a wide berth."

"That's what I'm aiming for. People glance at me, and they're intimidated. They don't come near me, and, by extension, you."

Families flocking to visit the sea lions avoided where he stood. A mother corralling her toddler steered him from Cassian's path, after shooting him a frightened look. My heart clenched even though her revulsion wasn't aimed at me.

"What's it like? Being feared?"

"Empowering," he said after a lengthy pause. "Isolating, I guess."

I wondered what they dreaded more: his standoffish

attitude or the wounds. Cassian hid his hands at every opportunity, and I didn't wonder why. Children gawked at them. Everywhere we went, crowds threw him pitying looks.

It must've felt awful. "People are dicks. I'm sorry."

Cassian pinned me with his ocean eyes. "If they stay away, my job is a lot easier."

"Yeah, but—"

"I don't care."

He did. Otherwise he wouldn't cover his scars.

The wooden planks groaned as I stepped into the bustling center of the pier. Cassian's attention snapped to the space surrounding me. He never relaxed.

"Nothing bad ever happens here. *Chill.*"

"Someone was murdered not that long ago." Cassian's hand engulfed my shoulder, pulling me aside when two teenagers ran beside us.

"I remember that. It was an accident."

"Right. The guy *accidentally* shot and killed a woman. Are you that naive?" His palm dropped.

Embarrassment mingled with my desire. The burn deepened when our gazes met. "Eventually, I'd like to date. Fat chance of that happening if you're nearby."

"Are you saying I frighten people, or that I overshadow the competition?"

Both.

Definitely both.

"I plead the fifth."

"Tell me why I'm intimidating, at least."

I passed a seagull perched on a trashcan, stabbing at an empty sourdough bowl. A yeasty smell saturated the air, and my mouth watered. "Are you hungry?"

"No. Answer the question."

I didn't know. Perhaps I feared his power, or my nerves when we held hands.

Yes, I was scared—of falling in love. Love was chaotic. It didn't care about logic. I'd seen what it had done to my mother.

But I couldn't tell Cassian the truth. He'd mock me, and I wasn't made of ice.

So I lied.

"You're a big guy, and you walk around with a fierce expression. On top of that, you're very blunt. Sometimes that's hurtful. I'm terrified of what you think of me."

"You shouldn't be. I have a feeling you'd be all over me if I told you what I really think."

Confidence was hot. Arrogance? Not so much. "You think pretty highly of yourself."

Cassian's bowed lips pulled into a catlike grin.

I roamed the pier, knowing he'd have to follow. "Since when do you flirt with me?"

"Since I discovered I had competition." The look radiating from him suggested he didn't consider Quentin a worthy competitor.

I squinted at him. "I don't understand you. What do you really want?"

"*You.*" He touched my back, and it zapped my skin. "And I know it's mutual, so don't lie. You tried to win me over with pastries."

"I was nice without expecting anything in return."

"You were bartering for my approval."

His heated stare sent a thrill between my clenched thighs. He made me *so* uncomfortable. I wondered how he'd look with a smile. A real one, not the jaded grins he gave me.

"I was trying to bury the hatchet. Why are you giving me a hard time?"

Cassian's smirk broadened as we crossed the street. "I enjoy watching you squirm. It makes my day."

"Hold a puppy, Cassian. You shouldn't find comfort in someone else's pain."

"I don't. Your pleasure gives *me* pleasure."

I flushed when his eyes cut to me. "Maybe you should stop with the flirting."

"Why? You love it, and it's fun for me." He strolled beside me, grinning. "What's life without a little spice?"

I wasn't ready to have my heart broken, and Cassian was out of bounds. A U.S. senator's daughter couldn't shack up with her bodyguard. "I want us to be friends."

"I don't do *friends*. Or any other kind of relationship."

Out of everything he'd said, that stunned me the most. "Why?"

"It's personal."

"That's the saddest thing I've ever heard."

He was a hot mess with more problems than that Jay-Z song.

"You have issues, Cassian."

We stopped at Market, waiting to cross the street.

"You *like* a man with issues."

No I didn't. "You're not my type at all."

"I know you want me, Rain," he sang as the sign beckoned us. "As I mentioned, I read people. You can't look my direction without blushing. That's why you baked me scones."

I *hated* him. "They were for you *and* Quentin."

"*Whatever*." He was giving me shit over sugar and flour.

"They were just scones! Eat them. Don't eat them. Set them on fire. I don't care."

"You do, though. That's what gives you away." Cassian gave me serious side-eye at another crosswalk, rush hour traffic almost drowning his voice. "Want to know how to get through to me? Honestly?"

His merciless teasing would do me in. "I'm sure it involves therapy and SSRIs."

Cassian's expression darkened. It was like a storm gathered over our heads. Adrenaline shot up my spine, extending the moment into snapshots. Light vanished. Sound disappeared. Alarm widened his gaze.

He body-slammed me.

We crashed. I collided with the ground, pain searing my flesh as it scraped concrete. His arms wrapped me as we rolled, crashing into a fence.

A monstrous roar exploded. It was ungodly, a thousand times worse than nails on a chalkboard. The metallic shrieking sliced my ears, followed by a mighty boom that shook us. I screamed. The fence trembled as he forced me down. Terrible sounds pierced my numb shock until a ringing blocked everything but my heartbeat.

Strong arms lifted me to a sitting position. I burrowed into warmth, clutching his chest, nose buried in the crook of his neck. I breathed in cedar, shaking as he patted my head, back, and limbs as though searching for injuries. He said things I couldn't make out—my hearing was still broken—and then he palmed my face.

Cassian pulled away, looking younger by a decade. "Rain, are you hurt? *Rain.*"

"What the *fuck* h—happened?"

I tried to stand. He dragged me down.

"Take it easy," he whispered. "Easy."

I winced at a sharp hissing returning to my senses. I looked in its direction. The sound came from an engine spilling purple fluid. From the mound of twisted metal, there was a crumpled hood, a tailpipe, a spinning wheel.

The car had smashed into the utility pole. The whole thing was crushed except for the driver's seat.

Right where I had been standing.

Horror poisoned my stomach.

Cassian stroked my cheek, beckoning my attention. "Are you hurt?"

"No, I'm fine." Blood streaked my jeans, but I didn't know whose it was.

"Let me see."

His gentle hands took my wrist and elbow. He turned my arm, frowning at a long, bloody rash. "Sorry about that."

He was *sorry*? If he hadn't pushed me, I'd be a smear on the pavement. They wouldn't have had enough of me to scrape into a coffin.

I almost died. If it weren't for Cassian, I would be dead.

He unpacked his first aid gear.

Tears flooded my vision. "You saved my life."

"Yeah, I did. I guess that means you owe me a pie."

The longer he held my gaze, the more my heart warmed. I couldn't fight it.

He was gravity, and I was caught in his pull.

Chapter Six

Cassian

I WAS A FUCKING MESS.

The car accident was the wake-up call I needed. Rain and I were headed for a wreck that rivaled yesterday's collision. If I tangled with a senator's daughter, I risked losing my career, the goodwill I'd earned with Richard, my reputation—*everything*.

I'd wanted paparazzi to capture our affair and destroy that bastard's campaign. When I accepted the job, I didn't give a fuck about the fallout. My world was already shattered.

The inferno had scarred my hands, but the aftermath had dealt the killing blow. Time didn't heal. It strangled hope. One by one, my dreams had vanished like the smoke that spiraled into the cloudless sky from my broken life. Eventually, the knife in my chest hit home.

I gave up.

I surrendered, and scar tissue spread to my heart. I'd screened my father's drunken calls. I'd stopped pretending to be a cop and enrolled in the executive protection specialist school. The work satisfied me, and sometimes I went weeks without thinking of the episode.

Then I accepted this job.

Senator Montgomery expected reports on his daughter's mundane activities. I forced myself to smile and pictured his agony when he realized I'd fucked his daughter, but even that lost its appeal.

I couldn't bring myself to hurt her, and the contact with Montgomery ripped the old wound open. Staying here rotted my insides, but abandoning Rain wasn't an option. Not now.

Deal with it, pussy.

I grabbed my phone and called Montgomery. He'd stayed in D.C. for the weekend, so at least I didn't have to look at him.

Chaos boomed through the speaker. "Senator Montgomery. This isn't the best time."

"There was an incident with Rain. Car accident."

"Do I have to fly back?" Resignation weighted Montgomery's words, not the blinding panic I'd have expected from a parent.

"She's okay, aside from a few scratches."

"How did this happen?"

I shifted the cell to my other ear. "The driver was under the influence."

"Of course. If there's one thing San Francisco doesn't lack, it's stoners and slackers." He relayed the news to a staffer. "How is she?"

Vulnerable. Lonely. Desperate for your attention. "A little shaken, but all right."

"Was there any press at the scene?"

How should I know? "No idea. I was helping your daughter."

Senator Montgomery's voice muffled as he spoke to someone on his end. "Get Lance to contact Mothers Against Drunk Driving. I'll promise them support for their endorsement. Also, find a photo of the wreck. Let's post it on Twitter and Facebook." Montgomery returned to the conversation. "Do you have anything else to report? Any fires I need to extinguish?"

You already did, you piece of shit.

I could've wrapped his throat and squeezed the breath out of him. He deserved to choke for air.

"Everything's fine."

"Good," he breezed without a trace of concern. "We have a major event next month, so I'd like you to make travel arrangements for Rain."

"I don't think she should attend. I've screened her mail,

and I'm concerned about a recent threat." I stooped over my desk and yanked open the drawer, grabbing the printed message that had been shoved into the mailbox. "It was very detailed."

"I'm sure, but I can't cancel this appearance."

"Sir, it would be unwise to go ahead."

"Noted." He ground out the word. "My security firm assured me they would take every precaution."

"Senator, your daughter's life is at stake. Is that worth gambling with?"

Static crackled until Montgomery's coolness broke through. "I've made my decision. She comes to the charity gala."

"Give me clearance to the event. I'll keep her safe."

Silence filled the other end. Montgomery wasn't in the habit of taking orders from the help. "Your services won't be necessary."

A click announced his departure.

I gaped at the blank screen as rage rippled through me. My stomach churned when people disregarded my expertise, but this was disturbing. Jeopardizing Rain's safety for a photo op?

He didn't *care*.

Rain's sweet smile materialized from the darkness, and my knuckles whitened on the phone.

The purple-haired beauty stood on my porch, her willowy shape wrapped in a jean jacket and black tank top. Midnight skinny jeans glided down her legs and gripped her ass. Her grin widened as I leaned against the doorframe, playing it cool even though I could've yanked her inside.

"For you." She offered me a round dish.

I tore my gaze from her pout. "What's this?"

"Turnips." She grinned, and then rolled her eyes. "It's a pie, silly. You know, for saving me."

Yesterday flashed through my mind in a montage of unpleasant images, but what stayed with me was her horror. All teenagers thought they were invincible, until they weren't. I'd realized that way before nineteen.

"You didn't have to do this." As I took the dish, we brushed fingers. A jolt ran down my belly. "I was joking about you owing me."

Pink patches burned her cheeks. If she didn't have a crush on me before, she had one now.

Good. Hot and bothered was easier to handle. "Thanks. I'll have a piece after dinner."

"Oh, it's not a dessert. I stewed ground pork and veal in beer, and added mashed parsnip with a bunch of spices."

Damn. That sounded up my alley.

"I can't remember the last time anyone cooked for me." Steam from three slits in the golden crust spiraled into my nose. "Smells incredible."

"You should eat while it's warm. It's low-carb. Honest to God. I went on a paleo forum and everything."

She was trying so hard, and it was cute. Really cute.

"You don't owe me anything. A simple 'thank you' is enough."

Rain shrugged. "It's no big deal."

I studied the uneven crimping of the crust. "First, it was scones. Then it's a meat pie. If I save your life again, what's next? A roasted pig?"

Rain pretended to ruminate. "Maybe I'll make Beef Wellington. Or brisket. But you'd have to do something truly over the top."

"I'd throw myself in front of a bus for free barbecue."

She laughed.

I backed into the door. "Come in."

Rain strolled inside, her flip-flops smacking the floor. She followed me into the kitchen and drifted to the houseplants. Her fingers brushed the soil. She tsked as she watered them.

I inhaled cloves and garlic; the tantalizing aroma would've dragged Quentin from his room. "You're lucky Quentin isn't here."

She arched an eyebrow. "Why?"

"Because he'd demand you bake him one, too."

"You could share."

I sure as hell wouldn't. "He's not getting a crumb."

She heaved a sigh, slipping the jacket from her shoulders to fling it over a chair. "You're such a caveman."

"You can't expect me to behave when you bring me food. Especially while looking like that." I slid the dish on the table, facing the far more delectable Rain. "You're too sweet."

A shy smile curved into her apple cheeks as I approached, backing her against the counter. Heat licked me where she stared.

Her hand flew to her throat. "Cassian, you can't."

"Can't what?"

My hands wrapped her tiny waist, and she gasped at the contact. A raspberry-pink flush blossomed over her breast where a golden string bounced with her heartbeat. I fished out the chain, dragging the embellished R from her cleavage. She'd gone still. I don't think she breathed.

"We shouldn't," she whispered.

"As long as you keep doing this, I'll try my damnedest to get you into bed." I released the necklace, sighing when it slipped between her tits. "You looked in the mirror before you came here, didn't you?"

"I just wanted to thank you."

"So you put this on after spending all day baking." I grinned at her embarrassment. "Rain, you don't have to jump through all these hoops. If you want to fuck, say so."

"I'm not trying to fuck you."

Maybe she was telling the truth. She could barely utter the word.

Rain palmed my pecs and pushed. I obeyed the pressure and backed away, giving her enough space to escape. Instead of leaving, Rain lingered near the doorway. Her gaze followed me as I grabbed two plates and cutlery.

"Eat with me."

"I made it for you. Besides, I baked one for myself already." She joined me when I sat, her husky voice cracking with emotion. "I don't know how to repay you."

"No need. I was doing my job." I didn't bother carving a slice. My fork stabbed the crust, slipping through an ambrosial blend of meat and parsnip. The savory taste demanded bite after bite. I ate like a starving man, demolishing a quarter of the dish. "Wow, this is amazing."

"I'm glad it's okay." Pleasure flushed her cheeks before the color faded to a dull pallor.

"Spit it out."

She frowned. "What?"

"Something's bothering you. Talk."

Rain looked mutinous but sighed. "Cassian, why didn't I see it coming?"

She needed to be comforted, patted on the back, whatever. I was the wrong person for that. "I was paying attention. You weren't. I'm supposed to notice things you don't."

She didn't look soothed. "What if Dad hadn't hired you?"

"Don't go down that rabbit hole, sweetheart." I pushed the pie aside, stuffed. "What-ifs are pointless self-torture. You're fine."

"Has anyone ever complimented your wonderful bedside manner? Because it's world-class."

I'm not here to coddle you. I almost said it, but Rain didn't need a second helping of cold, hard truth. "The car was a Tesla."

"What does that have to do with anything?"

"Teslas are quiet, and the dude was drunk. Sleeping at the wheel. That's not your fault."

She nodded, still looking like she'd shot a puppy. "I have to tell you something." Her eyes slid to mine. "You can't be mad."

"Yes, I can."

"Promise you won't."

I braced myself. "Yeah, I'm not doing that."

"I made plans to visit Mom," she blurted. "Dad okayed it."

Spineless asshole.

He ignored a death threat—strike one. He disregarded my advice again—strike two. Three meant I was done. No way was I compromising my career for someone who kept refusing protection. She ran to Montgomery instead of listening to me. He gave zero shits about whether she lived or died, but I had her best interests at heart.

I wanted to scream. "Overruled."

"That won't work this time." Rain fiddled with the tablecloth, casting me terrified looks. "I'm going."

No, you aren't.

"Pushing boundaries is juvenile." I grasped her chair and stood, towering over her. "Who just saved your life?"

"You."

"Who's in charge of your security, your well-being—hell, your entire schedule?"

She murmured an indistinct word.

"I can't fucking hear you."

"You." A bitter tear rolled down her cheek.

"You're damned right." I bent lower, seething. "And that better sink in because I'm not bowing to you, your dad, or anyone who hasn't been through my training."

Rain bolted upright, lips shaking. "Please, Cassian. I'd made arrangements before yesterday. I have to visit my mother."

"No. This conversation is over."

I headed out of the kitchen, but she blocked my escape. I would've laughed if I weren't so pissed. Did she think I couldn't toss her aside with a single sweep of my hand? She weighed nothing.

"She's the only family I have, and—and I'm lonely. I've never been so isolated. You don't know what that's like."

Yes, I did.

"So that's what this is about?" I gestured to her revealing tank top, and she flushed. "You put on the outfit, bat your eyelashes, cry, and I'm expected to say 'poor you'? I see through this act. I'm not some moron you can manipulate to get your way. If that's all I am to you, then admit it. Tell me, so I can quit."

"God, no. You have the wrong end of the stick. It's not like that at all."

I wheeled her toward the entrance. "You need to leave."

"Wait."

Hell no. My attraction to her had forced me do stupid shit, like pretend to be her boyfriend. This had to stop.

"It's not what you think. I swear."

"You're doing this so I'll reverse my decision about your mom."

"If that were true, why would I manipulate *you*? You're unyielding. There's an easier option. Q."

Fair point.

My head swam with suspicion. "Because you've succeeded once."

"Cassian, you know I like you." Rain's cheeks burned tomato-red at the admission, a promise burning in her potent stare. "You were right. I-I want you, too."

Shaking, she closed the distance between us and grasped my neck. I grabbed her hands, intending to fling them off, but my resolve shattered. Blood stirred in my groin as she slid to my jaw and cupped my face. She dragged me down, angling for a kiss. Without thinking, I seized her hips, fingers digging into her curves. Her breath hissed against my lips as she bounced on her toes.

If she kissed me, I wouldn't be able to stop.

"Leave." I ripped from her grasp. "Go on."

Confused, Rain stepped back. "What? Why?"

Because you're a damned liar. "I'm tired, and I'd like to be alone. Get out."

My rejection shone in her eyes. Pain.

"Cassian, I am sorry."

"No, you're not," I snapped.

But you will be.

Chapter Seven

Rain

Whiskey slicked Cassian's mouth as he slammed back two shots, his face registering zero pleasure. I could've wiped his shining lips, or better yet, *licked* them. He wore cement gray slacks, outclassing every man in the restaurant. A dark blue polo covered Cassian's broad chest, the short sleeves barely containing his biceps. He scowled, but he didn't have to smile. Cassian had the broody-but-gorgeous vibe down pat, scanning the crowd and glaring at anyone who strayed too close.

He looked at me and frowned. Was he annoyed with me? The butterflies in my stomach swooped low. Their wings kicked a whirlwind of desire and confusion. He'd won me over, but I hadn't chiseled through his rock-hard shell.

Finally, he spoke. "What?"

"Are you okay? I've never seen you drink."

"You've also never seen me piss, stroke my cock, or fire my weapon, but I do all those things too."

"Me-*ow*. I'm just asking."

"I don't usually." He growled, averting his gaze to the empty glasses. "Only when I'm goaded past endurance."

He was angry, and I couldn't fault him. Cassian had instructed me to stay away from Travis, and I'd defied him. I'd begged Cassian until he agreed to come on his terms. Meeting my mother at a Tex-Mex restaurant was a fair compromise. Nothing would happen.

"Doesn't do fuck all, anyway." Cassian shoved the drinks aside, hissing. "When are they coming?"

"Any second."

It was the bastard's forty-sixth birthday, and he demanded my chronically in debt mother to take off work. Before my trip to D.C., I wanted to squeeze in another visit with Mom. That meant dragging a grouchy Cassian to a strip mall in Concord.

"Why do you want me here, Rain?"

"Travis expects my boyfriend to be here."

Cassian's mouth twisted, his temper rippling off his shoulders like black smoke. "If I have to sit here for hours and put on a show, you owe me the truth."

I thought that was obvious. "He's not so horrible when you're around. Can you blame me for being selfish?"

"No, I blame you for being naive." Cassian's growl faded to a whisper. "This is a mistake, Rain. People don't change because you want them to."

He was so goddamned sure of that.

"I'm not an idiot. I have a plan. Once my arrangement with Dad is finished, the first thing I'll do is relocate Mom. Get her out of the ghetto and somewhere safe."

He snorted. "How noble of you."

"Are you making fun of me?"

"I'm mocking your faith in your father. You've known him for what, two years? He won't give his ex a dime."

"They're not—they were never together." My cheeks flooded with shame when Cassian's puzzlement grew. "My mom was a flight attendant. They met on a layover in Philadelphia. It was one night. I was an accident."

"Does that bother you?"

Of course it does.

I didn't answer, but Cassian must've read the worst on my face. "It shouldn't. Life is a series of complicated accidents."

"I don't want my entire existence based on a random encounter."

"Why?"

"Because I want a family. I want to belong, really belong, not this pretending whenever my dad's surrounded by voters. He owes me. Mom could've used his help when I was younger. We moved every year because Mom juggled rent hikes and her deadbeat boyfriends. I had to sue my dad just so he'd acknowledge me. Do you have any idea what that's like?"

"No." Pity shined from his gaze. "He's a piece of shit, Rain. A man is defined by his actions, not his promises to his constituents or a string of photo ops."

"At least he's making an effort. Maybe I should be happy."

"Sweetheart, he's not involved because he doesn't care."

Cassian's razor-sharp words cut into me, and his colorless voice dredged tears to my eyes. My throat closed as I slid from the stool.

It was the cruelest thing he'd ever said.

"You're such a jerk." Blinded by mist, I couldn't discern his expression. "All you know how to do is—"

"—save your life. Believe it or not, I'm trying to protect you. You can hate me for it, but I'm right. And I'm out of patience."

I wiped my face, seething. "Leave."

"Excuse me?"

"Go outside. You're in a shitty mood, and I won't let you bring me down or ruin my relationship with my mother. I'll give them some reason you couldn't show."

Cassian stood, looking as angry as I felt. "I am not leaving you alone with him."

"There's a restaurant filled with people if I need help." I sighed with frustration when he looked mutinous. "Stay at the bar. Keep an eye on me from a distance."

"I stand out. They'll see me."

"I don't give a *damn*."

I whirled, nearly crashing into a waitress balancing a tray of drinks. I squeezed into a booth near the windows, the vinyl sticking to my thighs as I slid across the seat. Tacky decorations plastered the walls of the Chili's knock-off, and a Justin Bieber track whined from the speakers.

I avoided searching for Cassian and dried my tears. Crying was pointless, but I couldn't stop. He'd hurt me more than he knew. He was wrong. A bitter man like Cassian saw the world in sepia tones. If he never found love, I wouldn't be surprised.

Two familiar shapes breezed into the joint. I waved to get Mom's attention, hoping my cheeks weren't flushed. She grasped Travis' hand. He spotted me, frowning. I hugged Mom, hating how bony her shoulders had gotten. A white dahlia perched in her raven hair, which twisted in an elegant knot down her robin's egg–blue blouse. She was way too beautiful for the crow beside her.

An Oakland Raiders hoodie drowned him in black cotton. His face burned red, and an aroma of stiff drink followed him like a cloud. His goatee twitched as he took in my appearance. "Hey, Rain. Where's the big guy?"

"Um—he couldn't make it. Last-minute job."

Mom patted my arm, her grin wavering. "You look upset."

"I'm fine." I faced the boozy Travis, working up a smile. "He wishes you a happy birthday, though."

Travis squeezed into the booth with a groan. "Too bad he's not coming. I was looking forward to shooting the shit." He snapped at a passing waitress. "Menus."

Already drunk. *Lovely.*

This would be another painful evening of Mom and me distracting Travis from ordering more drinks. Anger throbbed low in my throat, but I dampened the fire.

"What's new with you?"

"Landlord's a pill," Travis grumbled, cutting across my mother. "Keeps threatening to serve an eviction notice."

"What?" I glanced from him to Mom, panicked. "You're being evicted?"

Mom shut her eyes. "I told you not to bring it up, T."

"She deserves to know her mother is broke." Travis' fiery gaze slid to me. "In case you wanted to help out."

"I wish I could, but I have my hands full."

"With what?" Travis seized his cocktail when the waitress returned with a tray. "When I was your age, I worked all summer to pay my parents' bills."

I seriously doubted that.

"No. That's not happening." Mom faced him, testy. "She's my daughter."

"Jesus, okay." Travis drained the tumbler before grabbing the waitress. "Slow *down*, hon. Don't you see my empty glass?"

The server did, but she also objected to his touch. "Let go of my hand."

Travis obeyed, slapping it into her palm, winking at her. "Get me another, and *she'll* have a Diet Coke."

Classy.

Mom turned crimson at the exchange. "I think you've had enough to drink."

"Bullshit. It's my birthday." Travis opened the menu, looking bewildered. "I'll have the sizzling steak fajitas."

Knowing Mom couldn't afford the rent, I ordered a side salad. She squinted at me. "That's all you're having?"

"I'm not hungry." It wasn't a total lie. Travis' presence had ruined my appetite.

"Order food, Rain. It's my treat."

Why did she do this?

Why pretend everything was fine?

Oblivious, Travis smacked the table. "Babe, she said she wasn't hungry. Let her starve."

The harassed server brought more rum. He barked after her. "Where's our chips and salsa?"

Alcohol slipped down his pointed chin as he drank, too wasted to drive home, but he'd pitch a fit if anyone took his keys. I dreaded the end of the night when I'd have to call the police—again—to tell them he was drunk driving.

A pitiful bowl of iceberg lettuce and shredded carrots sat in front of me. I picked the tasteless leaves as Mom stabbed her entree with zero interest. Travis noticed nothing. He gulped alcohol, swore, and made passes at me.

When Mom excused herself to the bathroom, Travis seemed delighted to have me alone and in his crosshairs. "You look beautiful, hon."

Knowing this was a prelude for even worse commentary, I stayed mute. If I didn't talk, he couldn't find ammunition to hurt me.

A sympathetic frown replaced his indifferent expression. "How's your relationship with Cassian?"

"*Fine.*"

I winced at my tone.

Travis was a bloodhound for weakness, and his grin widened like a shark. "Uh-oh. I hope you're not fighting."

"We're not," I ground out. "Thanks for your concern."

"To be honest, I am worried. You'll never get a better man."

I stared at the table, refusing to rise to the bait.

"You're a leech," he rasped. "A lazy, entitled teenager without a lick of sense. Marie is lucky I'm here. I'm saving her from you."

Flames crawled up my legs and consumed my skin. An

awful impulse seized me. I wanted to lash out—to tell him what I thought of him.

He was the fucking drain.

"Nothing to say?" Travis snorted, shaking his head. "The silent treatment. You are such a sullen brat."

"No, I'm not."

"You are." Travis' gaze slanted with malice. "And you're a terrible daughter. You won't help your mom."

I stabbed at a leaf, imagining it was Travis' face.

"The apple falls far from the tree."

His words sliced through a chink in my armor, cleaving my heart in two. My flesh burned. Tears slipped down my nose, splattering the wood. I'd never liked the taste of alcohol, but I'd drown myself in a vat of booze if it numbed me from this. Before now, I never understood why people hid from pain. Appreciating life was impossible without pain. But there was no beauty in this. Especially when my mother stood a foot away, white-faced. She'd heard the whole conversation.

I glared at her. "How can you be with him?"

Mom flinched against the accusation. She opened her mouth as a smooth voice cut across her.

"Sorry I'm late." Cassian slid into the booth, wrapping an arm around my shoulders. "Hey, babe."

He kissed my cheek, and the shock of something so wonderful forced a sob from me. I crushed a napkin against my face as Cassian rubbed my back.

"What the hell happened? Rain?" Cassian cupped my cheeks and took in my agony, his menace zeroing in on Travis. "What the *fuck* did you do to my girlfriend?"

Travis shrugged, regarding Cassian warily. Even in his liquored state, he must've known Cassian would destroy him.

Darkness rippled from Cassian. He balled his fists, his scars whitening, his jaw ticking with tension. "I asked you a question. I expect an answer."

"Nothing," Travis said, avoiding his gaze. "She's overly emotional."

"Insult my girl again, and you'll see what happens when I'm *overly emotional*." Sliding from the seat, Cassian hugged me and pushed me toward Mom. "Wait for me outside." Cold fury blasted from Cassian as he wheeled to Travis. "Not you. You stay there."

I passed Mom, grabbing her when she showed signs of wanting to interrupt.

She fought my grip as I charged us through the glass doors. "Slow down. You're hurting me."

"He's a bastard," I snarled. "Why do you tolerate him?"

Mom shook, looking over her shoulder at Travis. "What do you think he's doing?"

Killing him, hopefully. "I don't give a shit. And neither should you."

"Rain, he's my boyfriend." She tried to search for them through the windows. "He's not—he's not all bad."

I dragged her attention back to me "You heard him. Don't pretend you weren't behind him. You didn't stand up for me. Why?"

Mom looked on the verge of crying. "Sweetie, it's complicated."

"That's a shitty excuse."

"I love him. I didn't want to fall for him, but I did. He takes care of me. I know it doesn't seem like it, but he does."

"No, he manipulates you."

"That's an exaggeration—"

"Look what he's done to us! We never used to fight, and now we spend all our time arguing over that lousy drunk." I grasped her arms as a sob wracked my chest. "I want my mother."

"Babe, I'm always here for you."

"Only when he allows it. What if I stop coming over?" I released her, shaking. "What if I disappear from your life?"

A tear slid down her cheek. "What?"

"If you keep dating him, that's what'll happen. You have to choose. Him or me." I refused to cave as Mom pleaded. "It should be an easy decision. Him or me."

"I can't," she whispered, tears falling like rain. "I can't."

A hand gripped my shoulder, gently tugging. His

thumb dug into a knot. His scarred flesh would've horrified some, but it gave me a wave of relief.

Mom abandoned me on the sidewalk. Watching her rejoin Travis' side was a knife twisting in my heart. It hurt more than anything Travis had said.

Cassian took my hand. He squeezed, and I followed the pressure. I stared at the ground as agony shook from me. A breeze dried my cheeks as we headed to the parking lot.

He joined me in the backseat of the car. "Do you want to talk about it?"

Emotion tightened my throat. I didn't need to hear that he'd told me so. Honestly, I wanted solitude.

"Rain," he prompted.

"Please go." My voice shuddered even though I was determined to be firm. "I can't always be bubbly."

Cassian crossed his legs at the ankles, his slacks revealing an inch of coarse, dark hair. His heartbreaking beauty twinged my chest. He'd rejected me the other day. I'd tried to kiss him, and he pushed me away.

"You were right. She won't leave him."

Sympathy burned from his ocean eyes. "I'm sorry."

"I've been through so much with Mom. It hurts. How could she pick him over me?"

"She loves you, Rain. But...some people are bad at love."

Wasn't that the truth? "Will she ever come back to me?"

"I don't know."

A wave of misery crashed over my soul. "What did you say to him?"

"I put the fear of God into him."

I laughed through my tears. "Why?"

He grabbed my palm. "Because he hurt you."

No light shined in this darkness, but a glimmer of hope sparked when I held his hand. Happiness was possible, but I had to choose it.

Slowly, I crawled into his lap. Cassian stiffened as I linked my arms around him. As though afraid I'd bolt, he wrapped me in a fierce embrace. My head sank into the space between his armor and neck, craving his warmth. Cassian stroked me, gripping my body like he needed this, too. I sagged into him as I let him hold me, accepting his comfort.

His hair tickled my forehead. His mouth hovered close, his sigh feathering over my skin. Cassian's thumb brushed my cheek, and then he pressed his lips to mine.

I seized his jacket and pulled him tight. His mouth caressed mine before he angled his head and deepened the kiss. My heart pounded as his full lips seared, nipped, and claimed me. I swept my tongue across his, Cassian filling my senses. His cedar scent surrounded me.

Cassian raked my head, smoothing my lilac mane to

cradle the small of my back. He shoved us closer, so much passion pouring from him that I didn't understand how I'd ever found him cold.

He moaned into me like I was his first breath of air. I leaned into him, kissing him fiercely. Desire fluttered within me like a hummingbird's wings. I had imagined this many times, but I'd never given an inkling of thought to how I'd *feel*.

Safe.

Free.

Kissing him triggered an avalanche. Bliss crashed down, obliterating my misery. I unbuttoned his shirt, my hands seeking his skin because—God, I needed more of him *now*. I grabbed the thick barrier between us, yanking on his body armor.

Cassian moved back, rewarding me with a glowing smile. He'd never looked so happy. It suited him. He tangled his fingers in my hair and pulled.

"I want to touch you," I sighed.

"I want to let you." He tortured me with another soft, barely there kiss. "Not here."

I closed my eyes when his breath tickled my lips, but when I leaned forward I tasted nothing but air.

Chapter Eight

Cassian

I HATED ANNIVERSARIES.

Every April twelfth, I relived the nightmare. My subconscious dragged me through burning halls. I choked on acrid smoke, and I broke the bonds tying me. Horror clawed my stomach as I searched the house, finding a door ringed with fire. Flames everywhere. Bright orange ate the carpet and walls, crawling over a pink comforter—

Stop it.

I couldn't. It didn't matter if I blocked it out, booked my schedule solid, or tried to convince myself it was the thirteenth. Nothing worked. Today was always the worst. Suffering was inevitable.

Sometimes I binged through comedies and drank, or I

reflected. Most anniversaries, though, I allowed myself to feel. It proved I was human. That redemption was possible.

I rolled out of bed and ignored the horrifying reel in my mind. A chime blasted from my cell as I tossed dirty dishes into the sink. Richard's name blazed across the screen. I usually steered clear of people, but it might've been important.

I answered. "Hey, Rich."

"Hi," he said, water running in the background. "I'm cooking mahi-mahi and kimchi. Want to come over?"

I couldn't see anyone. "No thanks. I have plans."

"No, you don't, liar. Q told me it was your day off."

"You got me," I sighed. "I'm under the weather."

"Your lies are becoming worse, not better. You need to up your game, bro." Richard hissed. "You should hang out. Vicki's doing a chick flick marathon weekend with her friends. I could use the company."

Lead settled into my throat. "Thanks, but no."

"All right, but you can't avoid me forever." Richard coughed as his stove sizzled and spat. "So, how are things? You—ah—getting along with the client's girl? Is she a pain in the ass?"

"She's all right," I muttered, opening the fridge. "She made me pie."

Which was gone. Despite the note claiming it as mine, Quentin stole a slice. *Thieving bastard.*

"I figured you'd have begged me to reassign you by now. Interesting."

"What is?"

"You rubbing elbows with a senator's kid. From my experience, kids of politicians are the worst. Entitled little shits, harping on about being the son or daughter or so and so."

"She's not like that," I admitted, grabbing a carton of egg whites. "She's pretty cool."

Richard inhaled sharply. "Did you just...compliment her?"

"Let's not make a big deal out of it."

"I feel like I should." Awe crept into Richard's voice. "Who would've guessed she'd thaw Cassian's ice heart."

"Spare me." I banged a skillet onto the counter, thought better of it, and drank the egg whites. "I'm not thawing."

"You are. I saw the photograph, Cass. You and Rain."

Of us kissing?

My stomach lurched. "What?"

"I texted it to you, which you'd know if you bothered to keep in touch." Richard broke off, coughing. "Stupid throat."

I thumbed through the text messages, finding an image of Rain and me walking through Concord, my arm draping her shoulders. The photo captured her misery as I led her from her mother. The attached article didn't comment on the bodyguard's unprofessional proximity, but Richard had noticed. A heart emoji accompanied the picture, followed by a wink.

Awesome. "I see it."

"Give me the juice, you sly dog." Richard sounded more intrigued than forbidding. "Tell me everything."

"Nothing to tell. She was upset. I comforted her."

More silence. "Really?"

"What was I supposed to do? Ignore her?"

"Yeah. What does a rich senator's daughter have to cry about?"

A lot. "She has no one to talk to, and her mother's boyfriend is an abusive dick."

"Well, well, *well*. Look at you, getting all protective."

"It's my job. She's nice." My unjustifiably angry voice boomed in the kitchen. "I like her. Is that a crime?"

"Anything that gets you to open up is great. I wish she weren't our client's daughter."

Too late. Already crossed that bridge. "Whatever."

"This is the longest conversation we've had in months, and it's about a girl. I think it's good she's rubbing off on you."

"Will you shut up?"

"If you come over and hang out, I won't pester you with questions."

"No," I barked. "I'm hanging up."

"Wait—"

I ended the call, hating how well he read me. He was right. I changed when I was with her.

Rain.

Kissing her was reckless and stupid. It was also the highlight of my week.

Fuck that, highlight of my *year*.

The way she'd responded felt brand new. Her lips were petal-soft.

And God, she was so eager.

It blazed a line of arousal down my chest and torso straight to my stiffening cock. Pulling away from her swollen mouth and hands as she was trying to rip my clothes off was a challenge. Driving with a raging hard-on was even more difficult. We didn't talk about the kiss, and I worried it gave her the wrong idea.

I wanted to fuck Rain, but I refused to hurt her.

It would never amount to anything more than a fling.

I drifted from the kitchen, stomach growling with raw egg whites that would probably give me salmonella. I sat through five minutes of TV before giving up and tossing the remote aside.

Pathetic.

I couldn't handle one fucking day inside my head.

A gentle tap echoed. My attention lurched toward the half-drawn shades where the curtains warped a silhouette.

Please don't be her.

"Cassian? It's me," Rain shouted. "Open up."

I worked up the willpower to kick her off my porch because I couldn't be around her while memories ravaged my soul. I yanked the door.

Her radiance smothered my resolve like water on flames. A dress wrapped her petite body. The fabric was a burnt orange that clashed beautifully with her purple hair. Frilly sleeves brushed her shoulders, and her neckline dipped so low it invited my tongue. Rain stepped closer, her lips a vibrant red that also begged for a kiss.

Goddamn it.

"You called in sick, so I made something." Rain's brilliant smile flattened the longer she held my gaze. "What happened?"

She carried a covered bowl.

"Nothing." My grip tightened on the doorknob. "I'm not feeling great."

Alarm raised her brows. "I can tell. You look sad."

Thank you, Captain Obvious. "Nope. I'm sick."

Rain pushed past me, squeezing inside. "I'd believe that more if you faked a cough, and even then I'd be skeptical."

"Please go away." God, I *sounded* depressed. "I mean it, Rain."

"I'll just be a second," Rain said, beaming. "Promise."

Whatever.

I didn't have the heart to force her outside, especially when she brightened the space. Rain strolled into the kitchen like she lived there and slid the bowl over the table.

"Chicken soup for your nonexistent cold."

She had no boundaries, but I was hungry.

I yanked my hand away from the hot bowl I dared graze with the tip of my finger. She grabbed a spoon from a drawer, dropped it beside the dish, and ripped the plastic off the top. Steam spiraled in lazy circles, filling my lungs with ambrosia and warmth.

Why was she so kind?

"Rain, you're not my girlfriend. You don't have to do this."

"I know I'm not," she sighed. "I like cooking for people. It makes me feel good."

I didn't want to argue. "Thank you."

The smile fell off her face. "No smartass remark?"

"I don't have it in me today. Just go."

Wearing a sympathetic frown, Rain sat next to me. She rubbed my shoulder. "What's wrong?"

"Nothing." I forced a grin and tried the soup.

Creamy, golden liquid welled, burying the spoon. The savory flavor of a carrot lump sizzled my tongue but failed to give me pleasure.

"Cassian, I hate seeing you like this."

"I'm off the clock. Entertaining you isn't on my list of priorities. If you have something to say, say it." Resigned to her presence, I ate. "It's delicious."

"Careful. You're in danger of becoming a nice guy."

I snorted. "Maybe it sucks, and I'm powering through it to get in your pants."

She arched an eyebrow. "Then I guess you've made decent progress on your goal. Bravo."

Nothing I said would turn her away. She drew closer with every exchange. Rain clutched my neck, fingers tickling my skin. "You have a beautiful heart. Stop pretending."

She was wrong. "You're mistaking lust for decency."

"You can talk to me."

She was joking, right? Doe-eyed, innocent Rain couldn't fathom my misery, and explaining it to her would rip her apart. She'd never see the world the same again.

I wouldn't do that to her. "Did you come over to talk about feelings? Because the door is there."

"Honestly, Cass," she drawled. "This alpha male posturing is beneath you."

Pain lashed my face. "Please don't."

"Don't what?"

"Call me *Cass*. Ever. I can't stand hearing it from you."

Puzzlement shined from her gaze. "Why?"

"None of your concern."

"But I am concerned, so spill."

I groaned, frustrated by this woman's relentless prying and my inability to carry her outside. "Not everyone is a free-loving hippie who shares private details."

"Why do you act like a cold jerk?"

"Why do you pretend to be cheerful?"

"I'm not faking it," she insisted. "I *am* happy."

"*Right*. You have a shitty father and an even worse stepdad."

"Ugh, they'll never get married. He's my mother's flavor of the year. Her infatuation with him will pass."

I finished the soup by ripping off a chunk of bread to soak up the juices.

"I made the stock. I might as well use my dad's state-of-the-art kitchen because nobody else will. Karen can't fry an egg to save her life." Rain fiddled with her hair. "Thank you for standing up for me. Again."

"Always count on it, Rain."

I never said her name like *that*, with a caress as smooth as velvet. Rain noticed. She straightened. Then she reached for me. Her fingers laced with mine, squeezing so hard my skin blanched. Rain's thumb brushed my knuckles, the sensation torturous because I couldn't reciprocate.

"Talk to me, Cassian. You were there for me. Please let me be there for you."

Air vanished from my chest as my last defenses crumbled, no match against her compassion. My disgusting scars wrapped her flawless skin as I gripped her.

"My sister called me Cass. She died today, sixteen years ago."

"I'm sorry." Pain flickered across Rain's features. "What was her name?"

"Claire." I resisted the tug of memories. "I love her. I never moved on."

"What happened?"

Bright orange flashed over Rain's tense face, and I shut my eyes against the image. "I won't talk about it. Ever."

"Okay. I just want to help."

"I know you do, but reliving the past doesn't make it better."

"You don't have to carry the burden alone." Rain leaned closer, kissing me. A tear from her cheek transferred to mine. I almost smiled. Rain had so much empathy that she cried over someone she never met.

"I'd never do that to you." I ran my fingers along her jaw, sinking them into her silky hair. Vanilla clung to her and the scent intoxicated me. "My story would fuck you up, sweetheart. It'd destroy you, and the world's bad enough as it is. It needs more people like you, not me."

"That's not true. *I need you.*"

That did it. My last thread of resistance snapped.

I yanked her forward and pressed my mouth to hers. Our lips clashed as I dragged her onto my lap, hands wrapping her ass. I stood as Rain caught my shoulder and gasped.

Weeks of pent-up attraction burned, obscuring everything but her. We bumped into a side table and a wall, knocking a picture frame to the floor. I grinned into her kiss. She grabbed my waist, bucking against me as my tongue swiped her mouth.

God, she wanted to be fucked so badly. Her frenzy proved that she'd told the truth.

I need you, too.

I pulled her tighter, deepening the kiss. She groped my chest and slid up, cupping my cheeks. She moaned as I sucked her delectable lip and nipped it. We migrated closer to my bedroom. My spine hit the door before my subconscious slammed on the brakes.

Not now.

Right place. Wrong fucking time.

Sighing, I let her slide to the carpet but held her close. Rain dove into the crook of my neck. I tucked her head under my jaw, wishing I could squeeze her inside of my heart. She was made for me. Every curve fit into my embrace, singed my nerves. Her hands glided as she swept up, fingers grazing my collar. Her sigh blasted my skin as she dug into my hair.

"I'm so sorry for what happened."

I pulled from her grasp. "I don't need your pity."

"Not trying to give you any."

She was a rose growing deep within soil, seeking cracks to spread her intoxicating happiness. She soothed me without touch. The urge to drag her over my bed sheets gnawed at me.

I wanted her so badly I could scarcely breathe. "Sunshine. That's your real name."

"Why?"

"Because you're not rain. You're sunlight."

I'd never call her Rain again.

Chapter Nine

Rain

IF I WAS SUNSHINE, Cassian was lightning.

When he met my gaze, the air between us changed like the crackling in the air before a storm. Desire struck me. It charged me with a strange obsession.

I smiled into my pillow every night, tossing, turning, and thinking of the kiss that could've been more. My dreams took it further. Waking from them became torture, and so did sharing his presence.

Cassian gave no hint we'd enjoyed anything more than a pleasant conversation. I expected a text. A wink. Something. Maybe I was one of his hookups. Perhaps he only liked the chase or he was sick of me.

God, it consumed me—even as we idled in a car

beside my father's private plane. Visiting my dad meant I had to fly, which terrified me. I'd rather spend that time licking concrete than board an airplane. My bodyguards had spent the last hour inundating me with statistics. When that failed, an impatient silence smothered the SUV.

Cassian hunched in the passenger seat, brows furrowed as he browsed a classic car restoration forum. He switched off the cell and jammed it into his pocket. Huffing with obvious boredom, he looked at me through the rearview mirror.

His cobalt blues narrowed. "How much longer do you need?"

Quentin stopped drumming the steering wheel and shot a glare in Cassian's direction. "Asking that every five seconds doesn't help."

"Neither does sitting here." Cassian's sigh raked fire down my spine. "She needs to grit her teeth and do it."

"No problem. I'll hand-wave a lifetime of paralyzing fear, and we'll be on our way." For an emotionless rock, flying was no big deal, but even just looking at the damned jet gave me heart palpitations. "Sound good?"

"Perfect," Cassian drawled. "Let's go."

"It's been thirty minutes." Quentin turned, golden hair cascading in his face. "Ready?"

Horror gripped my stomach as he motioned toward the drenched concrete where the plane waited. It glistened in the emerging sun, the staircase rolling from the airplane to the tarmac.

"I'll never, *ever* be ready. Just less terrified." I balled my fists until nails pierced my skin. "People willingly climb into these things. That boggles my mind. Nothing separates you from a horrible death but a couple of pilots and a strip of steel."

"And physics." Cassian released a derisive snort. "They review dozens of preflight checks. Get over it."

"I can't. I'm scared."

"You have better chances of dying from a bee sting," Cassian grumbled. "Or having your neck broken."

I'd heard it before. It made no difference.

"No other form of transportation is as monitored as commercial aviation." Quentin swatted my knee, his playful grin widening. "You'll be fine. I promise."

"I know." I spoke around the lump in my throat. "The storm worries me, though."

"That's drizzle, not a storm. It's safe." Cassian held up two fingers. "Scout's honor."

I'd hoped he'd say otherwise. "I won't take any unnecessary risks."

"Says the girl who threw a tantrum when I canceled her concert because of safety concerns." Cassian fidgeted in his seat, his patience waning. "Are we doing this or not? Every hour we waste is another four hundred taxpayer dollars."

Quentin grimaced. "Way to be a total dick."

"If I'm cranky, it's because my ass is falling asleep." Cassian glanced into the rearview mirror. "We've gotta go."

Nausea lashed my stomach. "I'm trying to work up the courage."

Quentin opened the door, throwing his legs outside. "I need to stretch." He swept from the Lexus, his jacket blowing open as he stepped onto the windy tarmac.

My attention snapped to Cassian, whose ocean eyes pinned me to the leather. Disapproval radiated from him.

"*What?*"

His eyebrow arched. "Are you that scared?"

"*Yes.* Fear of flying is common, especially when you've never done it before."

Ironically, I once had the opportunity to fly to D.C. for a class trip, but I'd chickened out. Never thought I'd have the money to travel, so I followed people on Instagram who made it their job. Drooling over their photos took the sting from never traveling.

Cassian's forehead wrinkled in confusion, as though I spoke in a foreign language. "You'll live."

"When we land, I'm finding the thing you dread most in the world and shoving you into a room filled with it. Then we'll see how brave you are."

"Good luck with that." He smirked, reaching for the handle. "Let's go."

"Give me a moment."

"You've had more than one." Cassian left his seat and yanked my door. "Outside. *Now*."

A blast of cold air stung my cheeks. I drew my legs together, frozen. He grabbed my shoulder. When I refused to move, he snarled.

"Come *on*. The longer you make us wait, the worse California's deficit gets."

I shot him a glare. "That was mean."

"Just trying to get your ass moving." His mouth tugged into a wicked smile. "I've tried the stick. I suppose it's time for the carrot."

I was about to ask what the hell that meant, but was struck dumb as Cassian stooped into the car.

"There's a bed on the plane, Sunshine."

Jesus. "Meaning what?"

"I'm not suggesting we join the Mile High Club, but there are plenty of things we could do."

I said nothing, hoping to discourage him, but Cassian was bolstered. His knuckles grazed my chin as though he found my behavior cute.

"Two days ago, I pried you off my cock. I'd be amazed if that slipped your mind for ten minutes."

He was right.

I told them I wanted to see my father in D.C. early. Honestly, I couldn't stand another second alone with Cassian. Now that I'd made out with my bodyguard twice, I needed to leave. Staying in San Francisco was courting disaster, but it didn't matter where I ran. Cassian's hands and soft lips haunted me.

"Why do you believe that?" I asked.

"Because it's been on mine nonstop. Ever since you looked at me with those big, pretty eyes, I knew. You and I are inevitable. We're destined to fuck, darling."

"Careful. I'll swoon and hit my head. Then you'll have to write a report to Dad."

"Honesty is a virtue, Sunshine."

"Not when you wield it like a toddler with a gun. You have zero self-control."

"If that were true, I would've ripped your clothes off the other day and gone to town on your tight little body."

"*Cassian.*"

He chuckled, pulling away. "Never pegged you for a prude."

"And you weren't supposed to be such a vulgar ass."

"We both want this," he hissed. "Why fight it?"

Why, indeed.

Weeks ago, I pitied that damaged mess wrapped in a suit. When he didn't blaze through my boundaries, his overprotective antics drove me insane. And yet, I couldn't stop fantasizing about him dragging me into his bed. I could've let him, but I was a virgin. He didn't know.

I was too mortified to tell him. "Because you'll get in so much trouble."

"I can handle it."

"I won't be the reason your career is destroyed."

"Not going to happen."

I melted like an ice cube in his palm. "My father will *kill* you."

"Only if he finds out," Cassian countered, a smile hitching on his face. "Even if he does, I'm twice his size. I like my chances."

"Now who's playing dumb?"

"Montgomery doesn't scare me," he rasped. "Nothing does."

I glanced at his scars, unable to say it out loud. *Even fire?*

He noticed my stare, shrugging. "I'm not afraid of fire. Never was."

How is that possible?

Curiosity piqued my interest as I stood beside him, searching his features for a lie. His sister's death gouged his heart. He patched the wound with a Band-Aid. It was a matter of time before something tore it, and then nothing would stem the bleeding. Behind his constructed facade, a reckless fury burned.

"Are you using me to punish yourself?"

Cassian groaned. "My God, Sunshine. You'd make a shit therapist. No, I'm not self-destructive, insane, or careless. I just don't give a damn. You can't hurt if you're dead."

Wow. "That's pure nihilism."

"It's how I've survived all these years."

"It's extremely unhealthy."

"I am telling you *my* truth. It doesn't extend to you." He shut the car door and took my arm, speaking in a low murmur as we walked toward the airplane. "I know I'm fucked up. Learning to live with it is a work in progress. I'm okay with who I am."

How could he be?

Alarm bells warned me to stay away, but I craved him as much as oxygen. He couldn't hold me the way I wanted here, in full view of Quentin and the flight crew, but his gaze smoldered.

"We've already crossed dozens of lines. Might as well finish what we started."

"What *you* started."

"We'll talk more in private. When Quentin falls asleep."

"Are you saying this to get me on the plane?"

"I'm serious." His smirk flattened to the disaffected frown he carried everywhere, but his voice was velvet on my skin. "Let me worry about the consequences."

Cassian palmed my back as I throbbed head to toe. As we climbed the steps to the jet, I thought only of his touch. Five uninterrupted hours with Cassian made me feel just as nervous as walking on the jet. All I knew was confusion and bittersweet warmth. Whatever this was, it couldn't last.

You're not rain. You're sunlight.

I clung to those words, wondering what they meant and why I felt like he'd dipped me in liquid heat. The man was eleven years older and employed by my father. Dad didn't have a say in my love life, but I'd made a lot of sacrifices to appease him. They would be meaningless if I fucked this up.

A flight attendant in a navy skirt and scarf greeted us as we stepped into the interior furnished with cream chairs and a modern sofa pushed against the wall. Quentin took an aisle seat, ears already covered with Dr. Dre headphones. I chose a spot near a window, mashing the button to darken the display as Cassian stowed my luggage. He wore a carelessly buttoned white shirt tucked into denim that gripped his sculpted thighs. The fabric buckled as he sat, revealing a sliver of his sinewy chest. I drank in more details because it was safe to study the angular lines carving his face and his midnight hair, which had the perfect amount of messy curls. Five hours beside him would be a challenge because I couldn't look at him without remembering how he tasted.

"Your cheeks are so red I could fry an egg on them," he chortled. "What's up?"

"My bodyguard propositioned me."

"You make it sound dirty when it's just harmless flirting."

I slipped the buckle over my waist. "You're many things, but harmless is not on the list."

"Don't put out the signals if you can't handle the heat. You kissed me with tongue, and you *loved* it."

So we'd arrived at the kiss. "I got caught up in the moment."

He chuckled. "You sure did."

"It won't happen again."

"Oh, it will. Our hotel rooms are next door to each other." Cassian barely looked up when the waitress offered him a preflight hot towel.

I balled mine in my fist, the warmth burning through several layers of shock. An image flashed through my mind —a shirtless Cassian knocking on my door. In my room, nobody could walk in unannounced. We'd be locked in silence with our undeniable chemistry, and I wouldn't be able to refuse him.

Sitting next to him was torture. "I'm going somewhere else."

"See you later."

Cassian watched as I squeezed past his legs and walked down the aisle. The bedroom was ahead, but fuck that. I sat beside Quentin.

The younger bodyguard removed his earphones and beamed. "Hey."

"Okay if I sit here? Cassian's driving me up the wall."

"That makes two of us." Quentin thumbed his iPhone, shutting off the music. "What'd he do now?"

"The usual."

Quentin reclined his seat, his button-up shirt wrinkled and his sandy waves disheveled, but somehow pulling it off. He rocked a beachy, SoCal vibe. He was the definition of effortless good looks. Dude looked hot in a hoodie and ragged jeans. Handsome *and* nice. A killer combination, but it didn't do it for me.

"Cassian's got a stick up his ass," Quentin drawled, not bothering to keep his voice down. "You're lucky you don't live with him. He's constantly on my case for leaving the kitchen window unlocked, so I started pissing with the door open."

Guys are so weird. "Over a window?"

"He's hella paranoid. Like, I get it. I'm a vet. I've been through hell. Used to have panic attacks at the grocery store. Took me a long time to adjust to civilian life, but Cassian's not ex-military. What's his excuse?"

I glanced at Cassian, whose back faced us. "His scars."

"Do you know what happened?"

I shook my head, deciding against telling him about Cassian's sister. It wasn't my secret to share. "He doesn't talk much."

"Tell me about it," he grumbled. "World's most boring roommate. Has nothing to say unless he's chewing me out for eating his food."

"Typical."

"I've never seen him take a shine to a protectee. The pet name is a dead giveaway." Quentin's electric gaze danced over me. "Not that I blame him. You're easy to like."

"You too, Q." Fear zipped my spine as the seats groaned with the plane's movement. "*Crap.*"

"Try to relax. Don't freak out."

I ground my teeth and shut my eyes, focusing on Quentin's drawl.

"By the way, there's a band coming to D.C. Fleet Foxes."

A sliver of excitement joined the terror. "I *love* them. They're on tour?"

"Yeah. I scored tickets. We could go together."

A concert would break the monotony of D.C. "What about Cassian?"

"We won't tell him. Otherwise the bastard will stop us from attending."

Doubt squirmed in my chest as I met the older bodyguard's glare. He frowned. It was as though he'd read my damned mind.

"I don't know. I'll catch so much shit from him." A fresh wave of hysteria drowned all thoughts of Fleet Foxes as we picked up speed. "This is crazy."

Quentin's soft chuckle fueled my anxiety as he gripped my palm. Calloused fingers brushed against mine, the texture softer than Cassian's damaged skin. Still, it was a lifeline I seized.

My back pressed into the cushion as the jet launched

forward. The wheels lifted as the plane shot into the air at a sharp angle. I cringed at the sudden drop of pressure from the ground, the weight molding me into the seat. Outside, San Francisco shrank into a marble. Then we disappeared into the fog, the oppressive whiteness consuming the wings.

It wasn't that bad.

I released him when the seatbelt sign dimmed. Quentin wrung his wrist, laughing.

"Sorry, but you took my armrest." Shaking with adrenaline, I stood and tried not to whimper like a complete wuss. "I need to dive under some blankets."

"See you later."

My legs were Jell-O as I walked past the sofas and opened the door to a circular room decorated in crème and gold. Plush carpet led to a platform mattress covered with a snow-white comforter and pillow. Drawers glided along the walls, ending at two mahogany nightstands with bolted-in lamps. It was nicer than my old place in Concord. Sandstone tile plastered the adjoining bathroom, which encased a shower. After a couple of years of living in the Presidio Heights mansion, wealth still felt strange.

I chewed my lip as I surfed the news. An article quoted my father condemning a congressman indicted for wire fraud. The charges against him included siphoning his campaign funds to pay for luxury vehicles, lavish vacations, and a jet-setting lifestyle paid for by Ohioan voters. I closed my phone and stowed it.

I threw my ratty purse on the bed and sat, struggling to get a handle on my nerves. My feelings for Cassian stabbed deep. I couldn't stop wanting him, but I *had* to. We were destined for disaster. *You can't hurt if you're already dead.* I mean, Jesus. I knew better than to tangle with that.

He was too dark. And intense.

I pounded my pillow as the adjectives became more complimentary. Filthy-hot. Charming. *Gorgeous.*

A man's throat cleared.

I whirled. I was so lost, I hadn't noticed the door opening and closing.

Cassian stood inside, his shirt untucked and his eyes burning. He pressed a finger to his full lips, grinning. His knee sank into the mattress, his hand dangerously close to my leg.

I yanked the sheets over my body. "What are you doing in here?"

"You and I have chemistry. We're two fireworks crashing into each other." Cassian fixed me with a stare that pooled desire between my legs. "I want you every day and night until my contract is finished. Don't act like you didn't bat your eyelashes the *second* I got here. The scones. The damned pie. You needed to be on my good side so I'd be your fake boyfriend."

Hearing his unfiltered opinion hurt. Cassian had it all

wrong. I did those things because I liked him.

"I don't blame you in the slightest." A smile carved dimples into his handsome face. "But I'm taking it a step further. I want more. Your tits in my hands. Your mouth on my cock. *You*."

I'm a virgin.

Tell him!

"If I refuse?"

"Then find another man to handle Travis. Do we have a deal?"

"No!" I struggled to speak. "I'm not ready to jump in bed with some random dude."

He arched an eyebrow. "We've been hanging out for weeks."

"That doesn't mean we aren't strangers."

"This would be a fling. Sex with no strings," he clarified. "In exchange, you get me. Whenever you like—*plus*—I'll help with your family drama."

"That sounds messy."

"It's reasonable. Having dinner once in a while with that asshole won't kill me."

"No." I drew my knees tight. "That won't work. If it's an arrangement for favors, I'm out. I'm not a *whore*."

"Of course you're not. Does Sunshine sound like a stripper's name?" Cassian chucked me under the chin. "I've told you what I need. Now it's your turn."

"I want this," I said, my arm outstretched toward him.

"*You.* No exchanges. No bartering."

His eyes gleamed. "Fair enough."

"And if we agree to do this, you can never be near my mother and Travis again."

"What—why?"

"Because it's wrong."

Confusion wrinkled his brow. "I'm *offering* my help."

"That's why it's off the table forever. I won't—" I swallowed hard, building up the courage. "I will not have my first time ruined by you."

Cassian pulled away slightly, absorbing my confession. "You're a virgin."

"Yes."

My voice was small, barely a whisper, but he heard me. Cassian moved closer.

His thigh brushed mine as he touched my cheek. "Why would I ruin your first time? I'm not a monster."

"I know, but if—if you're involved with my family, I'll wonder if you're doing it because we're having sex."

"It's not like I haven't helped you before."

"Yes, but it was against your will. I won't be obligated to the guy sleeping with me."

"Are you serious?" His voice darkened when I confirmed. "Why do you have to complicate something so simple? We're attracted to each other. Protecting you is my job."

It wasn't the answer I wanted to hear, and we both

knew it. "Those are my terms. Take it or leave it."

"Are you kidding?"

"Make a choice."

"This is unfair," he growled. "I have to compromise your safety, but you don't have to do anything."

I smiled. "Either way, I win."

"Not if someone hurts you."

"Q will be with me."

"Quentin." Cassian's nostrils flared. "That makes me feel *so* much better."

"He's always been professional. I trust him completely."

"Did he save your fucking life?"

"I'm not doing this to punish you, Cassian. I'm looking after myself. I won't get attached to a man who doesn't do relationships."

He bowed his neck and frowned at my comforter. Finally, he met my gaze. "I accept."

"You—you do?"

"Yes." He swallowed hard, his Adam's apple bobbing. "As long as you understand that I'll never love you."

That hit me harder than I expected. "Fine by me. I don't want love."

His eyebrows arched. "Really?"

"Love wrecked my mom. It's ruined her credit, strained her relationship with me, and might make her homeless. If that's what I'm in for—not interested."

Cassian was silent for several moments, and then he raked his hair. "Wow."

"What?"

"Love *happens*. You can't control when or how." He laughed, shaking his head at me. "The fact you think you can—like it's an infection that needs antibiotics—proves how clueless you are. That's not how it works."

"If that's true, how do you know it won't happen to *you*?"

Cassian looked taken aback. "I'm not capable of it, but you are."

"Whatever. You're not an authority on the subject."

"All that shit with your mom won't happen to you."

"Cassian, I've seen what it can do. No thanks."

"That's so cynical," he whispered. "Sunshine, this isn't like you."

"Stop with that stupid pet name." I'd rather not give Quentin more chances to goad Cassian. "And quit telling me what I am."

"Everything you said contradicts your nature. I don't know who you are anymore." But it didn't seem to bother him at all, because he pulled the sheets off my body and leaned into me. "Who knew the purple-haired chick had a dark side?"

"Everybody does," I teased. "Just like you must have a heart."

His arm wrapped my waist, and I willed my pulse to

slow. I couldn't look into his eyes because I'd fall into them. His hands snaked up my back and seized my hair. I gasped as his sigh blew over me.

"When my boss showed me your picture, I assumed you'd be trouble. I expected a brat, but what I got was *you*." He angled his head for a kiss. "You're not the girl I thought you were. Not even close."

His lips crashed into mine.

Sweet Jesus, yes.

He acted so dead, but here he was passionate. He molded into me, claiming the gasps that escaped. I glided over his knees and lap as I deepened the kiss. Warmth slowly coiled in me as I pressed into his steel pecs, loving the contact of his bare skin.

I licked the corner of his mouth. He dragged my lip between his teeth and sucked until it stung. Then he pushed me backward. I settled into the mattress. Cassian's broadness trapped me, but I'd never felt safer. He'd always protect me.

Always.

I'd never been in bed with a man. It gave me a sharp thrill to yank the buttons hiding his perfect physique. They unlatched, revealing slabs of muscle, carved shoulders, and a deep chest sprinkled with black curls. I skimmed through them, marveling at how manly he was. It must've been so hard to temper all that strength, but Cassian made it look effortless.

He ripped the shirt off and tossed it aside, pausing. "What is it?"

"You're beautiful. That's all."

Most men would've smiled. Cassian's expression flashed dark amusement as he lowered himself to his elbows and traced my jaw. The strange texture of his scars rubbed me. He looked like he ached to touch more of me, but couldn't bring himself to do it. I wanted to show him I wasn't afraid.

I grabbed his finger and stuck it into my mouth. I sucked.

That finally earned me a wide grin. "You sure you're a virgin?"

"Yes." I slid him in and out. "Hours of porn, Cassian."

"So I'll have to smash all your unrealistic expectations." He slipped from my lips and kissed me softly. "I'll go slow."

"Are we—are we having sex?"

"Sunshine, you're not ready to be held down and fucked—not even close. And I'm not taking your virginity in a goddamn plane."

"Cass—"

"Hush. You don't understand what you're begging for."

"They'll hear us, won't they?"

"I don't care." Desire raged a bitter battle with self-control behind his eyes. He grasped my neck as he silently appraised me. Then he grabbed my breasts. The contact startled me. Over my shirt, he drew circles.

"Cass—Cassian."

His soft movements peaked my nipples into nubs, and then he pinched. Sharp arousal tugged near my navel. I moaned, Cassian grinning at my reaction. Slowly, he undid my blouse. His palm flattened over my stomach, my nerves firing all cylinders until he groped my breasts.

The sensation was pure ecstasy. "You feel incredible."

"Just the beginning, darling."

Cassian chuckled as I arched into his hands. I sighed as his chest touched mine, comforted by his warm weight. His bruising kiss shoved his tongue so deep I couldn't inhale. I gasped when he allowed me a respite, kissing my jaw and collar. If I suffocated, that'd be fine. Dying in Cassian's arms seemed like an amazing way to go.

My legs clenched as he slid his knee between them and didn't stop until he nudged my pussy, dialing my pleasure to eleven.

"Cassian. *Cassian.*"

He disengaged from me, breathing hard. "What?"

"You're intense."

"Good or bad?"

"Good," I murmured. "*Too good.*"

"No such thing. Are you too shy to tell me something?"

I was. "No. Okay, yes. I don't want to orgasm."

The room boomed with his laughter. "Why?"

"Because it'll end."

"Oh, Sunshine. You'll come many times before this is over."

He took my head, forcing me to yield to dirtier kisses. Then he caught my hips, massaging my ass before hooking my jeans. Slowly, he undressed me. The last stitch of fabric tore from my legs.

He widened my knees, his voice rolling with bliss. "Such a sweet girl. So wet for me."

I had no time to feel embarrassed because Cassian stroked my naked thighs. He caressed, squeezed, and swept closer. Paralyzed, I waited. He massaged the inner curve and tapped my clit.

A fierce moan burst from me. Cassian smiled into my lips, demanding silence in between kisses. How could I be quiet when I rode an emotional roller coaster? Pleasure skyrocketed from one moment to the next, and I only had Cassian's back and shoulders to cling to.

He moved his fingers in small circles, tapping around the place begging to be fucked. Ecstasy zinged my skin, running its electric current up my spine. I bucked, wanting, needing, *craving* more, but he wouldn't relent.

"Please! I can't take this."

"What a needy girl." Cassian dipped into me and circled to my hood. "This might hurt a little."

A finger slipped inside. Discomfort made me clench, but as he pulsed I loosened. He slid completely out, and the ache throbbed. My walls latched on his finger as he pushed in, wetness gathering as he pumped. Arousal swirled my belly.

I was close. So damned close.

My breath hitched. Cassian fixed me with a heavy-lidded gaze as a sleepy smile staggered across his face.

He was happier than I'd ever seen him. "Come for me."

A second digit joined the first, and both curved as they thrust. My thighs twitched as the wave of anticipation peaked, flooding me with euphoria that sharpened into frustration.

I ground my hips into his hand, all dignity forgotten.

"That's it. Show me how much you want it." Cassian rubbed my clit and yanked off my blouse and bra. Then he leaned forward, his tongue lashing my nipple.

I cried out, slapping my horrified mouth. "Sorry."

"Scream for me, babe. Don't hold back."

Cassian licked my nipples as he worked me ruthlessly, fingers curving into me. A high-pitched whine tore from my throat. Pressure built behind my lids. I came, stifling my cry on my fist. My walls clenched on him, but he wouldn't stop.

"I can't," I panted. "No more."

"You don't decide how many orgasms I give you. Open."

"But it's so dirty."

"Your body is beautiful, not dirty." He stuck a finger between my lips. This time, I opened my mouth. Cassian's eyes fluttered when I sucked. "I wonder if they'd ground the plane if I went down on you."

"Probably," I gasped.

He kissed me again. "Take out my cock."

Shaking, I slid my arms from his neck, wondering how I became someone who not only tolerated demands, but followed them.

His erection strained against his pants as I grasped his bulge. Somehow, he was hotter there than everywhere else. I wrapped my hand around him and caressed his length. Cassian melted into me as I unzipped him. He helped me push his jeans, revealing a bed of trimmed hair. It darkened at his groin, where a large vein ran into his massive penis. I touched him, surprised by the smoothness as I jerked up and down.

He took my palm and guided me. I gripped the base and pumped. Pleasure rippled in his blue flames.

"Fuck yes. Keep going."

He balled his fist in my hair. I made out with him, my face fever-hot. He met my thrusts with lusty rolls of his hips. He bit his bottom lip, taking control. Faster and faster, I worked him as he swelled in my hands until he clutched my wrist and held me still. Cassian groaned, the tension dissolving from his features. Thick ropes of cum shot out, blanketing my body in liquid heat.

He stroked himself, hand over mine, eyes shut. A rapturous peace wiped his expression blank.

When his eyes shone out of half-closed lids, he smiled. It was his first real one. Not a hint of melancholy seeped through.

He looked happy and young as he descended. His fingers dove into my hair as he kissed me, no longer fueled by lust. I responded eagerly, desperate to fill the ache in my chest.

Gradually, he untangled from me. I grabbed his arm, not ready to let go.

Cassian gently disengaged as he dressed. He zipped his pants and tucked in his shirt, his smug, just-came appearance so mouthwatering I could've launched at him.

"Don't leave."

"Miss me already?" he teased. "Staying in your bedroom would be a bit obvious."

"But I want more."

Cassian grinned. "Be good, and maybe I'll visit you in a few days."

"Days?"

He cracked the door and peeked out, swinging back at my indignation. Dimples carved into his cheek before he winked. When he disappeared, I groaned.

If this was how I felt after second base—what would sex with Cassian be like?

Chapter Ten

Cassian

I stayed in her room too long.

My wrinkled clothes screamed guilty, as did my shit-eating grin. So I ducked into the bathroom and hid the evidence. I splashed water on my face, wiping all traces of Rain from my lips. I buttoned my shirt to the collar, covering my flushed skin. My pulse raced as though I was balls-deep inside her, but nobody would know unless they grabbed my wrist.

Insane. I hadn't been this excited over a hand job since I was a teenager.

Get over it.

I couldn't. My cock ached. I resisted the temptation to rub one out and returned to the main cabin. Quentin lounged on the white sofa, chatting with the flight attendant, who shot out of her seat at my approach. He gave the brunette a rakish smile before she zoomed to the back. Then he brought his hands together in a slow, golf clap.

"What?"

Quentin let his arms fall, slapping the leather. "You were in there a while."

"She wanted to talk."

"That's what you're going with?" Quentin's smirk was predatory. "I've lived with you for weeks. You're the world's worst conversationalist. You banged our client's daughter under my nose."

"No, I didn't."

"You're also a terrible liar." Quentin pushed himself upright, an edge creeping into his voice. "And a hypocrite and a huge douche."

Fucking Quentin. The few times we interacted, his demeanor shifted from cold indifference to barely constrained hostility.

"What's your point?"

He bared his teeth. "You're a cock-blocking asshole."

"Pissed that I beat you to the punch? I had no idea you liked her."

"You knew I did." Quentin stood, tossing his red earphones aside. "The concert was supposed to be our thing, and you swooped in like an overprotective boyfriend and fucked me. You're not her boyfriend. You're the help."

"So are you, dumbass."

"Give me one good reason I shouldn't go to Montgomery as soon as we land in D.C."

"The girl is mine. You lost."

His tanned face widened with a grin. "What makes you think I'm done with her?"

I saw myself throwing him against the wall in a chokehold. "I'm not dating her. Neither are you."

"Oh, so you only want to bang her. I wonder how she feels about that."

"It's none of your damned business."

"When you screw up and hurt her because you're *you*, I'll be there." He winked. "She'll need a shoulder to cry on."

"And you'll need a surgeon to fix your face after I break it."

"I'm amazed at how deluded you are. Can you teach me to ignore reality, too?"

"The hell are you babbling about?"

"You know what I mean." Quentin closed the distance between us, his features thick with rage. "You got on my case for getting too close with a client. I was jobless for a year because of you."

"You beat her ex into the hospital."

"Like that piece of shit didn't deserve it. I did the right thing."

"You went overboard." The photos of the guy after the

beating weren't pretty. "Sunshine isn't yours to mess with. Drop her or I'll make you."

"Listen to you," he chuckled. "You're drooling over her like a dog."

I brushed past him and returned to my seat, refusing to let him ruin the glow of coming over Rain's perky tits. Light from the window warmed my skin. It was all down to her. The way she kissed me, gripped my cock, and later my arm when I had to leave.

God, I needed her again. I was a man clawing desert sand for water, and she was an oasis. For the first time in years, I felt good.

Good enough to look at Quentin and smile. "I don't care what you think."

∼

Senator Dickhead gave me a bonus for saving his daughter's life. He slipped the bill into my hand after meeting us at the hotel. Fifty bucks. I wondered if Montgomery's constituents knew what he thought his daughter was worth.

Not much, apparently. Despite the threat assessment report from his security firm, he'd doubled down on attending the photo op, which was more about milking money from the senator, but still. A slew of articles reporting on an indicted congressman for wire fraud had Montgomery shaken.

Seeing him rattled was nice. I never had the support of millions of disenfranchised people I could access with a Facebook post. The sharks were closing in.

I strolled the Potomac, sidestepping joggers and tourists as I headed to the National Mall. Pink blossoms were piled under trees lining the river.

Concession stands filled the air with salt and sugar. A food truck beckoned me with roasting meat, the warm breeze carrying a dozen scents. Maybe I'd eat lunch while considering my next move. I moved from the walking path and headed toward the line of trucks standing on the green, and then a flash of purple stole my attention. A woman in cutoffs and a blouse patterned with small blue anchors burst into giggles. She held a hand to her deep red lips, trying to stifle her mirth as the man beside her grinned.

Rain was with Quentin.

Warmth leached from my skin as she turned bright red with the effort of not laughing, giving Quentin a playful punch. He absorbed the blow, his face rapt with admiration.

It looked real.

They weren't close enough to be confused as a couple, but what worked venom through my veins was her laughter. He made her happy, and it riled my insides. Their faces tipped to each other as Quentin removed a blossom from her hair. She smiled. It was polite, not the heavy-lidded stares she gave me, but I hated seeing them together.

I made a beeline for them, bulldozing into their discussion. "Hey."

"Cassian!" Rain brightened when she noticed me. "How are you?"

I pulled her into a one-armed hug, smirking at Quentin over her shoulder. As I disengaged, a fierce blush burned her cheeks. She wanted me, not Quentin. The asshole knew it, and wouldn't leave her alone.

Why?

I ignored Quentin, facing Rain. "Want to get lunch?" I wasn't planning on a date, but I wanted to crush whatever he was trying to start. "It's an hour until my shift."

"I'd love to!" she said. "Is that allowed?"

Quentin forced a grin. "Not really."

"Oh. Maybe we all could go."

"Three's a crowd." I didn't care how this looked. I needed her away from him. "Don't bother following us, bro. I've got it covered."

I took Rain's arm, but she resisted. "Q and I were in the middle of a conversation."

"It's all good," Quentin relented. "I'm sure we'll hang again."

Fuck off.

Her smile dropped as he melted into a crowd of senior

citizens with floppy hats and walking sticks.

"Geez. He looks mad."

"At me," I said. "Not you."

Wind played with her hair, obscuring her widened eyes. I pushed it behind her ear. We were in plain sight, but I couldn't stop myself. I brushed petals off her shoulder, and her blush darkened.

"Why is he upset?"

"Because I blocked his cock."

"Cassian." Rain's expression was torn between exasperation and amusement. "Just because you and I fooled around doesn't mean I belong to you."

"Then I'm making it a rule," I growled. "You're mine while I'm fucking you."

"Technically, we haven't done the deed."

"You're mine."

"That's awfully possessive from a guy who doesn't do relationships."

I palmed her back, the only part of her I could touch while standing in the heart of D.C. "Sunshine, I am not big on sharing—and that's putting it lightly."

"No kidding. You wouldn't even share a pie. You think I have a crush on Q?"

"He's doing everything to win you over."

"I'm a virgin, Cassian. Put yourself in my shoes. You're new and overwhelming." Her husky voice cracked like it always did when she went quiet. "You're all I can handle.

And the only man I want."

Rain tipped her head as though she expected a kiss. Her presence draped me like a warm blanket, and I was half-drunk with it.

People flooded the Mall. Among them, there might've been a photographer, but I didn't give a fuck. Rain leaned into me, palms sliding up my armor to anchor at my shoulders. She plastered a clumsy kiss on my chin before I dipped to meet her, warmth spiraling in my chest as our mouths touched. She sighed, giving into the passion and wrapping her arms around my neck.

I circled her waist and gripped her tiny curves. She dragged her fingers through my hair. I devoured her red pout. My tongue lashed her. She moaned, digging her nails into my skin. I pushed her behind the row of food trucks where generators hummed, drowning her sighs. She backed against the truck, purple strands fanning against gold paint.

We made out like two teenagers at school, but only one of us was nineteen. Where the hell was my restraint? Dead on the ground somewhere.

I kissed a senator's daughter on the National-fucking-Mall.

Rain pressed into me. She fluttered air as she gasped for breath. She pulled me close and kissed me as though she couldn't stop.

But... someone had to be the adult.

I took her wrists, hoping she didn't feel my goddamn erection.

"This is insane." My heart hammered. "Insane."

And yet, I couldn't let her go.

She breathed hard, looking equally startled. "What are we doing?"

I didn't know.

Whatever it was, it was headed for a spectacular crash.

Chapter Eleven

Rain

Mom's sobbing tore at me. Listening to her cry always pained me, but this made me murderous. It took five attempts before she enunciated one word.

Evicted.

"Rain, I don't know w-what happened," she bawled. "Everyone woke up with notices on—on their doors."

"What do you mean, everyone?"

"The triplex. Travis is beside himself. It's been awful."

I snatched my keys before remembering I was in D.C. "Did you get a Notice of Intent? Have you talked to your landlord?"

"He's not answering his phone."

I paced the room, restless.

Asshole thought he'd get away with this, did he? "He's using the Ellis Act."

"The what?"

"The Ellis Act. He probably wants to raise rents higher than he's allowed. It's illegal. At least, I'm pretty sure it is."

Landlords invoked the controversial law to avoid the area's restrictions on evictions. The act was supposed to give them a way out of their business, but most used it as a loophole. By kicking the whole building out, demolishing the property, and turning a single-family home into condominiums, they could put everything back on the market and skyrocket the rent.

Mom would be homeless in four months. Meanwhile, I sat on the twenty-third floor of a luxury hotel that overlooked deep green lawns and the Potomac River. Horrible, bubbling guilt ate away at the pit of my stomach.

I grabbed my laptop. I opened dozens of windows, pulling up several eviction lawyer websites.

"We'll fight this. Hire someone who knows the ins and outs of tenant rights. There are cases like this every day." I waited for her to stop crying, but the wracking sobs wouldn't quit. "I'll charter a plane."

"No. There's nothing you can do, and I don't want to get between you and your father."

What could I do besides be a shoulder to cry on? I'd already researched and given my mother notes she hadn't read, which dug at me. I'd spent a lot of hours in the cold basement of a library, but she'd refused to help herself—story of my life.

"What's Travis doing about it?"

Concern thickened her voice. "He sent a rude email to the landlord. You know him. He's not the best communicator."

I slapped my forehead, groaning. "Let me guess. It dropped the f-bomb too many times."

"Worse," she murmured. "My landlord complained to the police."

My throat tightened, and I battled a wave of sadness. "I'll send you a list of lawyers. They offer free consultations. You should call today."

"Yeah, maybe."

"Mom, you need to contact them." I pushed my computer away, frowning. "This isn't the time to be shy. You're losing your home. You have to do something."

"Well, Travis says we should move to Davis."

Most people thought of San Francisco at first mention of Northern California. The snob in me didn't consider anything north of Sacramento worth visiting. West of Sac was a flat, boring college town—Davis. Lots of farmland. I'd toured the university, but the brown landscape, dotted with livestock and the persistent stench of cow dung, failed to impress. Not exciting. And it was far.

"That's a two-and-a-half-hour drive. I'll never see you, which is exactly what he wants."

"No, sweetie. It's about cheaper rent and fewer restrictions on renters."

My frustration sharpened into anger. "Oh, you mean landlords willing to deal with a convicted felon. Mom, this is a terrible idea."

"I don't think so."

I could've screamed, but I bit my tongue. I'd learned to shut my mouth after years of poking at the truth—that my mother had horrible taste in men. She couldn't understand how they conned her with beguiling smiles. Thin promises. Oily grins. Cardboard men that hid insecurities under backhanded compliments. I saw through them, and it drove me mad that she couldn't.

Cassian had noticed, too. He took five minutes to clash with Travis after he insulted me, under the guise of a compliment. That was one reason I liked Cassian. He didn't bullshit me. He respected me.

I never worried about ulterior motives. Cassian spelled out what he wanted—sex with no strings. Mom chased passionate affairs with rollercoaster emotions. I wouldn't tolerate insane highs and lows. I needed stability, and Cassian was a rock.

However, my poor mother was a slave. She'd made one bad decision after another in the name of love. Mom treated relationships like a functioning alcoholic. She limped through life until it imploded. Breakups threw her into a well of despair, which I inevitably had to handle.

Guilt pitted in my gut. "Mom, you won't have to move. I'll ask Dad for help."

She groaned. "Your father wants nothing to do with me."

He didn't. "Dad won't say no. He can't."

"Even if he did, I don't want it."

"Why not?" I barked, my raised voice bouncing off the ceiling. "You don't have other options."

"Travis wouldn't like it, baby."

"Who the fuck cares?" The man gave me a goddamned ulcer. "Is he paying the rent? Does he make you happy? When was the last time he wasn't a complete asshole?"

"I—I'm sorry," Mom said, tearful again. "I shouldn't have called you."

"I want you to call me! I don't want you to waste your days with that arrogant prick when you could do so much better."

After a long pause, Mom's sobs broke through the speaker. "He's not that bad."

I ground my fingers into my temples. "Are you serious? I'm honestly curious if you believe that. Your daughter's feelings toward your boyfriends should be a red flag!"

"You've never liked him."

"I hated him the second we met," I snapped, bulldozing the walls I erected when Mom refused to take my opinion seriously. "I've hated all of them. Want to know why?"

She didn't, but I'd tell her anyway.

"Because they're losers."

"Rain."

Mom's sharp intake of breath added fuel to the fire.

"I've never told you the truth because you mope for a solid week before finding another loser. You only have yourself to blame! You. Mom. You've been a horrible judge of character, but now it's gone too far."

"I'm sorry I've failed you."

"You're not sorry! Because if you were, you'd dump him. You'd choose me, your daughter, over that sack of shit. Enough is enough!"

My frustration boiled as I confessed every dark feeling I'd repressed, shut down, or buried. As the rage passed through and pooled at my feet, horror clawed my throat.

I didn't talk like this to anyone.

Silence crackled as I clamped my mouth shut, my eyes stinging.

"Rain, you're right."

Light beamed through the darkness. I was? My thoughts scattered as well as any words I tried to string together.

I'd gotten through to her.

I suppressed a whimper of relief, wishing I could throw my arms over her. We'd hug until it didn't hurt anymore. Our relationship would heal, and once it did, we'd be stronger than ever.

"Mom, are you okay? I-I'm sorry I was harsh. I didn't mean to hurt you. Mom, are you there?"

The black screen mocked my patience.

She wasn't. She'd hung up.

I dialed her. She didn't answer. I called, and it shot to voicemail. Voicemail. Five minutes crawled by. I tried again. Voicemail.

Obviously, I was wrong.

This wasn't an accident. She was ignoring me. Why? Because I'd told the truth? Anger throbbed in my heart, followed by a razor-sharp ache. I dropped the phone, sickened.

I'd upset her, and now I paid the price. I'd lost the only person who loved me. Who else was there? My father, who reluctantly allowed me a room in his house? He didn't care.

My world caved in.

It was too much.

My cries built into panicked sobs. I shouldn't have said any of it. I was too honest, and she'd slipped further into that bastard's clutches. I caught my breast—inhaling stabbed my ribs as though glass filled my lungs.

The door clicked. A pair of boots jogged inside, but I didn't glance up from the carpet. A man's hand rolled over my shoulder and squeezed. He knelt and tried to get my attention, but I was inconsolable. His arm slid around my waist, and I dove into a steel chest. He locked me in his grasp, stroking my hair. My head nestled in the crook of his neck, and I breathed in bergamot and jasmine.

"What's wrong?" he asked, stricken.

Quentin.

I wanted Cassian. "It's my mother."

"Is she sick?"

"No." I dug into his back, breaking down. "Why is she doing this? I love her!"

"I'm here for you, Rain."

He held me, and his embrace didn't fill me with desire, but it was safe. So I hugged him, naive to the damage it'd cause.

Chapter Twelve

Cassian

Montgomery acted like a helicopter parent on steroids, calling me nonstop about his daughter. The moment we landed in D.C., he lost his mind. Overbearing as fuck. If she stepped a foot outside the geo-fence radius, he freaked. One blip in her schedule, and he demanded answers. He expected Rain to shoot up heroin when she was anything but troubled.

The idiot spent more energy worrying about how she would embarrass him, and not enough fretting about the political journalists, paparazzi, and other members of the press hiding in plain sight. Public opinion hung like a dark cloud over the nation's capital as they indicted more congressmen in the wire fraud scam. People were out for blood. A dirty senator made a hot story, and Rain had plenty of fodder.

So did I.

In this town, everybody knew everybody. Rain's hair attracted reporters like flies to honey. He needed her to hide, but she wasn't a toddler or a pet that could be locked in a room. So his texts flooded my cell.

What's Rain doing?

Where is she going?

Has she been with anyone?

Yeah. Me.

My pocket buzzed. I slowed my jog as rays broke the horizon. Light flared in brilliant shades of orange and teal across scattered clouds. Water lapped to a tour boat where a cork popped. I grabbed my phone and cursed Montgomery as yet another text flashed the screen.

Need to talk

About what? Rain gardened to pass the time, for Christ's sake. Sometimes I caught her whispering to plants or petting roses like a dog's head. The gentleness threw me more than talking to flowers because I'd worked for countless politicians and their children. I never knew *one* I could stand. Rain had agonized over offending me the day we met.

Did he know her at all?

Montgomery gave a damn about Rain only when it suited him. He wanted his wholesome image untarnished, but never included her in his brand. Instead he kept her at arm's length, which confused and hurt her. My hands ached to strangle him.

I dialed his number. "Cassian."

"This is Lance," drawled Montgomery's chief of staff. "Can you fill in for the senator's two o'clock at GWU?"

I ground my teeth. I'd take a knife for Rain, but not a scratch for Montgomery. "No. I'll send someone."

"He requested you."

"My schedule is full, but I'll text you a colleague's information." Refusing a job from a politician was a big no-no, but *fuck* it. "He's professional and reliable."

"The senator also wants to know if you can be at the photo op."

Now he wanted me there? "Thought I wasn't necessary."

"He was unhappy with the firm's estimate for the event."

Translation: You're the cheaper option.

"He can't slash the budget." Montgomery could eat shit and die, but his daughter was innocent. "It's an open space, and that means lots of risk."

"Senator Montgomery had his own risk mitigation specialist evaluate the area. They said four guards would be sufficient."

"Four? How the hell am I supposed to build layers of security in a parking lot with *four* guys? You know what—

never mind. I'll do it, but I'm not leaving Rain's side. I'll escort her to and from the photo op. Understood?"

"Fine," he replied. "Just be there. I'll forward you the details."

"Good. Anything else?"

"Yes, unfortunately." Lance sighed, cursing. "Senator Montgomery is letting one of you go."

"*What?*"

"He's reducing expenses. Rain's protection is paid for by the senator."

Sell your luxury cars, asshole. "Quentin and I are a team. Without him, my shifts increase from twelve to twenty-four hours. That leaves me with no time to monitor her social media accounts, review any hazards, or plan for her schedule."

"There have been no incidents with Rain."

"Yet," I ground out.

"He's not convinced she needs bodyguards twenty-four/seven."

Rage lodged in my throat. "Have you read my reports?"

"They don't have photos of known stalkers. Or license plates. Want to keep your job? Prove that we need you."

I'd listened to the same speech from countless clients, but hearing it from Montgomery's chief of staff stewed my blood. "My presence deters threats. People see me, and they leave her alone. If you take away her guards, you make her vulnerable to attacks. And for what? So he can save a few bucks?"

My shouts echoed off the distant bank. The complete lack of professionalism made me want to punch myself.

Lance didn't speak for several moments. "Do you have any data, or is this your intuition?"

"My *intuition* saves lives. It's already saved her life." Contempt bled from every syllable. "Tell the senator—"

"—I'm not telling him anything. This is his decision, Cassian. I'm sorry, but I have to go."

The call dropped, and I stared at the blank screen.

How did I become her *only* protector?

We needed to talk. I'd explain everything. She'd understand. Rain, thank *fuck*, was a reasonable person. Far more than her asshole of a father.

My pulse raced. Too edgy to exercise, I returned to the hotel. I did a double-take over a guy in a parking lot. His oversized suit, grim expression, and disheveled hair chimed alarm bells. My hand strayed where I hid a Glock in an inside waist holster.

I approached him, smiling. "Can I help you?"

The man raised his head, his blue eyes piercing my chest. His familiar features sank my stomach. Dread consumed me, legs to torso. His face was mine, if I were to spend ten years wading in alcohol. Ashen skin stretched taut over bones that jutted from his hollowed cheeks. He'd gone entirely gray, and the lines under his hooded gaze had deepened. Salt-and-pepper stubble covered the hard-set jaw we shared. Too much reflected what I saw in the mirror, except an aura of desperation clung to him like cologne.

He'd found me. No idea how, but he found me.

His pores seemed to leak vodka—one reason I rarely drank spirits. After Claire died, all he did was drink.

"Dad, what are you doing here?"

"Had to see you. I called your boss and asked where you were. Said it was an emergency."

Richard.

I never told Dad about my contacts in the various security agencies I worked for. Why the hell would I? His drunkenness had ruined so many goddamn Christmases that I'd never introduce him to a colleague. I screened his phone calls and occasionally answered an email. He must've stalked me on LinkedIn.

I groaned. "You shouldn't have done that."

"I had to. You wouldn't respond to my voicemails."

"No shit."

"You look good," he croaked, drinking me in. "I—I'm glad."

"Dad, let's cut through it." Suddenly, everything about him pissed me off. "What do you want? Money?"

"To be with my son."

I headed to the hotel, sighing. "Right."

Dad flinched. He couldn't fault me for the cold shoulder. When Claire passed, he checked out of life. Disappeared for days at a time.

"I lost a child—"

"—and you ignored the other." Christ, not this again. He wouldn't boo-hoo about Claire to me. "I was thirteen. My hands were destroyed. My sister *dead*. I needed you. You weren't there. I fended for myself, and what did you do? Drink."

"I've made mistakes. Terrible mistakes." He bowed his head, tears clinging to his lashes. "But I love you, son. I love you, and I'm sorry."

His eyes slid in and out of focus.

Fucking drunk. I could easily become him.

Ignoring that, I grabbed the door and slipped into the lobby. "I can't talk to you when you drink. And that's all you do."

He followed like a dog that wouldn't leave, no matter how many times I smacked his nose. "I'm not the only one still fighting demons. Cassian, what are you doing here?"

"*Working.*"

"Don't lie to me." He approached until I noticed every spiderwebbed red vein. "I saw you with Montgomery's *daughter*. When I came across that picture, I had to find you."

Anger pulsed in my chest. He'd seen through me, and I ground my teeth. "It's just work."

"*Cassian*," he pleaded.

"I loathe him."

Dad took my shoulders. "Does he know who you are?"

"Of course he doesn't." I shrugged from his touch, but couldn't tear my gaze from his.

"Cass, what are you planning?"

This looked bad. I'd booked the position under false pretenses, hoping to shit all over Montgomery's life. Dad believed I was mad with grief—capable of harming Rain. The only person I wanted to maim was Senator Montgomery.

"Let me help," he demanded. "I need this as much as you!"

"Get the fuck away from me. If I see you again, I'll have you thrown in jail. Your restraining order applies to his children, too."

He blanched. "You wouldn't."

"I will," I said, voice darkening. "Drink water and don't leave until you're sober, or you'll be charged with another DUI."

"I'm sorry. How many times do I have to say it?" He blocked my path. "I love your sister, and I love you, too."

I can never be him. "Save it."

"You don't understand what it's like to lose a child. Not all of us can compartmentalize."

"I think about her every damned day." I fisted his shirt as heat licked my neck. "What she'd look like. Where she'd work. If she'd be married. I've always blamed myself for letting her die."

"Cassian—"

"I blame you, too."

A tear rolled down his cheek. "There was nothing we could've done."

Smoke crawled up walls, and gray wallpaper blackened. Flames ate the carpet, wrapping the bed frame, and shackled to the brass was a foot—*Stop.*

I released him as pain shot into my hands. Something must've shown on my face because he looked stricken. I stared into my father's eyes. They used to be so full of life. filled with happiness, the hopes and dreams of his children, and laughter, but now they were empty.

I didn't see him anymore.

I saw my future.

"Get away from me."

"Don't do this, son."

I clutched my cell. "Go. Or I call your parole officer to tell them you're violating your restraining order."

He didn't answer. I stormed from my dad and disappeared through a door, climbing five flights before my rage banked into an inferno. I'd spend a few nights tossing and turning over what I said, but I still thrashed against my memories. My lungs screamed for oxygen even though there was no soot. Phantom fingers latched around my throat, squeezing.

I climbed to the twenty-third floor, my pulse jacked. When I burst into the hall, I searched for room 2305. The sight of her room arrested my heart. The door hung open.

Dread bottomed my stomach.

Where the fuck was Quentin?

He should've been outside guarding the entrance. Nausea gripped me as I walked into the flames of my past. I stepped inside, gun drawn.

Please let her be okay.

A deep sob shook from a woman's chest. I swung into the bedroom, where she had collapsed.

Locked in her embrace was another man.

Fucking Quentin.

Chapter Thirteen

Rain

"What did you do?" a man thundered from the entrance. He sounded violent, the last adjective I'd use to describe my bodyguard, but Cassian stood at the doorway in a muscle tee and track pants. He stowed a small gun in his waistband, and though his eyes passed over me, no glimmer of recognition shone. A chilly breeze seemed to blow in with his presence.

I shivered.

Quentin's embrace slackened. He pulled back, leaving his arm draped around my shoulders, and took in Cassian with a raised eyebrow. I couldn't blame Quentin for shielding me when Cassian's body language screamed murder.

"Quentin, I asked you a fucking question. Why is she on the floor?" Cassian roared, loud enough to shake the dust from the ceiling. "What happened?"

"Relax, man." Quentin yanked me upright. "You're freaking her out."

I wanted to tell him it wasn't true, but I flinched when his cold fury zeroed in on me. A beet-red color spread from his collar to his neck. He spoke like he could've ripped Quentin's head off, but he looked odd. Something made him resemble the way he was on that day—the anniversary of his sister's death. A hollowness gaped within him, sucking all warmth from the room.

"You okay?" he demanded.

No. Are you? "I'm all right. Just sad."

Quentin glared at him, annoyed. "See?"

Cassian peeled me from Quentin's side. His feverish touch scalded and bit into my skin. "What's wrong?"

"F-family drama." *Putting it lightly.*

"Tell me."

I stared at my wrist, which he grasped even as Quentin absorbed the exchange. Cassian palmed my cheek, and I felt a pull at my navel when I met his gaze. It was like he reached into me. I'd be fine. As long as he tethered me to the ground, I'd live.

He was gravity.

Quentin's throat cleared. "Sorry to interrupt what's clearly a moment, but I have to say something. You guys are not subtle." He shrugged, wearing an apologetic grin. "Anybody with eyes sees you have a thing for each other."

"I don't fucking care," Cassian barked.

"Then you're a moron. Your fling with the senator's daughter will get us blacklisted from every security firm. I'll never work again if Montgomery finds out you're banging Rain."

Shame engulfed my cheeks, both at Quentin's assessment of our relationship and the idea that I was ruining his career. "I'm sorry."

"Don't apologize to him," Cassian snapped. "You didn't hear how he talked about you."

"Cassian, leave him alone!"

He ignored my plea and approached Quentin. "Keep your mouth shut."

Quentin's dimpled grin widened. "You gave me shit for what happened at the other job. Now look at you. You've compromised everything. Your reputation. Her innocence. Hell, even her safety. How far you've fallen."

Ouch.

Cassian's lip curled. "Says the man who left the door wide open!"

"Yeah? At least I didn't trap her in an airplane to have my way with her."

Cassian shoved Quentin against the chest of drawers and drove his fist into his stomach. I gasped, clutching my torso as though I felt the blow. Quentin doubled over with a loud grunt, but Cassian seized him and tossed him into a wall. Quentin recovered and ducked under Cassian's next swing. His right hook smashed into Cassian's jaw with a wicked crunch.

I winced at the sound. "Guys, stop!"

They exchanged blows, two vicious titans slamming into each other. A lamp toppled from a nightstand. The television wobbled from the console. Picture frames crashed as Quentin cracked the glass. Cassian restrained Quentin with a hand wrapping his neck and threw him backward.

I walloped Cassian. "Stop *fighting*! Are you out of your minds?"

Distracted, Cassian loosened his grip. Quentin broke free and hurled his fist. The punch skimmed air over Cassian. He grabbed Quentin's waist and launched him. Quentin stumbled, his shirt hanging out from his pants. Blood spilled from his lip onto his chin. He wiped the long streak of bright red.

"The *fuck* is the matter with you!"

"You're done." A bruise welled on Cassian's face, but he squared his shoulders. "You're *fired*!"

I grabbed Cassian's bicep. "No!"

"Quentin's not a bodyguard anymore," Cassian snarled, whirling at him. "Hear me, asshole? I'll make sure you never get a job again."

"For telling the truth? Or touching her?" Quentin

barked with laughter, his mirth rising to the ceiling despite the crimson sprinkling the carpet. "You're out of control, man."

God, he *was*. All this over a damned hug? "I agree with Quent—"

"You left the door open," he said, cutting through my words. "You made her vulnerable. That's more than enough reason to fire you on the spot. You could've gotten her killed."

Quentin stared at him, wide-eyed. "It was five seconds!"

"It's my decision."

"Cassian, be reasonable." I clutched his elbow, but he ignored me. "He came in because he heard me crying."

"Quentin had one responsibility, and he failed. I don't need to explain myself to you or anyone. He's finished. End of story."

"He isn't fired, you unbelievable ass! *You're fired!*"

Cassian's lips tugged. "Right."

"I'm calling my father the second you leave this room!"

"Good thing I don't plan on going anywhere." Cassian's amusement grew as he blocked my way out. "Even if you did, he values my opinion more than yours."

That hurt.

Tears stung the backs of my eyelids. I headed out, but Cassian stopped me with a thick arm.

"Move," I ground out.

"I don't take orders from you." Cassian jerked to the exit. "Quentin—go!"

My cheeks burned as Quentin obeyed. "I'm so sorry! I'll make this up to you. I swear."

"It's not your fault, Rain." Quentin's smile became a sneer. "Cassian has no idea what he's started."

"Get the fuck out. Now!"

Quentin disappeared. The door slammed, walls shaking in his wake. I gaped at the bodyguard who always kept it cool, who'd never made me feel threatened or unsafe. Cassian slid the deadbolt and palmed the wood, his color returning to normal. After a while, he turned around.

Tension knotted his features. His scowl darkened when he locked eyes with me.

I couldn't believe what he'd done. "What the fuck is wrong with you?"

"A lot of things, Sunshine."

"Don't call me that stupid nickname!" I shoved him—well, I tried to. His body refused to bend, and I couldn't raise my hands against him. My fists shook, and he eyed them with a smirk, as though amused by the idea of me striking him.

"Go ahead. I'll enjoy the foreplay."

"Stop it!" A frustrated scream balled in my throat. "Don't try to change the subject. You crossed the line. You're not firing Q!"

"Yes, I am." Cassian lowered his voice to a deadly

whisper. "I walked into the hallway and no one was at your door, which was ajar. You don't understand what went through my mind."

"F-fine. You were worried, but then you spotted me and Q."

"*Exactly.*" He glowered. "You were in the arms of another guy."

I ignored the thrill of his jealousy. "That doesn't give you license to lose your marbles because a dude hugged me."

"I lost my temper. There's a difference."

"You acted like a *child*." I paced the room, hating the way he tracked me with his eyes. "Tell me what's wrong with you."

"I told you—a lot."

I grabbed my phone and texted my father, but Cassian seized it and tossed it onto the dresser. Butterflies somersaulted when he enveloped my hands with his. He brought them to his mouth and kissed my knuckles, and my anger gave way.

No. "Cassian, we're done."

"Not even close, sweetheart."

"*You hit Quentin.*"

Cassian shrugged, his touch gliding up my arm. "Quentin goaded me. He's been after you since the beginning, and he was fucking rude."

He traced my collarbone. Pleasure seeped through my

skin, rapidly cooling my anger. "If I want to hug someone, I *will*."

"Fine. I *overreacted*. Is that what you want to hear?" Cassian held my face, his thumbs brushing my jaw. "And I had a shit day. Seeing you with him pushed me over the edge."

"You can't blow up at me. *Ever*."

"I wasn't angry with you." Cassian swallowed hard when I didn't answer. "Don't you believe me?"

I did, especially when his words stroked me like his hands. I wanted to lean into his touch and soothe my ache. Temptation slowly worked its way through anger as he sat on the bed, dragging me with him.

I resisted. "We can't."

"Why not?"

I opened my mouth, but said nothing. He'd shoot down my feeble excuses. My rage melted the longer we touched, as though an invisible current passed between us, dragging me forward.

Finally, he smiled. It stopped short of his eyes, but at least the scowl was gone.

"Come here."

Cassian took my waist and pulled me over his lap. His head tipped toward me as his fingers dove into my hair. I wrapped him in my embrace, seduced by a heady cedar scent. I grabbed his neck and yanked him closer, but we didn't kiss. My blood still boiled and Cassian's smirk worsened my temper.

He squeezed my hands before sliding them to his chest. I slid them downward, digging into the cotton, feeling the ridges of his abs through the fabric.

I should make him apologize.

When his breath tickled my skin, all thoughts of making Cassian do anything but kiss me disappeared. He claimed my mouth, his tongue teasing with quick swipes. I glided up his body, tracing every muscle that made him strong enough to pick me up, one-armed, as the other ripped off his holster. He slammed it on the dresser before lowering me to the mattress, where he deepened the kiss.

He knelt at the bed, his stare so potent my thighs clenched. Cassian looked younger by a decade as he slid my blouse off, dragging my bra with it. They slithered from me, cold air stinging my erect nipples. I hid myself, face burning.

Cassian kissed the shell of my ear. "You're beautiful. Don't hide."

I melted like ice in a Californian summer. Ecstasy lit his face when he uncovered me. He kissed me with a ravenous hunger that dimmed my memories of all the annoying shit he'd done. When his lips blazed a path through the valley between my breasts, I stopped breathing. His wet kisses trailed the sensitive skin before claiming my nipple. He lashed, arousal slamming into my groin.

"I'm still mad at you."

"I don't care," he grunted. "So long as I get a taste."

God, was he serious?

Cassian tongued my other breast before continuing the torture downward. He sucked a hickey on my hip as he unbuttoned my pants, which he inched off. My panties joined my jeans on the floor as Cassian's searing kisses scorched down my stomach and over my mound.

"Open wide," he growled, eyes filled with dirty promises. "If you try to close your legs, I'll stop touching you. I don't want to be nasty, Sunshine. So keep that pussy exposed."

He lowered between my thighs.

Oh my fucking God.

My embarrassment guttered out the moment Cassian pressed his hot lips to me and caressed my seam, dragging his flaming touch to my clit. *Fuck* how filthy this made me. I needed this every day. I bucked into his mouth and moaned.

Cassian pleasured me in ways I never imagined. He reached back and curled into my wetness, eating like a man delirious with hunger. I chased his tongue with my hips as shamelessly as I did his fingers.

He slid his palms under me and squeezed when I whimpered. His thumbs parted me, and then he kissed me.

My pussy contracted so hard that I thought I orgasmed. I arched. I clenched, and that's when a sudden blow caught my ass cheek. Cassian palmed my burning skin, pulling away to fix me with a stare that penetrated me.

"What did I say? Keep them open."

All that escaped was a tortured moan.

He dove in, fucking me with his tongue as I balled my fists in the sheets and tried not to scream. My calves twitched as he buried himself as deep as he could. I loved every movement of his wet heat pressing into my clit. Pressure ramped in with every fierce kiss, until it released. I came with a shuddering groan. Cassian thrust into me, his thumb working me as pleasure submerged me under overwhelming waves.

God, was it over?

No. Cassian flipped me to my stomach.

Kneeling, I waded in the glow of my orgasm. Cassian dragged me against him. Digging into my ass cheek must've been his cock, because *fuck*. It felt like a huge rock. I wanted him so badly my teeth ached.

"Mad at me, babe?"

What had he done? Didn't remember. Or give a shit.

He rubbed his erection into my side, and I lost all interest in his question.

He squeezed my ass before he spanked me. Thought I'd hate it, but it was hot. I loved when he manhandled me. Nothing he did while he was in this state would bother me.

"Answer me."

"Still mad, yes." I grinned, bowing my head. "Maybe you need to do it again."

"You're a greedy little virgin, aren't you?" He fucking loved it, judging by the thickness grinding into me. "Awesome, because I haven't gotten my fill of your sweetness."

Spreading me with his thumbs, he licked me from behind. I dropped to my elbows as he sucked, swirling over my clit. He fucked me with his tongue. I chased the ecstasy, and he yanked me into him, encouraging me.

He taunted me as he caressed my pussy in tight circles that shoved me toward the edge all over again. "I know you're a good girl, but be dirty for me. Come on my tongue."

He slid back inside and seized my hips, locking me so I couldn't escape the mounting pressure. A thrust of his finger ripped another moan from me, and I clenched hard.

I collapsed onto the sheets, thighs slick with my arousal. Cassian unzipped himself and circled his hard-on with his thumb and forefinger, slowly bringing himself to his own climax. Then he moved to my side and flipped me, his cock thrusting in his palm. I grabbed the base of him and helped, emboldened by Cassian's deep sighs and the way he sucked in his lip. I felt a surge through his cock, and then his seed spilled across my breasts. Cassian shut his eyes, his loud groan ricocheting off the ceiling.

"You like doing this to me."

"It's not as fun as being balls-deep in your pussy, but

it'll do for now." Cassian stripped from his muscle tank and wiped my body. Then he pressed his lips to my ear, smiling. "Next time, you'll take it in your mouth."

∽

DAD SIPPED his single-origin coffee and fiddled with his phone. The man was married to the damned thing. Unless it was in his hands, he fidgeted like a child. He grunted one-worded replies to my questions as he tapped emails. I fantasized about smacking it out of his hands.

We sat in the Capitol Building's stainless-steel cafeteria, where congressmen and women ate their fill of carbs before the caucus or whatever.

I played with my visitor badge. "What do you have after this?"

"A call with a UC Berkeley professor about an oil spill. After that, a whip meeting."

"I read somewhere that senators spend fifty percent of their year begging for money. Is that true?"

"Fundraising. It's called fundraising." A small smile curved his cheek, a peace offering I took.

"What made you go into politics?"

Dad paused in between typing a text, his pale blues flicking at me. "Tell me the real reason we're here."

I gave up on my Philly cheesesteak and pushed the

plate aside. I wanted time with my father, but I couldn't pretend I didn't have an agenda.

"It's about Q."

He frowned. "Who?"

"Quentin, my bodyguard. The young guy," I clarified when he looked lost. "Please don't fire him. He's been great."

"You prefer him over the other, Cassian?"

I shook my head. "I don't want them to lose their jobs."

"You don't *need* two bodyguards. That's why I told the big fellow I could only afford one."

No wonder Cassian was so hell-bent on firing Quentin.

I slumped in my seat. "That sucks. They're both very nice. I'm close to them."

"They're not your friends, Rain. Don't mistake their politeness for anything more than that. Those men are paid to protect you." Dad drummed his fingers on the table. "Well, if you're finished...I have a mountain of emails to answer."

I seized his hand. "Dad, I want to know the father who's been missing for all my life."

He stiffened, somehow more remote than Cassian, who was carved from concrete. "Of course."

"I don't expect you to believe me, especially since I—I have to beg you for a huge favor. I tried handling it myself, but I'm overwhelmed. There's nobody else to ask for help."

Dad blanched. "You're pregnant?"

I groaned. "No."

"Whatever it is, we can fix it. I'll call my publicist and campaign manager. I saw nothing in the press, so if we head this off we might have time to—what?"

"It's not me. My mother's being evicted."

"Oh." Dad slipped from me, the tension dissolving from his features. "Why is that my problem?"

"She's the mother of your *child*, and she'll be homeless if you don't do something." When he looked unmoved, I leaned forward. "You can't give your back to my mom. She raised your daughter on her own with zero support."

"I never knew you existed."

Liar. "Mom contacted you many times."

"How was I supposed to take her seriously? A woman I didn't remember was pregnant with my baby." He pinched the bridge of his nose, releasing a tense breath. "That's in the past. We made a deal. You live with me for three years, and—"

"Yeah. I get it, but I've barely seen you, which makes me wonder if the whole act was a publicity stunt. You don't seem to care about knowing me."

"Rain, that's not true."

"Name one thing you've done that wasn't selfish."

Dad stopped glancing at his phone and narrowed his pale eyebrows. "I hired the best bodyguards and assigned them to you."

"With strict instructions to monitor my activities and keep me out of trouble. What else?"

He stayed mute, his lips whitening. "What do you want?"

"My mom to have a home."

Dad sipped his water as though it were wine. "Marie should learn to save her money."

"She's being used by her boyfriend. She won't talk to me anymore."

Dad's mouth curled with disgust. "Wonderful."

"Please. This isn't for me. It's to help my mom. She's a decent person."

He snorted. "Well, that's a matter of opinion."

"But I haven't asked you for anything. Ever."

"You sued me," Dad snapped. "You put my marriage in jeopardy. Strained my relationship with my boys. You've almost derailed my career. Having you at my house has cost me, Rain."

I was right.

He didn't think of me as his daughter. I was the stain on his record. Even now, he looked at me as though wishing I'd disappear.

"I'm sorry for screwing up your *perfect* marriage and family, but I will not apologize for being born."

"Lower your voice." He searched the room for anyone eavesdropping and faced me. "I could use my Swiss bank account. No one has to know."

"You will be paying for a woman's apartment. That's hardly a scandal."

"No, but it'll destroy Karen and I. What's left of us, anyway." Dad's blank expression betrayed zero emotion. It was as though he sat at a negotiation desk. "I want something in return. You'll come with me to events and play the dutiful daughter role. You'll appear in photo ops, on my Instagram, and give interviews to support my campaign."

A small sacrifice to pay for housing my mother. "I'll ask my college for a leave of absence."

Dad towered over me as his phone chimed, marking the end of our half-hour appointment. "And you'll dye your hair. Blonde. Brunette. I don't care what, as long as it's normal."

I gritted my teeth. "Fine."

"I'll be in touch. Patrick will help you with everything. No need to call me."

"Okay."

He rapped the table and then buttoned his jacket, sweeping out without so much as a handshake.

What was wrong with him?

Why couldn't he show me a fraction of warmth?

Sometimes I watched my dad on YouTube. He displayed a surprising amount of excitement during his rallies—banged his fists on the podium, yelled, screamed hellfire. Spittle flew from his mouth when he got going. With me, he was a damned robot.

A twenty-year-old aide led me from the Capitol Building through the visitor's entrance, where I relinquished my pass. I strolled into blinding sunshine and descended the searing-white steps, ignoring a man who cast a massive shadow over mine. He took my arm, but I ripped it from his grasp.

"Meeting with Dad sucked?" Cassian snarked. "Can't say I'm surprised."

He kept doing that.

Occasionally, I'd caught his snide comments regarding my dad. I assumed he hated him for his politics, but Cassian wasn't the type to rave about the news. Insulting Dad was cheap. Cassian had issues, even if he gave amazing oral.

I crossed the street into the sprawling green of the National Mall.

Cassian followed. "What's wrong?"

"Why?"

"You look upset."

I stopped. Cassian bumped into my back. He righted me before I stumbled.

I brushed him away. "You're pissing me off."

"What the fuck?"

"Q was let go because of you."

"Nope. Your daddy was sick of paying for two guys, so he offered me the choice. Should I have given him my name?"

"You treated him horribly. Q didn't deserve that. He's been sweet and kind and—"

"Stop while you're ahead."

"Right," I sneered. "Wouldn't want to make you jealous. Who knows what you'd do?"

He grabbed my elbow, dragging me into his arms. "What crawled up your ass? I apologized, didn't I? Or do you need another reminder of how I made you come. *Twice.*"

Of course he'd bring up that, but all it took was his smile to shove the memory into my brain. That tongue. Those lips. I wanted him to lick me now.

"Quentin's fine," Cassian promised. "I wrote him a good recommendation."

"That doesn't erase what you did." I tore from him.

As I wandered the endless green lawn, I pictured the upcoming weeks. Candid smiles with the senator. Handshakes with men I'd never see again. Interviews where I'd laud my father for whatever bullshit young voters cared about. I'd bleach the purple. A small sacrifice, but I'd ripped so many pieces of my cardboard heart. I felt like a shadow of my former self.

"I have to dye my hair," I blurted.

"Don't." Cassian's fingers glided across my back, fanning my locks over my shoulder. "It's beautiful, and it suits you."

"Thank you." I glowed from the compliment. "But I have to change."

"The man is not worth your time."

I glared at Cassian. "Why do you hate him so much?"

"Because you cry after seeing him."

I bit my lip. "I'm not right now."

"A ringing endorsement."

I hated how he pointed out every-goddamned-thing. "Would it kill you to lie to me?"

He laughed. "What?"

"I don't want brutal honesty. I want comfort."

"Oh." Cassian shoved his hands deep in his pockets, something he did when I caught him off guard. "What if I took you on a date?"

"That's not funny," I snapped. "Goading me about Dad is mean, but dangling promises you can't—won't keep is downright cruel."

Besides, I couldn't stand Cassian's face at that moment.

"Jesus, Rain. I'm serious."

He dragged me to a halt. A few weeks had made a world of difference on Cassian. He still dressed in a black suit and crisp white shirt, the jacket always unbuttoned, but he smiled more.

He lightened while I darkened.

"Where will you take me?"

Cassian drew closer with a Cheshire cat grin. "Somewhere you'll fucking love."

Chapter Fourteen

Cassian

Concerts were a pain in the ass, and I hated them.

Usually, I manned the exits or kept overenthusiastic fans from the stage. Always wore earplugs. Without them, my head ached. No bodyguard likes a crowd, but for her, I compromised.

Fuck, I did more than compromise.

I met with the security director of the venue, scoped the place, sweet-talked him into letting me carry a concealed firearm, and ushered her into the VIP entrance. My contract wouldn't end for another couple of months, and I wanted to spend it inside Rain. It was worth the two-hour snoozefest. I'd listened to enough ballads about trees and nature to last a fucking lifetime. To pass the time, I scanned the docile attendees for threats.

When it ended, I escorted her through the back exit, and we piled into a car. Everything went so smoothly that I felt guilty for canceling her Gorillaz concert weeks ago.

Rain gripped my arm when we left the SUV, in the hotel lobby, and all the way to the room. When the door snapped behind us, I sighed.

Her fingers buried in my dress shirt. "How did you know I'd like them?"

With Rain's curves molded to me, every mental process ground to a halt. I thumbed the strap that fell and pushed it over her shoulder. My dick pulsed as I grazed her soft skin. All night she'd clung to me, bobbing with the mellow guitar music. She'd dragged my attention from the crowd to make out with me, tongue thrusting into my mouth, and I'd somehow held it together. Until now.

"Cassian?"

She's a virgin. Slow.

Slow wasn't normally in my vocabulary, but I tried for her. I threw my jacket onto a chair and flashed her a grin as I unbuttoned my shirt to remove my armor.

"Sorry, what was the question?"

Rain seemed at a loss for words. I put a lot of effort into my body, so her silent awe boosted my ego. I took her hand and slid it over my chest. Her cheeks flushed as she stroked me.

"I—I asked how you knew I'd like them."

Rain traced my arms, squeezing my bicep. Then she roved my abs, over the hills and valleys of my muscles. The further she went, the faster my heart pounded.

"I checked their YouTube, and figured you'd appreciate hippie songs about trees."

"Well, you were right. Next time we'll go to a band of yours."

"That was my first concert."

"Wow. How come?"

Because I'm a shell of a human. "Don't like crowds."

"It's fun, isn't it?"

"Watching you dance was nice. You're a feast for a starving man."

Her moss-green gaze met mine. "Meaning, you like me?"

"You know I do. Fuck the music and people, Sunshine. I want *you*."

She dove into me, hugging my middle. Rain buried her face in my neck and exhaled. Her nails dug into my skin as she released shuddering breaths. I kissed her shoulder.

God, she was gorgeous.

"Wait," I sighed, hating myself. "Let's talk."

Rain masked her pain with a tight grin. "That's not your thing, remember?"

It wasn't, but she'd bulldozed through my rules. All of them.

I cupped her cheeks. It's said that eyes are windows to the soul. I lived by that, assessing everyone, analyzing every detail.

Vulnerability shone through her. She was scared.

"Tell me what happened to your mom."

"No."

"You'll feel better. It's eating you up inside."

"I won't say anything until you give me something." Rain backed from my touch and sank onto the bed. "Quid pro quo."

Why on Earth did she want to know me?

Rain's feet dangled off the mattress as I bit my inner cheek.

I sat, my thigh brushing hers. "My dad visited the other day, but I want nothing to do with him. Part of me hates him because we look so much alike. Your turn."

"I get no follow-up questions?"

"Quid pro quo," I parroted.

"Fine." She stared at the wall. "My mom stopped talking to me after I gave her an ultimatum. Travis or me. She chose him."

I wished I hadn't seen this coming. "I'm sorry."

Rain shook her head, emotionless. "I can't think about it. The good news is my father will pay for her apartment, provided I become his lapdog."

"You don't have to change for him."

"Unfortunately, I do."

"Fight the eviction," I growled. "Hire a lawyer."

"With what money?"

I thumbed her chin, my blood pounding when her eyes bored into mine. "I have a friend—a client who owes me a favor. He'll represent you."

She leaned forward as though caught in the same magnetic pull, but paused. "No, I can't let you do that."

"You're not. I'm offering." I hated to see her so crushed. "Jesus Christ, Rain. I want to do this."

"You promised not to interfere."

"It was a dumb promise."

"Not to me, Cassian." She brushed away my touch, motioning between us. "This is the only thing in my life that isn't fucked. I won't ruin it."

"I'm older than you. Trust me on this. Take my help."

Rain still looked unsure. "You might be older, but I'm not sure about wiser."

"Smartass."

A tentative smile broke her melancholy. "You don't have to."

"Yes, I do. You're more fun when you're safe and happy."

"That's sweet of you, Cassian. Thank you."

Nobody ever called me sweet, except her. Only she had reason to like me because I went out of my way to support her. I couldn't use my drill sergeant voice around her. I was incapable of being harsh, and she brought my guard down constantly.

It was a problem.

I had to establish hard boundaries, get my shit together, and stop caving every time she blinked in my direction.

She dropped her head on my shoulder and intertwined her arm with mine. She kissed my cheek, warmth gliding over me. Her fingers teased the seam of my jeans, straying close to my groin. She tiptoed over my waist and traced the outline of my cock as she pressed her mouth to my ear.

"You know, I've never given a blowjob."

"I've been told I'm an amazing teacher." I grabbed her thigh and slipped under her skirt. I nudged the edge of her panties and sucked in my bottom lip. "Are you already wet for me?"

Pink patches darkened her cheeks.

Aw, she's embarrassed. "There is nothing shameful about your feelings."

"I'm not ashamed. Just shy."

I hooked my finger inside her underwear, gliding along her wetness. Rain shivered as she felt me, green eyes wide with anticipation. Starting at her waist, I raised the tank top over her belly and ripped it over her hair. She had the most gorgeous skin, and I marveled at how much she loved my touch. Rain beamed when I twisted the clasp of her bra. She enjoyed having her tits played with, and that was great because I loved touching them. Purple spilled across her chest in a shimmering wave.

"I'll fuck the shyness out of you, Sunshine."

I tugged the skirt and thong off her ass. Bearing witness to Rain's naked body was a mental exercise, because restraining myself took every ounce of concentration. She was small-boned and delicate, with a flat, smooth stomach and teardrop breasts. Damn, I wanted them in my mouth.

Focus. "On your knees."

Rain hesitated before sliding off the bed. She knelt at my feet and tentatively unzipped my jeans. The fabric snagged my hips. I stood to help her, and then she freed my cock from the briefs. It bounced out at full mast. She gripped the base and gave it an experimental pump.

A thrill jolted to my groin. "You don't have to squeeze so hard. Light, consistent pressure."

"Okay," she whispered, staring at my length. "Do all women do this?"

"Everyone you know has oral sex. I promise." I smiled when her forehead wrinkled in disbelief. "Rain, there's nothing wrong with giving pleasure to your partner."

"You're right."

I tried to remember how anxious I was my first time. I was more worried about disappointing the girl than anything else. Rain probably felt the same. It was my job to soothe her fears and make this fun.

"You're doing great."

"I am?" Relief washed over Rain's features as she caressed me with a slow, one-handed movement.

"Yeah. Touch the head."

She brushed it with her thumb, and I twitched at the contact. "It moved!"

I laughed. "It does that. Use both hands."

I showed her how, pulling the skin and wrapping her around me. Her other hand worked my dick. Anticipation leapt inside my chest as she parted her lips. She licked me, and ecstasy zinged up my spine. I buried my fingers in her hair, heart pounding.

She tasted the underside, tonguing the sensitive membrane that shot fire down my cock. I wanted to plunge into her, but I held still.

"That's good," I forced out. "Don't stop."

She drew away, smirking as she fisted me. Rain leaned forward, mouth open. Wet heat smothered my dick.

"Squeeze gently and suck." The first tug ripped a groan from me. "Don't be afraid to use your tongue."

With encouragement, Rain tested herself, inch by inch. She played, swirled, and sucked. I closed my eyes, losing myself in her lips and tongue dragging my arousal forth. She bobbed like a champion, pushing herself further.

My breathing hitched. I gripped her head. The desire to come slammed into me. My hips thrust as she tightened, sucking hard.

"Slow down." I made a ponytail with her purple mane, watching my bulge in her throat. "I'm getting close."

Rain took me out, gasping. "Don't you want to orgasm?"

"Yes, but you might not like it in your mouth."

"I'll decide that."

She winked at me before swallowing my cock. Rain moved quickly, rotating, her wet heat dancing underneath me. I focused on the pressure building in my balls, her sweet mouth, the cum that she'd devour.

"Fuck, I'm coming. Take it out if you don't—"

Too late. She grasped my ass and yanked as pleasure knocked the air from my lungs. I moaned, forcing her to take my thrusts until every drop spilled. My thighs shuddered as she glided my length. Ecstasy blinded my vision.

"Shit. That was fucking heaven. I feel like you drained my life force." I lay back, my heart hammering as she wiped her face. "You were amazing, Rain. I—Where are you going?"

Rain paused in between getting up. "Aren't we done?"

"Hell no." I seized her arm and pulled her to me.

Did she think I'd leave her high and dry?

Giggling, she fell into my arms. She avoided me until I grabbed her chin and pressed my lips against hers. Blood still churned to my groin, keeping me hard as I kissed her. It'd be so easy to spread her thighs and sink inside.

I sucked her bottom lip until she gasped, making my

way down her body. I kissed both knees before spreading them. Rain whimpered when my kiss landed beside her entrance.

I teased her clit, humming, blowing hot air, rubbing it with my thumb. Rain tried to reach me, but I palmed her belly. She sank as I flicked her nub. I plunged into her. She contracted, sending a jolt to my cock. She fisted my hair, pleading with long, drawn-out whines. I dragged her wetness to her nub. Her hips bucked, greedy little thing that she was.

I forced her down, sliding her leg over my shoulder.

"Open your eyes, Sunshine. Look at me while I enjoy you."

She peeked.

"No. I want to see those big, beautiful eyes. Do it."

Rain obeyed like the perfect girl she was as I kissed between her legs. She released a keening wail as I clutched her ass and lifted, diving as deep as I could. She clenched as I ate her, and then she arched.

"I'm—I'm—oh shit."

A fierce orgasm gripped my tongue, but it was over too fast. Didn't seem fair for a nearly ten-minute blowjob.

I flipped Rain to her stomach and slammed the mental brakes to keep from fucking her. She was the ideal amount of vulnerable and sexy, and it took every ounce of concentration not to sheath my dick. I draped an arm around her, grabbing her tits as I wedged my erect cock between her closed thighs. She gasped at the contact. I held her jaw, and she kissed me.

"Cassian, please. Just do it."

It was hard to ignore her, especially when her arousal spilled over me. It'd be easy to bury myself and go to town. She was too sweet. I thrust my tongue between her lips as she pushed, rubbing harder.

"Cassian!"

I dropped to the mattress and tugged her hips over my head. She resisted before I forced her to sit on my face. My tongue delved into her and her walls seized. I ate her out like a starving man, encouraging her when she descended. Rain ripped the bedspread, fists clenched so tightly they bleached, as though restraining herself from grinding on me.

I wrapped her waist and wrenched her. She tensed before coming again. She cried, digging her nails into the bed.

When she stopped shuddering, I rolled her to the side.

Rain wore a dazed expression. I shifted to the edge of the mattress and dragged on my jeans, forcing my stiff cock inside. It'd need another release, and I'd get one soon enough.

"Jesus." She moved beside me, leaning on my shoulder. "That was *incredible*."

I wiped my chin, taking a moment to taste the sweetness left behind by her, biting into my thumb to keep from yanking her legs apart and fucking her.

Rain's hair tickled my skin, and then she leaned closer, kissing me. "I want more."

"You'll have more. Later."

Rain wanted me to stay, her desire made clear by the way she clung to me even as I dressed. I didn't have the heart to brush her aside. Part of me wanted to join her under the sheets and fall asleep.

I caught her hand before she touched my cheek and kissed her wrist. "It's a damned shame."

"What is?"

I couldn't say it.

This won't last.

Chapter Fifteen

Cassian

Days later, I still couldn't sleep. I couldn't wipe Rain from my mind. I stared at the door separating our rooms, and the temptation nagged at me all night.

So did guilt.

When we said goodbye that evening, her eyes were sad. I left anyway, despite the deep reservations in my gut. I was such a bastard. Her downcast gaze stayed with me like a chest cold. I wondered if she was awake, too.

Was she okay?

Did I fuck things up?

My nightstand blared with a phone call. I groped for my cell, glaring at the screen. Richard.

I answered. "Hey."

"Are you fucking the senator's daughter?" Richard went straight for the jugular—as always.

I appreciated the bluntness, but not at two in the damned morning. I shifted the phone as I sat up in bed. "What kind of question is that?"

"A valid one, I think. Especially after looking at the other day's tabloid. You and your protectee are *pretty* cozy."

Fuck, not again. "Am I supposed to know what you're talking about?"

"Check your phone, asshole."

I did.

My stomach clenched as I enlarged a photo of Rain and me at the National Mall. It was damning. Her back pushed against the food truck, wearing daisy dukes and that white blouse patterned with anchors. I held her shoulders. Rain tipped her face toward me, red pout parted, eyes half-closed. Must've been snapped right before we kissed.

Busted. "That shot was taken out of context."

I winced at my deadpan delivery.

"Cassian." Richard sounded more exasperated than angry. "You and this girl get along too well."

True. "Look, I can explain."

"Oh? I'd love to hear this."

"I was just comforting her."

"You seem to do a lot of that lately," he said dryly.

"Which is amazing because I've never seen you care about anyone but yourself."

"Ouch."

"Stating the facts."

I should've gone to his damned barbecues once in a while. "I do nice things for people."

"Since when?"

"I donate to charity," I growled. "And I offer discounts to repeat clients."

"Wow," he snorted. "You're a saint."

I ripped the sheets off my bed, the fatigue wiped from my mind. I locked the door separating my room from Rain's, hissing into the speaker. "*Fine.* I'm a jerk."

"I'm not calling you to give you shit. Honestly, I'm worried. Your father contacted me recently."

"Yeah, about that. *Never* mention to him where I am. We don't have a great relationship."

"I see." Richard lapsed into silence. "May I ask why?"

"No."

"Come on. I tell you everything."

"Against my will."

Violent coughing burst from the phone. Richard recovered, wheezing. "Gimme a break. If you hated me, you'd hang up."

"What do you want from me? You're my boss."

"I know you, and vice versa. You need someone in your life. Call me, for God's sake."

"No." I bristled. "Again, you're my boss."

"So-the-fuck-what? Rain's your protectee," he countered. "Unless she's becoming more than that."

I switched the cell to the other ear, groaning.

Richard broke the lull with a gasp. "She is, isn't she?"

She was just a fling. Jesus, was I still lying to myself? Rain was so deep inside me that I couldn't get a good night's sleep.

"That is the dumbest thing I ever heard of. Why would I jeopardize my career?"

"No idea. Midlife crisis?"

Richard was so damned irritating.

I snapped the top off a water bottle. "I'm too young for midlife."

"You don't act your age. My eighty-year-old dad is more animated than you."

"Yeah? Well, I bet he doesn't see as much action."

"Oh, you'd be surprised. Nursing homes are sex compounds. Seniors swap STDs like business cards. They figure they can't get pregnant and they're dying, so why bother with condoms?"

I grimaced. "Wow. I did *not* want to know that."

"I do. Gives me some hope for the future."

Such a freak. "Rich, I'm not fucking her."

"I'll extend you the benefit of the doubt. Once. Only because I find it hard to believe. What do you have in common with a nineteen-year-old?"

I stared at her door, picturing her buried beneath her covers. Rain liked to sleep under a mountain of pillows and comforters. We shared none of the superficial things. Our political alignment was night and day. She loved romantic comedies. I watched *Ice Road Truckers*. She was as innocent as I was bitter, and our music tastes clashed horribly.

But I liked everything that made her different. She was fun to be around. She brought out the best in me. She was utterly selfless, and too beautiful to leave alone. Rain demanded my attention.

I'd give her my body, career be damned.

Richard's wet cough cut through my thoughts. "Jesus, this will not go away."

"Sounds bad. You should see a doctor."

"Yeah, I'll make an appointment," Richard wheezed, making me wince. "I won't say anything more about the girl. Only this—she'd better be worth it."

"Stop reading trashy tabloids."

"I mean it, Cassian. He's a *senator*. He can ruin your life."

Already has. "Bye, Rich."

I hung up and tossed my phone across the bed, stewing about the risk I took every time I touched the senator's daughter. My strange indifference over destroying my livelihood didn't extend to Richard. If his security firm lost clients because of my indiscretions, I'd feel guilty.

A soft knock tapped the door. I hesitated before

unlocking my side, revealing my protectee in striped pajama bottoms and an AC/DC shirt. Rain's sleepy smile widened when she saw me shirtless.

"Hello."

"What are you wearing?" I teased, brushing purple strands from the logo. "You weren't alive when they were popular."

"Do I have to be born in the decade of music I like?"

"What are you doing up?"

She shrugged. "I can't sleep. Heard you moving around, so I thought I'd bug you. Interested in a Jeff Goldblum marathon?"

I laughed. "How do you know who that is?"

"*Jurassic Park*."

"Everyone and their mother has seen *Jurassic Park*. Name another movie he's in."

She ticked them off her fingers. "*The Fly, Independence Day*, and *Earth Girls Are Easy*."

"I'm not familiar with the last one, but it sounds interesting."

"It's a sci-fi musical. Very cheesy."

I suspected she wanted me in bed more than a goddamned Jeff Goldblum marathon, which I'd suffer through if she weren't crushing on me. *Hard*. Ever since my lawyer friend had filed a motion to stay against the eviction notice, Rain clung to me like...well, like a *virgin*.

How would I let her down gently?

I'd *never* be her boyfriend. I couldn't give an iota of the affection she needed. I was terrible for her in every way. What would I do, toss her aside?

"We're supposed to have boundaries, Sunshine. Why are you such a rule-breaker?"

"You started this," she pointed out.

"Yes, I did, but I don't care about Jeff Goldblum."

"Cassian, I just want you."

I brushed my knuckles against her flushed cheeks, marveling at how she seemed to love my scars. Other women flinched or pretended not to be disgusted, but Rain melted at my touch like wax to a flame. She closed her eyes and tried to bury her joy.

I could play along.

Maybe I'd even enjoy it.

Soon, I'd have to break her heart, and something told me she wouldn't be the only one hurt.

Chapter Sixteen

Rain

Sweat broke through the thick makeup the artist insisted was necessary for the HD cameras. Another fifteen minutes under the punishing Californian sun, and all her hard efforts would slide off. I wilted, channeling Cinderella's stepsister, with my feet shoved in heels that pinched my toes and clothes that didn't flatter as much as hide my body.

My lips pulled into a taut grin as Cassian led me into the fold of assistants. Dad waved at me, beaming.

We were there to open a hospital wing my father had helped fund. I'd wondered about the work that went into photo ops, and now I had my answer. Every detail was meticulously planned, often months in advance. Aides hand-picked the children behind us from a pile of hopeful letters. Hospital security stood under the wing's awning, shielded from the harsh rays. A black SUV was parked nearby, the driver fanning his face as a bodyguard blocked its doors. Dad had booked them weeks before.

My outfit was prepared. They covered me in a crème tunic dress with sleeves. So not my style. I'd never wear it again, even if it wasn't July.

I patted my neck with a folded handkerchief, swearing when beige stained the cotton.

My makeup artist tutted, opened her kit, and stabbed the setting powder. Her brush attacked my skin, the bristles tickling my nose. I inhaled dust, sneezed, and dabbed my nostrils. She sighed, undoing the damage I'd done by wiping.

God, I needed out of here, but I'd given Dad my word.

Dressed in a navy blazer, white shirt, and charcoal slacks, my father screamed camera-ready. He didn't sweat. Nothing fazed Dad when his supporters surrounded him, but he gave my hair a disapproving scowl. His displeasure sat in my stomach like a rock. I told him I'd reconsidered our deal, but still wanted to help him.

I was *that* desperate for his approval. "Isn't it time for your speech?"

"Not quite." Dad draped an arm over my shoulder as men and women filtered into the event, lured by the campaign signs and multicolored balloons. "You remember what to do?"

"Smile. Look at cameras. Clap when appropriate." I shrugged. "Seems simple enough."

"Good."

I almost bit my lip. "Aren't you afraid they will see through this?"

"What?"

"The sick kids. Me in this schoolmarm outfit." I met his steady gaze, trying not to frown. "If you want to reach young people, this isn't how to do it. We sniff out insincerity like you can tell a Merlot from a Chardonnay."

"Rain, my social media manager knows what he's doing."

"I hope so," I sighed, fanning my neck. "So, I was thinking. Maybe we could hang out afterward?"

Dad gave me a thin smile. "I have meetings with my constituents, but I'll be home for dinner."

Another strained half hour with my stepmother?

No thanks.

"Guess I'll see you in a week. Or whenever your political strategist says you need a father-daughter photo."

His pale blues cut to me. "Now's not the time."

It never fucking was. "I'll wait for our twenty-minute heart-to-heart where we awkwardly stare at each other."

"Rain, I'm serious. I can't do this."

Acid stung my throat at his dismissal. All I wanted was

a chance to repair our broken relationship, but he never put in the effort. Two years ago, he'd promised to make us a priority. I'd believed him when he apologized for being absent, but he would've said anything so that I'd drop the lawsuit.

He treated his supporters more like family than his flesh and blood. He talked about them like a rock star waxes about their fans, with a shine that stoked the flames of my jealousy.

Dad squeezed my side before approaching a microphone stand flanked by bodyguards.

His supporters ceased vying for his attention and quieted. I swallowed my hurt feelings and grinned. I tuned out his speech. Cheers erupted as he navigated a bullet-point list of *I will do this* and *I will do that*. Empty promises. He'd sold me on the mother of all lies—*I will be there for you.*

When the crowd clapped, I brought my hands together like a marionette doll. Dad's speech ended with a burst of fanfare from the speakers, and then he mingled. Unable to stomach it a moment longer, I faced the children.

An olive-skinned girl wearing a fuchsia bow winced from the sunlight. "You have pretty hair!"

I stooped to her level, smiling. "Thanks. My name is Rain."

"Rain? That's cool. I'm Ayla. What color is your hair?"

"Hmm." I grabbed a strand and frowned. "What do you think?"

She scrunched her nose. "Purple?"

"Yep! Purple's my favorite."

"Mine too. My sister's favorite is pink." Ayla picked at her bow. "But they made me wear this."

"Oh, how awful of them. You know what? I think you'd look better in my glasses. Want to try them on?"

"Sure!"

I yanked the shades from my purse and handed them to her. "Here. Keep them."

Ayla mashed them onto her face and flashed a toothless grin. "Wow! Thank you!"

I liked the sunglasses, but they were a small price to pay for her smile. Members of the press asked Dad for sound bites. His responses droned in the background as I chatted with Ayla, six years old with acute lymphocytic leukemia. My eyes burned as she recited her hopes and dreams (to be cancer free and join the United Kingdom's royal family).

"You don't need a crown to be a princess, sweetie. Just the right accessories and you've got one already." I pinched her cheek.

"Will you visit me?"

"As long as your mommy says it's okay."

Ayla jumped and ran into her mother's legs. The

woman's gaze widened at something as Ayla demanded her attention. "Mom, you're not listening!"

Suddenly, the air charged. A thousand needles pricked my skin into gooseflesh.

A man yelled.

I whirled.

It was like a fight broke out. Montgomery's sheep were no longer docile. People shoved and tripped. They screamed expletives while shaking their clothes. Someone bolted through a cord running from the microphone stand. It tipped and crashed. Feedback from the speaker shrieked.

I covered my ears, wincing. I looked for Dad, but security had whisked him toward the SUV.

Why was he leaving? Shouldn't he break up the scuffle?

Swift movement dragged my gaze to a red sphere sailing through the sky. It exploded, splattering me with a bright, tacky substance. A water balloon? Who threw it?

I searched the crowd as my dad's SUV peeled from the parking lot. A hard blow smacked my temple. The balloon burst, drowning my hair with a thick fluid that streaked the concrete.

"Are you okay?" Ayla yelled.

"Ugh. I'm fine." I wrung my hands, inhaling the metallic stench. "Gross."

A strong arm ripped me from Ayla. Cassian yanked me

into the hospital as I dripped on the pristine floors of the new wing.

Lovely.

"Are you hurt?"

"Not at all." Aside from the brief sting, I felt nothing but disgust at the caustic scent. "I think it's paint."

Hospital staff and assistants swarmed me, bleating suggestions as I stared at the growing puddle around my heels. Someone handed me a towel, which I wrapped around my head.

A hospital security guard took one look at me and said, "What the hell?"

"A protestor did this," Cassian grumbled. "Police are probably detaining him."

"Cassian, take me to the house. I need to get this off."

"Hold on." He checked me for injuries, his nose wrinkling from the smell. Satisfied, he growled orders into his radio. "We're good to go."

"Is my dad going home?" I asked him.

"I don't know." He hauled me from the swarm of aides discussing strategy for how to play the failed photo op.

I followed him to the opposite end of the building.

Thank God there were no media vans. A Lexus was parked at the curb.

I paused. "Wait, I'll ruin the seats."

"Do you think I give a fuck?" Cassian yanked the door open. "Get in the car, now."

I slid inside, wincing as the vibrant red smeared the leather.

Cassian ducked into the passenger seat and barked at our driver. "Take us home."

"What happened?" I wiped my hands on the ill-fated dress. "God, what a mess."

"A teenager came to the event with balloons and had a field day." Tension dissolved from Cassian's forehead as we were whisked away. "Little jerk."

"Why would he do that?"

"He meant to hit your father." Cassian shrugged, unconcerned. "Police will handle it."

"Oh, is that all?" I deflated into the cushion. "We didn't have to leave. It's just paint."

"Escape and evacuation is protocol. His safety was compromised." Cassian perked up, smiling into the rearview mirror. "Plus, your dad's photo op was fucked. Probably doing damage control."

He sounded too happy, but I shut my mouth because I didn't want to annoy my only bodyguard. "Our first appearance without Q, and it bombed. Coincidence?"

"No," Cassian grunted.

Quentin had packed his things and left before we returned to California. I still texted him, but his replies were sparse. I hated that our last interaction was so ugly.

All thoughts of Quentin fled my mind when we reached Presidio Heights. The car rolled into the property and parked. Barefoot, I slid onto the gravel and listened to Cassian's low, pleasant voice as he thanked the driver with a fifty-dollar bill. Cassian generously tipped drivers, hotel staff, and anybody who held open doors. When I asked why, he said tipping was essential for his industry. Better service came with larger tips, and he was never reimbursed, so I'd pushed my dad to give him a bonus.

Cassian gave the driver a friendly wave as he pulled from the driveway. He could be personable or menacing, depending on the company. In the presence of colleagues —besides Quentin—he oozed charm. His chameleon-like ability to win people over made me envious. He'd stopped being a hardass weeks ago, probably because he figured chocolate worked better than broccoli.

But once the gates closed behind the Lexus, he dropped the smile. He zeroed in on me. "You okay?"

"'Course. Just some stupid guy." I gestured at his jacket blotched with crimson. "You're the one with the ruined suit."

"I don't care about my clothes."

He followed me to the side of the house. I grabbed the hose and sprayed my hands and feet. "At least it's coming off."

My hair was a mess. I drenched it in cold water, praying it wasn't damaged, but the oil slid from my strands and pooled on the brick path.

"I wonder what the kid was protesting. Was he against

children? Achievements in medicine? Maybe he hated my dress. Can't say I blame him." I flashed Cassian a smirk that he didn't reciprocate. His rising and falling chest was the only sign of life. "Are *you* okay?"

"I'm pissed," he grunted.

"At me?"

"At your fucking father. I said we needed a perimeter. Layers of security. More bodyguards. He brushed my concerns aside, and as a result, you were attacked. *You.* Not him."

Cassian's tortured gaze made me ache. My feelings for him kept growing, but I couldn't tell what he wanted. A whirlwind of confusion collided with the hummingbirds swarming inside.

"It's all right. I'm fine."

"No, it's not. Don't excuse it."

"What am I supposed to do? Cry? I've moped plenty, and I'm tired of it. God, I'm sick of trying so hard. You know what bothers me more than the stupid paint? It's me not belonging in this family. *At all.*"

"You don't want to mingle with a bunch of trust-fund brats."

"Yes, I do." I fought to keep a straight face, but my lip trembled. "Who the hell was I kidding?" I rolled my sleeves and laughed at my splattered dress. "This isn't me, Cassian."

"No, it's not. You're nothing like him."

Cassian's deadpan delivery and his brutal accuracy hit my abdomen with a sledgehammer blow. My stomach caved in as images I'd tempted myself with—snapshots of birthday celebrations and Christmases—erupted into flames. Dad and I would *never* have a fulfilling relationship. I'd flit in and out of his campaign events, but I wouldn't be part of his life.

My throat tightened on a lump, and I stalked toward the sliding glass door. Cassian grabbed my arm and spun me.

"I'm not insulting you. It's the truth."

"Why can't you let me be happy?"

"Because I respect you too much to lie, and it wouldn't help, anyway." Cassian closed the distance, his knuckles brushing my cheek. "You aren't him. So the fuck what?"

"He's my *father*."

"Montgomery treats you terribly. He makes you feel like shit, and he has you convinced you're not good enough because he's a bastard." Cassian made a scornful sound. "Screw him."

"But I—"

"I like you the way you are. You put everybody's happiness before yours, even with people who should mean nothing to you. You don't understand how special that is."

Tears slipped down my cheeks, and his thumbs caught them in gentle strokes.

"Really?"

"Yes. A greedy politician is pedestrian. I could spend a hundred lifetimes searching and never find a woman like you."

I didn't know what to say. Words seemed inadequate for what he'd said. "Why do you pretend to be cold?"

"I don't."

"Yes, you do. It's confusing. You—you can't say stuff like this and expect me to—"

Not to want more.

I gnawed my lip. If I finished that sentence, he'd end our brief fling, finish out his contract, and I wouldn't see him again. The prospect weighted my stomach.

What would I do when he left?

My eyes stung when I imagined a Cassian-free existence. I wouldn't look at the mother-in-law house without a pang striking my chest. He was my first. My pulse galloped when he smiled. When we touched, I melted into a puddle and became a stammering mess. My whole body ached for him. He didn't feel the same, and I suffered when he reminded me of his indifference.

I had to leave.

"You need more." Understanding dawned on his face, and then a heavy resignation. "But I can't give it to you, Rain."

Yes, he could. "You just don't want to."

"It has nothing to do with what I *want*—where are you going?"

I clutched the handle. "I can't do this anymore. Sorry."

I'd never be able to sever my feelings, which had rapidly outgrown their cage. My heart longed to be free, and it would always hurt in his presence.

"*Sunshine.*"

"We promised each other we'd end things if it got too messy, so I'm ending it. If I can't be with you—*really be with you*—then I'd rather be alone."

"Rain," he reasoned.

"I'm done."

"*Wait.*" Cassian's ragged tone stopped me. "Just wait."

Passion blazed through his dark blue eyes as he took a giant step into my space and grabbed my waist. Whatever he needed to say was lost when I knotted my fingers in his hair. Our faces tipped toward each other, pulled in by a magnetic attraction.

He claimed my mouth with a rough thrust as he pressed me against the glass. I yanked his shirt as Cassian stole my breaths. He sucked in my bottom lip, caressed it with his tongue, and bit.

I moaned, tugging the button-up from his slacks. The sliding door opened, and I stumbled backward. I palmed his hip, curving over smooth muscle that sloped to a powerful back. The other unzipped his Kevlar and worked through his buttons. Small, rough ridges glided under my palms. I swept them up a lean torso, his broad pecs sprinkled with hair. I tugged him to meet me. Ecstasy zapped my skin as he deepened the kiss.

We staggered further into the house, the sodden fabric trailing water everywhere. He lifted me, and the bright kitchen twirled. I hung onto his neck as he climbed the staircase, where he bumped into a random room with a king-sized mattress.

Alarm rode my spine. "We are not doing this in my father's bed!"

He swung through another door, and he made a beeline for the shower.

I dropped as Cassian removed my dress, tossing it in a sopping heap. He stripped me of my panties and bra. I shivered as he added his clothes to the pile. "C-Cassian. What if my dad comes home?"

"Then I guess he'll find me with his daughter."

I swallowed as he stepped out of his slacks, leaving his holster on the counter, more nude than I'd ever seen him. Cassian's gaze caught my eye. He winked.

I dared to hope. "What does this mean?"

"It means I don't want to let you go. We need each other. I need you."

My heart swelled four sizes too big as we kissed. Kissing Cassian while clothed was one thing, but while we were both naked with his hardness digging into my stomach? I glided on cloud fifteen.

Water shot from the nozzle as Cassian turned the

knob. When steam fogged the glass, he nudged me inside. The spray flattened his hair, and I enjoyed massaging his head, even though I stood on my toes to reach him. Cassian, in turn, washed my boobs. A boyish grin illuminated his face as he soaped them before turning his devotion to my ass.

"When are we having sex?"

"I'll fuck you in good time, darling. I'm in no rush." Mischief glinted in his eyes. "You're not getting rid of me, Sunshine."

Pleasure radiated to my bones as I crushed my lips against his. His touch ran down my curves like the water. Mist bounced off his shoulders until he knelt and seized my legs. Then he dragged me over his mouth.

I shook as he plunged in. A gasp ripped from my throat, booming across the bathroom and rebounding. I struggled. His flicking teased my clit, and God, I wanted to chase it with my hips. Cassian encouraged me, fingers kneading my thighs, so I ground into him.

I tolerated a few seconds of his greedy tongue before sparks ricocheted across my skin. My body clenched hard. I grabbed for a handhold as dizziness overwhelmed me. Cassian kissed my pussy, his tongue thrumming me as I rode an ecstatic wave. When he got up, he pushed me against the wall and mashed his mouth into mine. His body blocked the spray as he seized my head and shoved his tongue between my lips. Shock zapped my clit as my musky taste swirled all around Cassian's mouth. God, it was fucking hot.

When he had his fill of kissing, he turned me around. My palms smacked the tiles as Cassian thrust himself between my legs. He wrenched my body against his, sliding himself between my folds, but still not penetrating. He groaned as he glided in my slick heat, fisting my hair.

Hot ribbons draped my back as he came. The warm shower melted it away, and he hauled me upright. When we were both washed, we toweled dry and retreated into my bedroom.

He didn't climb into the sheets, but he pulled me into his arms. I nuzzled his bare chest, smiling. His lips tugged into a small grin when our eyes met. We'd never held each other like this. This would be my new favorite way to sleep.

~

A SHRIEK SNAPPED me from unconsciousness. I glanced at the nightstand, where my phone's screen blazed with *Mom*.

I sighed, debating whether to answer. When Cassian came through with the lawyer, Travis and Mom made a joint call to thank him. She apologized for ignoring me. I forgave her, but I couldn't forget.

"Pick up," Cassian prompted.

I mashed the phone against my face. "Hi, Mom. Everything all right?"

"Rain, oh my God, you have no idea how long—I'm so sorry, baby. I wanted to reach you, but Travis started listening to my calls and monitoring my email."

"Are you kidding?" I gasped into the receiver while Cassian's probing stare bored into my back.

"No. I tried kicking him out after the lawyer gave us the stay of eviction. I—it wasn't pretty."

Tears slammed into my vision. "Are you safe?"

"I am. I'm staying with a girlfriend, but eventually I'll have to go back."

"You can't go alone. I'll come with you—hey!"

Cassian plucked the phone from my hands. "Marie, this is Cassian. Rain is right. You shouldn't be alone. I'll send a colleague to escort you. Yes, I'm sure. He's a good friend. No worries. Bye."

Cassian ended the call and tossed the cell.

Stunned, I grabbed it. "What happened?"

"I'll contact my boss. He'll be at your mom's place soon. She'll be fine, Sunshine. He won't let anything happen to her."

My heart was caught in barbed wire. "I don't know what to say."

He rolled off the bed, tugging on his slacks. I helped him button his shirt when he fumbled, burning when my skin brushed his.

"Thank you." I clasped his fingers, stilling his movements. "Cassian, you weren't supposed to be involved with my family shit. I'm happy you did, but...what does this mean?"

"I'm not letting you walk away. I don't care what it takes. If I have to meet you halfway, that's what I'll do." He grasped my chin, silencing me with a fierce kiss. "You're mine."

He winked as he headed out, and confusion rankled my chest. I needed clear labels, but he'd never give me one because intimacy scared Cassian. He had no problem going down on me, but a fifteen-minute cuddle was too much.

I stood at my window as he strolled the lawn, jacket draped over his shoulder. He reached the mother-in-law unit and disappeared. The windows shuttered.

Cassian parsed out personal details like state secrets. He let nobody in, and he suffered for it. A reckless idea formed in my head. Something that would benefit him, if I pushed hard enough.

How could I get through to him?

The fire.

It would either bend us or break us.

Chapter Seventeen

Cassian

Fuck me with a rake.

This girl had me by the balls.

I replayed what I'd said as I ripped open my fridge. Half-assed promises wouldn't cut it with Rain. She'd leave if I never showed her affection, and I couldn't bear handing her to someone else.

The door smacked as it closed. Eating was off the table until I figured this out, because she was right. I was sweet on her, had been since the beginning, and I'd adjusted my rules a thousand times.

Why?

The answer was closing in like a bull at a matador. Lust didn't explain how I acted around Rain. No, this was stronger than attraction. Having her wrapped in my arms was peaceful, but still, I'd dragged myself from her room. I helped with her family. I was too involved. Meeting her gaze shattered my iron will.

And it didn't take a genius to figure out why.

I had feelings for Rain.

Inappropriate feelings. Emotions that made me question myself, because the overwhelming warmth clouded my judgment. My pulse raced at the thought of losing her, and it wasn't just her body I wanted.

Fuck.

In my mind, I stomped on them with a steel-toed boot.

I grabbed the cell from my pocket and dialed Richard's number.

"Hello?"

"Hi, Rich."

"Hey, Cass. How are you?"

"Not bad. You?"

He murmured, "Never better."

I listened to him drink, hating the sound of ice tinkling on the glass. It reminded me of my father's drunken sobs during late-night calls, but Richard wasn't an alcoholic. He always had his shit together. When he moped, something was really wrong.

After five minutes of monotonous chitchat, I caved. "Rich, what's the matter?"

Richard's sigh came through the line. "Vicki and I are separating."

"Damn. I'm sorry."

"She's been to a lawyer and everything. Doesn't want couple's therapy—can't say I blame her. Our marriage has been lackluster for a while."

Yeah, I might've caught that. "You didn't seem that happy with her, to be honest."

Richard sighed again. "No, I guess not."

"Did she move out or what?"

"Yes. She said she wasn't feeling it anymore."

"Sorry, man."

"Thanks," he mumbled. "You know what bums me out? That I'm not very upset. That fact bothers me more than my wife leaving me."

I walked the length of the mother-in-law unit as though a supportive phrase would swoop from the darkness. "Sorry."

"It's all right. Thank you for calling, but I think I'll go to the range."

"Is that a great idea?" I blurted. "I can hear you drinking."

"It's ginger ale, Cass."

If he was sober, I could still ask him.

Now or never. "Listen, I know this isn't a good time, but I need a favor from you. It's important."

Interest piqued in his voice. "A favor?"

"Yes."

"Wow." Richard shed his melancholy like someone removes a jacket. "Am I being punked?"

"This is serious. I have a possible domestic violence victim who needs protection."

Richard sobered at once. "A relative?"

He knew damned well most of mine were dead. "Sunshine's mom."

"Who the hell is Sunshine?"

I groaned. "That's what I call Rain."

The cell's speaker boomed with his laughter. "You have a nickname for her? And it's *Sunshine*? You're killing me."

I endured it as long as I could. "Lock it up."

Richard's hilarity dissolved into soft chuckles. "Oh, Cass. You have it so bad for this girl. When's the wedding?"

"I'm not marrying her."

"'Course not. You're her bodyguard."

Sharp frustration needled my chest. "I knew you'd make a big deal out of this."

"Shouldn't I? You're calling to ask a favor for your protectee, who you're definitely fucking. I ought to fire your ass."

"It's not what you—I'm doing everything I can to keep her safe." I ground my teeth, hating that I couldn't come clean. "You know me. I wouldn't take advantage of a woman."

That was perfectly true.

"You're skating on thin ice, fuck head." He talked as though he wore a smile. "You're not as slick as you think."

I squeezed the phone. "I'm just trying to help her."

"She has you wrapped around her pinkie."

"If you shut up sometime this century, I'll tell you why I need you."

"Okay, okay," he relented. "I'm listening."

"Her mother needs an escort to her house. She broke up with her boyfriend, but he won't leave the apartment. I've done a background check, and he has prior convictions. You've heard this story before. You know what'll happen the second she steps into that place. I'm worried."

"Why call me?"

"She's a decent person who deserves a chance, and if there's one guy I trust with cutting down an abusive prick, it's you. I wouldn't be half the bodyguard I am if it weren't for you."

Richard lapsed into silence.

"I like how you complimented me and patted yourself on the back at the same time. Well, all right. You've buttered me up. I'll do it."

"Awesome. I'll text you the details. Thanks, Rich."

"You owe me."

"Whatever you want. I'll be at every barbecue for a solid year."

"You better," Richard grunted, a sly note entering his voice. "Oh, and when you do marry the girl, I expect to be best man."

"Sure."

I rolled my eyes as we hung up.

Me and Rain, married. It was a ridiculous idea—until an image of Rain in a bridal gown steamrolled me.

Her, standing at the altar with a faceless stranger. Anger licked my heart, engulfing it in flames.

∽

Rain's skinny arms basked in the light as she drove the Lexus, dodging in and out of traffic as we left the bridge. Her hair had lightened to a silvery shade of purple. Giant sunglasses covered her face. She wore flip-flops and a semi-transparent dress that fell across her thighs. I palmed her leg, dragging the fabric to her thong.

"Distracting me is very unsafe."

She had a point.

"Rain, keep it under seventy."

"Uh-oh. He's using my name." Rain flashed a grin but eased up on the gas. "Is this a serious breach in protocol?"

"Not really. I can't stop you from everything. I just made you think I could."

"Not for long."

Too right. "Where are you taking us?"

"Somewhere important."

Odd thing to say.

After Richard scared off Travis from her mom's apartment, Rain wanted to go somewhere with me. She remained tight-lipped about where we were going, insisting on making it a surprise. I didn't do well with surprises but played along. She said it wasn't far. We headed east.

What the hell was here?

I mulled over the options as Rain intertwined her fingers with mine. Holding her slowly became second nature, but I couldn't bring myself to let her in. I'd hidden too many things from her, and I liked what we had.

"Crap. Need to change lanes."

SAN CARLOS AVE. 1 MI

My gut wrenched, taking me by surprise.

We were close to my old stomping grounds, and the backdrop of rolling hills dotted with trees sickened my stomach. I swallowed the bile.

It had to be a coincidence.

Rain took the exit, carrying out a series of turns that heightened my suspicion. My insides turned to stone when she pulled over, stopping at a green sign.

Wisteria Avenue.

I grew up on the palm-lined street.

It was also where my sister died.

A lump lodged in my throat. "Why are we here?"

"I'm sorry for lying to you." She cut the engine and faced me, blanching. "But I didn't think you'd ever agree to come here."

"No shit. Start the car."

Rain shook her head, her eyes wide. "No."

"What do you mean, *no*?" I stared at her, bewildered by this betrayal. "This has nothing to do with you. How did you even find it?"

"I looked up your name and found your previous addresses." Rain met my gaze, looking determined. "This isn't about me nosing in your business. I want you to face the past instead of hiding from it."

"How am I hiding?"

"You never reveal anything about yourself, only superficial details. If I didn't exist, you'd spend your days alone."

I leaned across the console, teeth bared. "Maybe I like my life."

"Liar."

"Who you are, my therapist?"

Pink tinged her cheeks. "Your girlfriend."

I rubbed my forehead, fighting to control my tone. "What does that have to do with this place?"

"I know a spark when I feel one, but it won't matter if you never open up. This will fade. We'll never have a chance if your history is a big question mark."

The street sign forced that violent night into my head. I clenched my hands to keep from shaking.

She didn't understand what being here did to me.

"You have no right to rub my nose in what happened so that you can satiate your curiosity! How could you do this?"

"Cassian, I'm trying to help." She clasped my fists, her eyes already misting with tears. "Because I care about you so much. I want to help you heal."

My voice chilled. "Heal?"

She snatched her palms, whitening. "Yes."

"You think I'm a broken man, is that it? That you—and you alone—can fix me? You're not Mother Teresa. You have no idea what you're forcing me to confront."

"How can I? You won't tell me anything."

"For good reason," I growled. "Have you ever considered that I might not want to be healed?"

Rain sank into a tearful silence. Her face crumpled in the rearview mirror. My lungs collapsed when she stifled a sob, but before I could touch her, she unbuckled her seatbelt.

"Rain, I'm sorry."

She didn't look at me. She left the car, strolling past my window without a backward glance. I sat, paralyzed, as she turned onto Wisteria and disappeared.

Why did I pour acid on her tender heart every time she tried to help?

It wasn't her fault for assuming my sister's death was an accident.

I'd crushed her.

If I let her go, I'd lose her forever.

I burst from the car. When I staggered onto the street, my lungs tightened. A bright blue sky offered a fantastic backdrop against the stucco houses leading up a gentle slope.

I searched for Rain. I'd drag her to the Lexus, apologize, and give her a version of the truth. Before that, I had to find her. There was nothing but rows of dilapidated houses, bars on windows, broken children's bikes lying on yellowed grass. I searched driveways and between backyard fence slats. My hopes were dashed when my destination was only five houses away.

Fuck.

I revisited that night multiple times a year, but this threw me into the deepest hell. Each step closer intensified the agony radiating from my hands. Orange flames jumped to the blackened sky. Fire was everywhere.

It surrounded me, leaping from the gloomy corners of my mind where I'd shoved Claire because thinking of her hurt. Because it was easier not to feel. Because I'd spent so long detaching from everything and everyone, that I'd forgotten the comfort of suffering, and now it choked me.

Numbers painted on the curb grew until they reached 406.

I balled my fists and quashed the fear. It was just four walls and plaster.

When my breathing slowed, I glanced up.

A two-story house perched on a dead lawn. I'd returned only once after the fire to salvage anything of my sister's when the crime scene techs had allowed us to root through the carnage. This modern construction looked nothing like my childhood home or the harrowing aftermath.

A chain-link fence separated the property from the neighbors'. The golden yellow stucco contrasted nicely with the dark brown tiled roof. It barely resembled the ghost from my past. All that remained was the giant oak.

Grief squeezed my throat. I pictured my sister's grass-stained jeans sprawled on the lawn, back against the trunk, her forehead wrinkled as she buried her nose in a book.

My eyes burned and misted. I turned my back on the house and dropped to sit on the sidewalk, the energy draining from my limbs. Several minutes passed before a pair of flip-flops smacked the pavement.

Rain's face was a mask of tears, but she made no sound. She couldn't meet my gaze. Her lip quivered.

I was certain she wanted to apologize, but I didn't need to hear it. "Sunshine, come here."

She hesitated. I reached for her hand and tugged her down. Her warm body pushed into my side. I wrapped her trembling waist and pointed.

"Claire read under that tree. I can still see her." I grinned at the memory, but my heart wrenched with pain. "God, I wish she were here."

"Tell me about her."

"She liked wearing my clothes. Used to steal my shirts and played dumb when my dad caught her. She hated that they didn't manufacture Teenage Mutant Ninja Turtle apparel for girls. She was fearless. Climbed into people's backyards, scaled trees, and beamed her way out of trouble."

She'd always be a little girl.

I'd lost her so young. We could've had decades.

Bittersweet anguish sharpened into anger.

"I'm sorry," she blurted. "Bringing you here was—was a mistake."

"It's fine."

"No, it's not. I hate that I hurt you. I'm terrified of losing you."

"You won't." I cupped her cheeks, and she leaned into my touch. "I have far more good memories in that house than bad ones. Thank you."

I pressed my lips into hers, and she sighed. It was a sweet, bolstering kiss. She hugged my neck, digging into my shoulders as though she feared I'd tear her off. I slid down her throat and pulled her close, relishing the citrus scent of her skin, her flying heartbeat, how my wounds knitted when we kissed.

We parted, but still clung to each other.

I opened and closed my mouth, trying to get out what boiled inside as Rain stroked my back.

"Couldn't save her. I tried, but it was hopeless. Claire was gone when I found her."

Shackled to her bed.

Rain's chest swelled. "I'm so sorry."

"Didn't put it together at first. I had to free her—stuck my hands in the fire and yanked her. The pain didn't even register. Then a firefighter grabbed me. Hauled me out of there. I fought him. I thought she had a chance, but then the roof collapsed."

"God." After a stunned silence, she spoke again. "And your father?"

Revulsion hit my guts. "He was already out."

Rain sensed the bitterness in my tone. "You blame him?"

"He should've saved us."

She tightened her embrace. "It wasn't your fault. Or your dad's."

"That's hard to accept."

"Bad things happen to good people, and most of the time there's nothing we can do. Don't punish your dad. I'm sure he feels horrible about losing his daughter."

"He does."

Rain disengaged, sympathy etched on her beautiful face. "She would've wanted you to live, Cassian. Isn't living life to the fullest a better way to honor her memory?"

"Maybe, but I can't let go of the guilt."

I could tell by Rain's furrowed brows that she didn't understand.

She curled on my lap and rested her head against me. I smoothed her hair, and she nestled in the crook of my neck.

"Are you furious with me?"

"No, babe." A megaton weight felt like it lifted from my chest. "You were right. It helps to talk."

Since we met, I'd broken every rule, and now she lived in my veins, changing the very fabric of my existence.

I cared about her, too.

And because of that, I'd forever keep the whole truth hidden.

Chapter Eighteen

Rain

GET DOWNSTAIRS.

I stared at Cassian's text as I flipped through channels. *What's up with him?*

His messages were impossible to dissect because he used the bare minimum of emojis and responded to my long-winded paragraphs with one word. Two nights before, I'd sent him this:

Me: Hi, Cass. Sorry for what I did. I wanted to help, but I took it too far. I haven't had a lot of experience, and sometimes it's overwhelming. But I hope you realize that I care about you deeply. You're the strongest person I know, and I'm proud of you. <3

Cassian: :)

He wasn't a texter. I was still coming to terms with it.

My thumb hovered over the screen, but I put it aside. Cassian preferred calls, so I tapped his name as I bounded off the couch.

My heart hammered when the call connected. "Hi there."

After what happened in San Leandro, I didn't want to force my presence on Cassian. I needed to process what he'd shared about his sister's death. And he probably needed space.

He'd burned his hands, that much was evident—but, God, the truth was worse than my imagination. Disturbing images floated to my mind, and I shut them down as I busied myself with household chores.

I didn't contact Cassian again. I was excited he'd reached out on his own.

"Hey. I'm taking you out."

I switched off the TV, nerves abuzz with pleasure. "Where?"

"Wherever you want, babe," he murmured, his voice mellow. "It's nice out. A walk through the Mission?"

"Oh, that's perfect! When?"

Maybe we could visit a brewery. My fake ID sat at the bottom of my drawer, where it stayed after I moved in with Dad. I hadn't used it out of respect for him, but I was dying for a beer.

"Now?" I raced upstairs, phone clutched to my ear. "Why didn't you tell me we had a date?"

"I am telling you."

"I mean like an hour or two ago!"

"We live in California, not New York," said Cassian, exasperated. "You don't have to wear anything fancy."

"If I poke my head out the window, I won't see you in a suit?"

"No." Amusement rumbled in his rich baritone. "I'm wearing jeans and a button-up. Bodyguards don't put on suits all the time. I only do it when the client demands a strict uniform."

"I had no idea." As I rifled through my closet, I ripped through racks of clothes. "What am I going to wear?"

"Something that shows a lot of leg. Or ass. Both?"

"Sleazy isn't my style."

I picked through summer dresses with diving necklines. I wanted a classy number. The same maxi dress I wore when I met Cassian slipped through my fingers. Dashing into the bathroom, I dotted my eyes with liner and slicked my mouth with bright, pale pink. I grabbed my fake ID and found a pair of chunky wedges before descending the stairs.

A gorgeous sunset washed the kitchen, turning every marble surface gold. The shimmer silhouetted Cassian's broad frame, which stood at the glass doors. My heels tapped the tiles as I approached, awed by the brilliant light.

I opened the door and fell under Cassian's shadow. Pleasure squirmed in my stomach. No one ever looked at me the way he did, as though he was looking at a treasure.

"Sorry, but I didn't take your advice. No butt, no legs."

"I don't care." Wonder lit his features. "You're stunning."

God, he was perfect.

He cupped my cheeks and kissed me, teasing with a brief peck. I palmed his shirt, eager to see him naked and feel his thighs gliding under mine. My nails dragged down his collar and scraped the body armor.

I pulled from him, heart pounding. "You're wearing this?"

"Of course. You're still at risk."

He was my bodyguard. I'd forgotten. The past few weeks had blurred our roles, but his responsibilities never changed. How would I react if something were to happen?

"Let's go."

He took my hand, even though we were in full view of the cameras on my father's property. We strolled the lawn and exited the gate, the air saturated with the promise of a balmy summer evening. I inhaled mown grass and charcoal.

Cassian called a rideshare car, which spirited us to the Mission. I pushed the scary thoughts of anything bad happening from my mind as we joined the sidewalks crammed with tech workers. It so wasn't his scene. Cassian was more of an Outer Richmond guy. I visualized him running into the freezing, white spray of Ocean Beach, conquering the riptides that drowned even experienced surfers. I saw him wrapped in a wetsuit and riding waves.

Stony-jawed, he led me down Valencia Street. Carrying on a conversation was impossible with the number of people jostling from bar to bar.

I tugged Cassian's arm as we passed the Wizard's Kettle, a bistro pub I'd been dying to try. "Can we stop here?"

He stopped, glancing at the guard. "Sure, but he'll never let you in."

I raised my eyebrows. "Watch this."

Opening my clutch, I seized the fake ID and approached the heavyset man guarding the entrance. His narrow eyes squinted at me. Beaming, I gave him the card. His wary gaze flicked from the photo to me. "This says you just had your birthday."

"Yep." I studied his tattoo sleeve and gasped. "Oh my God, is that the Gorillaz album art?"

He looked up, lips curving into a sheepish grin. "Yeah, I'm a fan."

"Me too! Did you go to their concert a few weeks ago?"

"Yeah." He handed the ID to me, smiling. "It was off the chain."

"I heard they played an unreleased song."

After a few minutes of chitchat, the bouncer waved me through with a smile. I tried not to look smug as an exasperated Cassian pulled out his wallet.

The Wizard's Kettle was a small, rustic dive, with tiny stools and tables. Knockoff Harry Potter wands filled the shelves behind the counter. Pinball machines flashed in the backroom. It was dark, cramped, and hot. Cassian would be uncomfortable, but there was nowhere else to sit.

He frowned at the VHS mounted on the walls and the television with a built-in VCR playing *The Dark Crystal*. Confusion knitted his brows as he stared at the flickering screen.

"Why are they using old tapes?"

"It's nostalgic." Although I didn't see the appeal of the pixelated video, either. "Millennials love reliving the nineties."

"Not me," he muttered. "You weren't even alive. God, that's crazy."

Cassian's bemusement grew as he scanned the draft list written on a hanging chalkboard. "Butterscotch Ale. A nutty, cracker-like malt flavor in front, ending with a sweet, scotch finish."

"They're copying the book series." I shrugged, rolling my eyes. "It's dumb, but everyone raves about this place."

"What kind of bar have you taken me to?"

"It's a highly rated microbrewery with five different IPAs and the highest IBU scores—"

"Wait, wait, wait. You can't even drink. How do you know so much about beer?"

"Because I read." I flagged down a blonde wearing a brewery T-shirt and ordered a flight.

"Give me a pint of your bestseller," Cassian grunted, turning away from the server. "I didn't realize you were into beer."

"I used to brew it in our garage. It started as a hobby. My mom's friend gave her a beer-making kit, which she passed on to me. It was fun, and weeks later, I got buzzed on my Hefeweizen."

"Wow. That is cool."

"Yeah, and then I needed to brew a kölsch. So Mom bought the supplies—the tubing, yeast, bottles—and I went from there. I wasn't getting drunk or anything. I enjoyed the process. I had to stop because of Travis. Bastard drank everything I made."

"Huh." Cassian mulled that over, studying me. "Interesting."

"You sound surprised."

"I'm impressed. I like a woman who makes me beer."

The waitress returned with our drinks, and Cassian stared at the six-ounce glasses filled with different ales. She dropped the opaque yellow IPA in front of him and left.

"Maybe that's your calling." Cassian sipped his booze and made a face. "Ugh. Too bitter."

"It's the hazy IPA. You said you wanted the most popular beer." I lined my tasters and began with the least hoppy ale. "And I'm not sure if this is a viable career."

"Yes, it is." Cassian attempted another mouthful, wincing. "But don't make this shit. It's like being punched in the tongue with flowers."

"The hops release that flavor when they're boiled. If you hate it, get a drink with the smallest IBU number. It's a scale of bitterness."

Cassian leaned over the table and pinned me with a piercing stare. "You're way too invested in this for a nineteen-year-old. Do you have any idea what I drank at your age? Warm, flat bilge at college parties."

"I can't imagine you at a party."

"It's where all the girls hung out." He shrugged, changing the subject. "Have you picked a major yet?"

"No. I have no clue what to do."

"I'll tell you one thing." Cassian moved his glass aside and took my hand, thumb massaging my palm. "You're like me, Sunshine. You weren't meant to sit at a desk."

"Really?"

"It's just my opinion," he continued in an earnest tone. "I would've appreciated someone planting that bodyguard seed in my head early on. Nobody did, so I became a cop. Total misfire."

Maybe he was right. Almost everyone in this city worked in tech, but I didn't relish a high-powered job or a ladder-climb up a company's executive chain. What I wanted was much more straightforward—family and happiness. Picking a business major felt like ticking off one of my father's boxes.

"How do you read me so well?"

"Because I watch you all day, Sunshine. I know your likes and dislikes. Your pet peeves. What makes you wet."

Especially the last. "I feel like I've barely scratched the surface on who you are."

"That's because I'm older and more mysterious."

I laughed, but he was right. It drew me to him at first. He was a dream-come-true. A dark knight who had finally lowered his gates.

We left the Wizard's Kettle and strolled more of the Mission. Several blocks away, we found a Mexican eatery packed to the gills with families. I chose a spot outdoors as Cassian settled in the queue that led into the greasy dive. He returned with a tray filled with carnitas, water for him, and a glass of horchata for me.

Pride smoldered inside me. He stood head and shoulders above everyone else, and unlike other people I knew, he didn't fill the silence with meaningless chatter.

"What's on your mind?" His graveled voice stroked my skin. "You haven't said much."

"I'm thinking about you."

"You could talk to me." A smile curved into his cheek as he ate the last of his tacos. "Stay with me, Sunshine."

"How—how do I compare to your other dates?"

"I don't date. I meet women, and if they're not crazy and resemble the person in their profile, I bring them home to fuck."

My fork slipped. It rattled against the table, and I clenched my thighs. My mouth went dry. I couldn't admit the fear rattling in my chest.

Suddenly, he brushed my forearm in a soothing gesture. "Hey, you're *not* them. I thought that was clear."

Was I falling for him?

Mom described love like a rollercoaster ride without brakes. It careened forward, no matter who was in its way. I couldn't tell whether or not my fascination with Cassian was infatuation, but our relationship matched Mom's description to a fault.

We did everything we could to be together.

Did he risk his career because he cared about me? Or was this simply a moment of pleasure?

Cassian seemed to sense that I needed to be touched. He lugged his chair close and pulled me on his lap so I couldn't escape the promise in his eyes.

Tonight, he was taking my virginity.

When the Uber dropped us off, Cassian moved me from the car and held me under his chin. We stood beyond the hedges surrounding my father's mansion, yet not out of sight from the security cameras. When I pointed them out, Cassian shrugged. He turned his attention down the gentle slope that offered a view of downtown. A thin, orange line still burned on the horizon, surrounded by a sky of cobalt.

We hadn't talked much on the trip back. Cassian communicated just fine with his hands and mouth. He knew when to hold me, and when my heart screamed for a kiss. He even sensed my reluctance to return home.

"Rain, we don't have to," he whispered. "If you're not ready, it's okay."

I was.

I wanted to give him everything, and that frightened me. He'd won me over weeks ago. He'd break me if I went along with this, but I couldn't resist him.

I met his deep blue gaze. "Cassian, I want this."

My nerves fired on all cylinders as we headed toward his mother-in-law unit. Cassian opened the door. I wandered inside, smiling as my teeth chattered. Cassian slid the deadbolt, throwing us in darkness.

He approached me in one stride, cradling me like he had outside. His hand dove into my hair, but he stopped short of kissing me. "You're shaking."

"I'm scared."

"I won't hurt you."

"Yeah, I know," I sighed, smoothing the lapels on his shoulders. "I'm—I'm worried. I'm afraid you'll ghost me right after you've taken my virginity."

"Why the hell would I do that?"

No idea. "It's just a stupid fear."

Cassian's voice boomed through my ribs. "I don't intend to have you once, Sunshine. For twelve hours, we'll do nothing but eat, sleep, and fuck."

A delicious shiver rode my spine. "Twelve...hours?"

"I waited forever to have you. If I wanted a piece, I could've gone to any bar. I have no intention of tossing you aside." His lips grazed my cheek and halted at my ear. "Anything else?"

Excitement coursed through my veins as I shook my head.

"Good."

Cassian lifted me. Colors danced on the wooden floors as we passed through sunlight. I clung to his neck, overwhelmed. My feelings for him blotted my nerves as he carried me into his bedroom.

He paused, holding me. "How did you picture your first time?"

"I—I thought it'd be unremarkable."

He laughed. "Mine was. Lasted ten seconds."

"How old were you?"

"Fourteen. I'll never understand how you made it to

nineteen." Cassian sank into the mattress, pulling me over his lap. "Guys must chase you across the campus."

"They tried, but I was looking for fireworks, and I haven't gotten them with anybody but you. Cassian, I wouldn't want it any other way. You're perfect for me."

"I'm not perfect."

My heart said different. "I can't stop thinking about you."

Cassian's mouth crashed into mine. It was as though he needed to silence my confession that I was halfway in love with him, falling deeper with each—searing—kiss.

I grabbed his shirt and unbuttoned, gliding it and the body armor off. Once he was bare, I wrapped his middle and squeezed, loving how we fit together. Cassian ground his lips against mine. His tongue pushed through, and I moaned because it reminded me of what he did between my thighs.

Slowly, he pulled my straps down. The sheer fabric tumbled to my waist. He sprinkled my collarbone with kisses as he removed my bra. He teased, claimed, and nipped my breasts. Light touches of his wet heat blazed when he reached my nipple. He sucked, and I dragged my nails into his scalp. It was like liquid, swirling a lazy circle of arousal.

Cassian's hands pursued my curves, and so did his mouth. He kissed the underside of my tit and my stomach, pulling the dress and thong off. As he climbed over me, I gaped at his abs. I'd seen him naked before but would never stop marveling at him.

Cassian was ripped. Beautifully built. Like a bigger Chris Hemsworth. I couldn't imagine anyone confronting him in a fight. Rippling cords flexed his arms, leading to the scars I loved. He unlatched his belt, sliding it from his jeans.

I sat up and helped him, kissing the inch of hard abs above his waistband as I unzipped him. Together, we removed his clothes. My kisses followed the pants as excitement burrowed in my chest. Cassian stroked my face, but when my lips touched his thigh, he fisted my hair.

Damn, that was hot.

I took him in, eager to see him lose control. I loved that I was his undoing. He shed all his rules, shucked his stony mask, and fucked me. He abandoned his calm nature when he hit my throat, and it was a thrill when he shut his ever-vigilant eyes, lowered his guard, and took the pleasure I gave him.

When I tapped his leg, he loosened his grip.

Cassian wiped his forehead. "I'd love to finish in your mouth."

"So why don't you?"

"I'm taking your virginity." He pushed me onto the bed, following me. "Tonight's not about me."

"I need you to have fun."

He cupped my cheek. "I am."

Cassian pressed his lips to mine, a gentle brushing that spiraled into a frenzied make-out session. As our mouths locked, he massaged my breasts and pinched my nipples. I arched my back and reached for his cock, but he pinned my arm above my head.

He tutted. "Patience. I'm not wearing a condom."

It was all I could do to not scream, *Fuck me without protection*. The ache between my legs demanded filling. I lost my sanity in the moment. My body wanted him now.

I groaned when he tongued my nipple, igniting a chain reaction of sizzling heat. His antics made me greedy. I couldn't control my hips when his kisses touched me down there. He lapped, blew hot air, and he sucked.

Too much. "Cassian."

He pulled away and wet his finger between my folds. My pussy seized as he drove inside. Pain stung deep, doubling when he added another digit. Then his mouth found my clit, and the sting melted into pleasure. My walls relaxed.

His tongue stroked my wetness to my clit. He toyed with me, sliding in. I was on fire, and the only way to douse it was with an orgasm. Whenever I was about to burst, Cassian stopped.

"Oh, you evil man."

"I want you to enjoy this, and we stand a stronger chance if you're horny and desperate."

God, I was.

I grabbed his shoulders and wrenched him toward me. Cassian yielded—or pretended to—his eyes laughing. I wrapped him, ankles falling down his back when he crawled forward. He disappeared, and the crinkle of foil ripping preceded his return. He rolled a condom over himself.

"It'll hurt, but then it'll slowly feel good."

I nodded, almost giddy with excitement.

Cassian lowered himself, touching his forehead to mine. It was like peeling the final layer of mystery, and this was the man beneath it all. Tension narrowed his gaze. A broad pressure slipped up and down my slit, grinding. Finally, it halted.

He kissed me and pushed.

So rigid. I winced from the pain, but he pulled out. Seconds later, he drove in deeper.

I grunted.

Cassian paused. "You all right?"

"Yeah." I grimaced. "It's tight."

"That's normal. It'll get better."

He nudged my boundaries with every stroke. My walls clung to him. Uncomfortable. It was like we fought a battle against my body, but gradually it began to ache less. Then it felt wonderful.

His arms on either side trembled. He bit his cheek, clearly fighting some instinct. His glacial pace was for my benefit. Cassian would rather suffer than injure me.

I was in awe of him. The effort was massive because his heartbeat slammed into my chest. I took his face and crushed my mouth against his. My tongue swept his lip, and his hips ground into mine with a sharp thrust. It smarted, but it nailed a deep pleasurable recess I didn't know I had.

I couldn't speak.

His thrusts were slow. He buried himself when my breathing subsided, the pressure riding my clit. I was sore, but pushing against him was amazing. I bucked. Cassian's pounding sharpened. I never knew the joy of Cassian's body gliding over mine, of his short gasps, of his rough kisses as he entered me.

Nothing was better than sex.

He cupped my breasts and deepened his strokes. He shoved inside me, the pain and pleasure so abrupt I yelled. He slowed until I dug into his shoulders. Cassian growled, seizing my waist as he pushed into me. I yanked him and kissed his full pout. I broke. It was as though all the molecules holding me shattered.

I nuzzled Cassian's neck and cried as my walls clenched. Ecstasy flooded my senses, putting all the orgasms I'd ever had to shame. His cock pistoned until his brows drew together, and he came undone with a loud groan. He held me close, sighing. Cassian melted around me. Our lips met again and again until Cassian's forehead touched mine, and a smile widened his jaw. It was the smile that split the heart of every unattached woman in a room.

"I've never seen you like this."

"I'm happy," he whispered, brushing my hair. "I'm with you."

Chapter Nineteen

Cassian

THIS GIRL COULD NOT GET ENOUGH.

In one week, I'd fucked Rain everywhere. I bent her over the kitchen island. Took her on the sofa. Ate her out on the coffee table. Fingered her in the spa. Banged her in the command post.

Nobody noticed I was balls deep in the senator's daughter. It wasn't like we were subtle. I made out with her in front of the security cameras positioned around the house. The footage caught me grabbing her ass. We had sex every day. I learned to pace myself because I wasn't a teenager. Rain didn't want to wait.

As a case in point, Rain teased me under the table. We were supposed to be eating breakfast. At eleven. The last time I woke up this late, I was in college. I focused on my untouched scrambled egg whites, but Rain's hand glided under the hem of my boxers. She grabbed my cock, and then breakfast turned into an impromptu fuck session.

Rain clung to me as I pressed her against the counter. Her legs wrapped my waist, and her dress hung off a shoulder. I buried my face in her tits as I came. She fisted my hair and released a shuddering moan. When my thighs stopped twitching, I slowly let her down.

"Cassian, your pulse." Rain palmed my neck, giggling. "It's so fast."

"That's your fault. Did you think I'd eat my eggs while you blew me?"

"I wanted to see how long you could resist."

"I didn't."

Rain adjusted her gown, glowing. She pecked my cheek and returned to the table. My forehead hit the wall as I breathed deeply. Then I tucked myself inside and stumbled to the chair.

Rain dipped a spoon into her cereal, mouth bulging. "Sleepy?"

"I might face plant into my eggs and sleep for a year."

A pleasant buzz sat in my throat when I looked at Rain, who was far more alert than she should have been.

She shrugged. "I could keep going."

"Are you trying to give me a heart attack?"

She wore me out with her late-night blowjobs, her

greedy hands seeking my dick at three in the morning, and her plaintive moans demanding more.

I needed to sleep for a decade.

"No way. You're too entertaining." Rain ate, her eyes wrinkling with humor. "What?"

I took her tiny hand and dragged it over my lap, not used to the comfort she gave me. "I'm glad you chose me to be your first."

Rain tried burying her smile. "Me too."

A comfortable silence lapsed between us, broken only by the lawnmower's buzz. Rain searched me, head resting on her palm. "You look different."

"We've had a lot of fun since last Sunday. I'm tired, but happy."

This week had been the best of my life, and it was because of her. Every minute with Rain soothed me. I felt better with her. I could think clearly.

Rain kissed my jaw. "Good."

She finished her breakfast as I wolfed mine down. "You should stay and catch up on sleep."

"Nope. You know the rules."

"You need rest." Rain checked her phone and swore. "Oh shit."

"What?"

She ran into the bedroom. I followed her as she picked random articles of clothing, dressing at lightning speed.

"Babe, what's the rush?"

"I have to meet my dad."

Great. I half-heartedly made my bed and lurched into the bathroom. Without bothering to wait for the heat, I turned on the shower. Icy spray hit my face.

"Get washed first."

"No," she moaned. "I'm already late!"

"Leaving in five minutes won't make you any less late."

"If I step in with you, we'll fool around."

I leaned on the tiles, groaning as the water needled my back. "We won't. Promise."

"Yeah, right." Her figure rippled behind the glass as she removed her dress. "You're easily manipulated, Cassian."

She opened the doors. Blood pounded to my groin when Rain's naked curves brushed against me, hair piled on her head. She pressed into my body. Arousal chased my bone-weary fatigue.

"All I feel like doing is *this* every day. All day." She sighed, playing with my stiffening cock. "Will our chemistry ever go away?"

"It might calm a little, but it'll never disappear."

I lathered my hands with soap and caressed her shoulders, admiring the hickeys marking her as mine. "My contract is ending in a month, but we should tell your father about our relationship."

Uncertainty flared from her eyes. "What happens to us?"

"Nothing changes, except I can't be your bodyguard anymore. I can't make decisions about your safety and fuck you all day. It's a conflict of interest."

"Fine. I don't want you risking yourself for me, anyway."

I cupped her cheeks, drawing her gaze. "No matter what, I'll never stop protecting you."

~

Sweet Jesus, make this end.

I stood outside Montgomery's study waiting for Rain to drop the bombshell, which seemed unlikely to happen, since Montgomery bullied her constantly. The man had suffered another defeat in the polls, which meant his confidence for securing the U.S. Senate Primary was shaken. He couldn't berate his trust fund brats, so he picked on her.

"Was I supposed to step aside?" Rain's tone got huskier with the rising tension. "Let the girl take a face full of paint?"

"Smile and wave," Senator Montgomery roared. "How hard is that? Are you incapable of following simple instructions? Or are you punishing me, yet again, for not being in your life?"

"Dad! Of course I'm—I'm not."

"All I wanted was a united front, not to be the laughingstock of the *Washington Times*."

"It's the Internet, Dad! They make fun of everyone."

"Did you see that article?" Montgomery demanded. "I'll find it—ah. Senator Montgomery Photo Inspires Hilarious Memes."

"Dad, you have to relax. This will blow over in a week or two. You just need to wait it out." Her voice dipped, so I strained my ears. "Are you on edge because of the wire fraud thing?"

"That has nothing to do with me," he muttered.

Shortly after the photo op, a picture of Rain and Montgomery went viral on Twitter. It showed Montgomery fleeing the event, surrounded by security, and his daughter with her arms around that kid. Montgomery's opponents seized the image and retweeted it. Montgomery resented Rain for it, like a douche.

God, I loathed him.

"Maybe you should do some humanitarian work. Don't invite the press. Get out there and help your community. Be genuine."

"Much as I appreciate the advice of a teenager, I think I'll stick with my manager."

Silence swelled between them, during which I imagined Rain nursed her hurt feelings. Then Rain spoke.

"Dad, do you love me?"

Oh, Sunshine.

The pause was deafeningly quiet, until he finally said, "Of course I do."

"Then why are you so harsh? I'm doing everything I can to support you."

"Support me?" Montgomery's exasperation suffused me with rage. "I'm constantly bribing paparazzi not to release photos of you. Look at this." They both went quiet, and then he growled. "Go on. Tell me you're sorry."

Rain choked, succumbing to tears. "It was once."

"You were drinking in a bar with your goddamned bodyguard. Do you have any idea what this would do to my career?"

I couldn't stand this.

Listening to her cry after these meetings always sickened me, but now it battered my heart. I opened the door and entered the study, a white office with hardwood flooring. Senator Montgomery glared at Rain, who leaned on his desk. She made eye contact with me and wiped her face.

Her shame twisted my stomach into knots.

Montgomery greeted me with a snarl. "What?"

"Rain." I crossed the room and pulled her in my arms.

"What are you-you doing?" She hiccupped surprise, casting terrified looks at her dad. "I didn't tell him yet."

"It's okay. I'll deal with him." I stroked her hair. "Run upstairs."

"But—"

"Go," barked Montgomery.

Rain glanced at her dad. She wilted like a flower without sun and slipped from me. She disappeared.

I faced her father. "I'm dating your daughter."

"Are you?" Montgomery's wizened features registered nothing but bemused contempt. He tossed a paparazzi photo at me. "I never would've known."

A candid shot of Rain and me kissing fluttered to the floor. I picked it up, studying our happy faces.

Jesus, I looked like a completely different person.

"I hope you had your fun," he spat acidly.

"It's not about that."

"Right." He threw his jacket over a leather-backed chair. "Spare me."

"I'm finished working for you."

"No shit. You're done. You're fired!"

I turned, heading for the door. "You need to hire someone else."

"Walk out, and you'll never work as a bodyguard again."

"Do you think that scares me?"

"I have no idea." Senator Montgomery slammed the desk with a surprising amount of strength for an old man. "But I'll reach out to every security firm and make sure you're blacklisted. Good luck paying your bills."

I couldn't care less. "Whatever."

"What the hell is the matter with you? Dead-eyed *freak*. Don't you care about your career?"

"How will you ruin me, exactly? You don't even know who I am."

"Carter," he blurted. "No, it's Caster."

"Wrong and wrong."

Montgomery's eyes narrowed. "I'll contact my aide and have everything about you delivered to me—"

"Cassian Grant. As in, Claire Grant."

Senator Montgomery's pale eyebrows furrowed. "Who?"

I'd fantasized about this moment. I'd imagined him breaking down into tears. Begging for my forgiveness. Reacting with rage. Denial. Anything but confusion.

It surprised me how much it hurt.

"Claire Grant."

He didn't react. The name meant nothing to him. Either he was the world's greatest actor, or he honestly didn't remember my sister.

How could he forget?

Why did God permit him that mercy, but I was forced to suffer?

I buried my fury for Rain. When I crossed paths with Montgomery, I suffocated my snarling thoughts and locked away my pain. I avoided being alone with him because I didn't trust myself, but now we were alone.

And I'd never felt so vengeful.

"I wish so badly it had been you, not her. Every morning, I pray for your death."

He staggered back and gaped at me. "Excuse me?"

"You killed my sister."

He looked at me like I was crazy and dangerous. "I think you have me mistaken with someone else."

"You never attended the trial, Senator." I approached him, violent images flashing into my mind. "If you had, you would've remembered these hands. This is what you made. You're the reason my dad hasn't been sober in a decade, and why I can't—to this day—step inside a building without finding the fire exits."

The senator slipped behind his chair. "What do you want?"

"Claire Grant," I bellowed. "What do I want? My sister to be alive. Tell me you forgot her name so I can beat the shit out of you."

He drained of color. His pupils reduced into dots. The asshole hid his shame under a thick blanket of denial.

A terrible impulse to strangle him seized me. He was old. It wouldn't take long.

My sister had suffocated and died. So should he.

"I—I have no clue who—"

My arm swept across the desk, upsetting picture frames and the laptop and shattering the paperweight, which cracked the floorboards. The door flew open, and two men restrained me before I lunged. Montgomery must've hit a panic button. He probably had one in every room—the bastard knew how people loathed him.

"Get him out of here!" Montgomery screamed, the fiery glow returning to his face. "Now!"

I fucking hated him.

The ignorance, feigned or not, stuck like a knife in my chest. He wasn't allowed to forget my sister.

God, I'd had him within reach.

I had him, and I did nothing.

I would've killed him.

I was sick.

Sick and broken.

Chapter Twenty

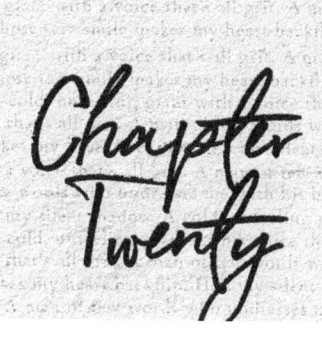

Rain

Why were they yelling?

I frowned at the vent filling my room with incomprehensible shouting as my father and Cassian had a screaming match.

I slid off my chair and cracked the door.

"Get him out of here!" Dad hollered. "Now!"

I peeked over the landing as Cassian was escorted by two guards. Dad followed, barking like a terrier, bellowing obscenities. I'd never seen him lose it.

What did Cassian say?

Dad slammed the door, and then he roared a ragged, "Fuck!"

Dramatic.

My heartbeat galloped as Dad seized his white hair, pacing and working himself up. He discarded his tie and rubbed his face. He collapsed onto the stairs, head in his hands. He stayed in that position, his shoulders curled forward in defeat. That sliver of humanity gave me hope.

I ran to the window as Cassian disappeared from the gates. He'd warned me this might happen, but watching it sucked.

I never wanted him fired, but somehow I'd accomplished that and jeopardized my dad's job. A guilty pleasure inhabited my soul to hear his anger on my behalf. I expected Dad to be annoyed with Cassian, but throwing him from the house?

Maybe he did care.

Suddenly, Dad's heavy footsteps raced up the stairs. He stumbled into my room, his wrinkled chest pulsing from the gap in his shirt.

Livid, he zeroed in on me. "You are never seeing that man again."

He had no right to break us up. The fact he'd stormed up the staircase to kill my relationship disgusted me.

"What happened down there?"

"None of your damned business."

"It is when you're screaming at the top of your lungs." I crossed my arms, frowning. "Save your breath. I'm not leaving Cassian."

"I won't have you under this roof if you're with him!"

"What's your problem?" I shouted. "He doesn't have tattoos. He doesn't get drunk. Cassian is the most responsible man I know."

"He brought you into a bar!"

"I took him there with my fake ID." I swallowed hard, his contempt sinking into my stomach. "It was my decision, not his. Don't blame him!"

"You will not see him again. If you want a relationship with me, you'll end yours with him." White-faced with fury, Dad slammed his fist into my wall. "I won't have it."

He was so ridiculous.

"This is about your pride. You can't stand that he dated me under your nose. Grow up."

"Leave him, or you are cut off!"

His rage blew through me like mist, because if it came to him or Cassian, I wouldn't hesitate to pick my boyfriend.

"Dad, I'm crazy about him. He's good to me."

I waited for him to break. A reasonable person would have, but my father trembled and shook with self-righteous anger. He asked too much from me and gave me fuck all.

I stepped around him, seized my duffel bag, and yanked open drawers. I grabbed my colorful silks, my loud blouses, every sequined top Dad hated, and packed.

"R-rain." His voice cracked. "Think about this."

I was done. "I don't need to. Cassian means the world to me."

"It'll never last," he reasoned. "You're nineteen, and he's thirty."

"We have better odds than you have of getting reelected."

"What kind of man dates a girl ten years younger than himself?"

Eleven, actually. "He's perfect for me."

"Men like him are only interested in one thing, and it has nothing to do with your intellect or your charm. Rain, he'll dump you as soon as he's sick of your naiveté, and weeks from now you'll look on this moment as your biggest regret."

"I'm sure that'll be you."

He clutched my wrists. "Don't do this."

"You're cutting me off because you hate him." I slipped from him and shouldered the heavy pack. "You're selfish. He makes me happy, and you never have."

"Rain, stay."

I kicked on my flip-flops and brushed past him. A strange calm possessed my soul as I ignored his bleating cries that I'd made a promise—that he knew what was best for me.

I looked back when I cleared the gate. Dad stood on the front steps, the door yawning inside his glitzy mansion. The brightness blended with his hair and skin. He was colorless, and I lived in a rainbow. Leaving him would hurt, but it was the sort of pain that would fade.

I wanted to love my father.

I couldn't.

~

My phone's battery was at ten percent, and I no longer had a bodyguard. Cassian wasn't answering my calls, so I took the metro to the East Bay and dragged my things to Mom's doorstep.

Cassian had told me his colleague scared Travis off, but it hadn't worked for long. Travis' Ford was parked on the street. He loved that rusted pickup. If I was malicious, I would've keyed it ages ago.

I hesitated before approaching the house.

Cassian wouldn't like me being here. He believed Travis was a violent criminal who could never be trusted. I didn't trust people. I relied on their behavior, and for all his faults, Travis had never raised a hand against my mother. Confronting him was my choice—not Cassian's.

I knocked. Several moments passed. Before my knuckles touched wood again, a voice boomed from inside.

"Marie! Are you deaf?"

Timid steps creaked the floorboards, and then the door opened an inch. A sliver of a woman peeked through. Mom's beautiful ebony hair that I always admired was coiled at her neck, brushed to perfection. She wore a jean jacket over a tie-dye shirt, black capris, and flip-flops.

She looked great. "Rain! What are you doing here?"

"Dad kicked me out."

"He what?"

"It's fine. I'm sick of living there." I spoke in a whisper, sure that Travis listened to every word. "Are you okay? Why's he still here?"

"He won't leave," she muttered. "I'm trying, honey."

Travis appeared behind my mom, wearing boxer shorts and nothing else. I cringed at his beer belly, which distended the faded, prison tattoos. Desperation hung around him like his rank sweat.

Mom's lips thinned. "My daughter's here."

"She's not welcome."

Her brows narrowed as she stepped outside. "Ignore him. He's been a jackass since I said we would never work. He refuses to go, and because we both signed the lease, I can't force him out."

"Is he hurting you?"

"No." Mom sank onto a patio chair. "He's just making my life hell."

I glanced inside, hating him. "Why won't he fuck off?"

"I don't know, babe." Mom gestured for me to sit, but I didn't want to take it easy while that asshole all but held my mother hostage. "Rain?"

"Going to have a chat with Travis."

"Rain, no!"

Ignoring her, I wrenched open the door and strolled

I pitied him, so I bit back hateful words. "You want to live in a place where you're miserable? Make yourself happy. Don't wait for someone to do it for you."

Travis opened and closed his mouth, stunned. He blinked and looked around as though surprised by the mess. Slowly, he turned off the TV and lurched from the recliner, heading for the bedroom. I followed him as he rummaged through drawers and stuffed clothes into a suitcase.

"Tell her I'll be gone soon," he said without glancing at me. "Five minutes, tops."

"Okay."

Happiness swelled in my heart as I bounded outside. I beamed at Mom, who paced the patio, phone mashed against her cheek. Her face lit with apprehension.

"Never mind," she hissed into the speaker. "She's fine."

"Mom, he's leaving!"

She stowed her cell. "What?"

"We talked, and I convinced him to go. He's packing his things. We should probably give him space."

"How did you do that?"

"I don't know." I grabbed her elbow and moved us away, so thrilled I could sing. "I must've gotten to him."

She tucked a strand behind her ear, distracted by a car rolling to the curb. "Oh, perfect, he's here. I called your boyfriend."

"You did?"

into the apartment. The boxes were gone, but an aura of stale grease clung to the living room. A pile of trash surrounded the recliner where Travis sat. A basketball game roared on the television, but Travis paid it no attention. He watched Mom through the window. Blue light from the screen cast his devastation in sharp relief.

He wiped his face of emotion when he saw me. "Come crawling back, eh? I'm not surprised."

"Me neither. I saw my mom dumping you years ago."

I expected him to spit the venom that consumed his body.

Instead he cracked. "Make her change her mind."

"No."

"Please. I have no one."

"You don't deserve her. I'm not sure you deserve anybody."

He drowned his sorrow in more beer, his fingers buckling the aluminum. "I did everything to keep her."

"That's why you lost her. You never considered what she wanted." My pulse raced as I stepped closer. "And now you need to leave."

"I'm not going anywhere," he bristled. "It's my home, too."

"Look at me."

He did. His alcohol-soaked eyes locked on mine, and they were fractured with pain. Maybe he realized that he'd brought all his agony on himself.

Walnut Creek was a quick hop from Concord, but Cassian must've floored it to reach Mom's house. He emerged from the Mustang and slammed the door. He blazed across the lawn, radiating raw power as he made a beeline for the house.

"Hey!"

"Sunshine." His stony features melted. "What are you doing here?"

I raised my eyebrow, objecting to his tone. "Dad kicked me out. I couldn't get ahold of you, so I came here."

A vein pulsed on his neck as he pinched the bridge of his nose. "I can't believe he did that. Sorry, Rain. I went for a walk, got into my car, and headed to my apartment."

"It's all right. I'm glad you didn't pick up because I wouldn't have come here. Travis is leaving. Forever."

"Seriously?"

"Yeah. I convinced him he was better off somewhere else."

He looked as though I spoke Greek. "How?"

"I pulled a Cassian." I shrugged, meeting his amused gaze. "Told him he had to go."

"Unless you threatened to kick his ass, I doubt you pulled a Cassian." He grabbed my waist, kissing my head. "Next time, wait for me. Anything could've happened."

He tensed as the door flung open.

Travis emerged in wrinkled clothes, blinking at the harsh sunlight. Cassian sandwiched me to his side as

Travis gazed at my mother with undisguised longing. Then he glowered at me. He seemed to want to say something but decided against it. Then he marched to his Ford. He stowed his suitcase, climbed into the driver's seat, and drove away.

Cassian gaped as the truck grumbled from the street. "I'll be damned."

"Surprised I did what your biceps couldn't?"

"I'm not. You're amazing." He kissed my cheek and then addressed my mom. "Mind if I steal your daughter for a second?"

"Of course not." She squeezed my shoulder, beaming. "I'll be inside, honey."

Cassian linked my arm with his, guiding me down the sidewalk. He turned onto the bike path that followed the storm drain. Weeds brushed our ankles as we strolled. Cassian said nothing, his face fixed in silent contemplation. He found a bench partially hidden in the shade, and we sat. Cassian pulled me close. I tucked my head under his chin, comforted by his steady heartbeat.

"Tell me what happened with Montgomery."

"After your meeting with him, he freaked out. He barged into my room and demanded I dump you. When I refused, he gave me an ultimatum. You or him. I chose you."

"Sorry," Cassian sighed. "I never meant for you to lose your father."

"Don't be. This is all on him."

"Are you all right?"

"It—it hurts that he was willing to throw me away." Tearing Dad from my life left behind a gaping wound. "What did you guys argue about? He was crazed."

"I told him we were seeing each other and that he needed to hire someone else. Then he flipped his shit."

"It's not like you're a reformed felon. His voters won't give a damn I'm with my ex-bodyguard." I couldn't understand my father. "Whatever."

"Where will you stay?"

"Here at Mom's."

He clasped my hand, drawing lazy circles in my palm that filled me with buttery heat.

"Move in with me."

Adrenaline shot into my chest. "What?"

"*Move in with me.*"

Was he serious?

I searched his stormy blues that always seemed so deep and vast, like a riptide pulling me forward.

"We just started dating."

"I want you all to myself." Cassian touched his forehead to mine, his full lips pulling in a grin. "Say yes, Sunshine."

"Yes."

Happiness spread like a flame under my skin. Love had blinded me. I hoped it wouldn't betray me.

Chapter Twenty-One

Cassian

Rain moved in. She'd invaded my being, and then she invaded my drawers. She packed them with photographs, textbooks, clothes, and makeup. Obscure band posters plastered the walls. Signs of her popped up everywhere in ostentatious displays that demanded my attention—a bright throw draping the bed, potted plants lining the balcony, blue pillows on my couch. Any color was shocking when you lived in grayscale, but I welcomed the change.

Before her, my apartment was blank.

She filled it with life.

The apartment became a haven instead of a depressing reminder of my solitude. We settled into a comfortable rhythm. I returned to Swanson's Jewelry for eight-hour shifts, and Rain registered for classes. School wouldn't start for another month, so she killed time by sprucing up the place. When she wasn't cooking, she baked. I never came home without a hot meal waiting for me, which made me feel guilty.

She did all kinds of shit for me, and what did I do?

Lie to her.

My key scraped the lock, and I pushed the door. I shut my eyes as I strolled inside. I wanted to remember what it was like to be loved by a woman I didn't deserve—because I suspected Rain's feelings had grown.

An ambrosial scent beckoned me into the kitchen where Rain had made a mess. Flour dusted every surface and a stack of dishes was piled in the sink. A plate of cookies sat on the table. Rain stopped scraping them off a sheet pan and bounded to my side.

"Hey!" She threw her arms around me, rising on her toes to peck my chin. "How was your day?"

"Same old. What's that?"

Rain plucked a cookie. "Try it. Fresh out of the oven."

"Carbs are the devil."

"That's why I used nut flour. Only six net carbs per serving."

I tore off a chunk as she held it to me, butter melting into my tongue. "It's amazing."

Rain beamed, still clinging to my middle. "You look grumpy. Did you have an incident?"

You need to talk to her. Say it.

"No."

Rain laced her fingers with mine as she leaned into my body. Pleasure jolted to my groin when her lips grazed my neck. Her smile blazed a path to my mouth.

"You're too good to me, Sunshine."

"No such thing."

Her feathered kiss teased me as she drew back with a suggestive wink and a widening of her electric eyes. Arousal tugged at my navel like swirls of heat, closing in on my cock.

"I mean it. You don't have to cook."

"You gave me a place to stay." Rain's touch gravitated toward my waist. When she slipped into my waistband, I inhaled a sharp gasp.

"Rain."

"You stopped an evil landlord, protected my mother, and saved my life."

"Rain."

"What?"

My brain cells failed as she removed my belt with a devious grin.

Stop this.

Tell her.

When I didn't speak, her lips curved. "Everyone needs someone, Cassian."

"You don't owe me."

"You're a wonderful person, and you deserve to be spoiled." She unzipped my slacks. "And I like cooking. It gives me something to do while you're risking your life."

"I don't know about my life, but I'm risking my chiseled ass if I keep eating your desserts."

She slid her hands into my pants and squeezed. "You're right. Feels soft."

"Soft?"

"Just kidding!" Rain let out wild laughter as I hoisted her into my arms. "Kidding!"

Blood pounded into my groin. Her ass-grab was enough for my cock. She barely had to work to get me hard. So unfair.

I marched her into the bedroom, moving her onto the mattress. Before I ripped off her clothes, she yanked my collar. Our foreheads touched.

"I've waited for this." She pulled me closer, her touch sliding up my neck and face.

Fuck, she was gorgeous.

I breathed into her mouth, nipping her pout as she arched and thrust her tits into my chest. She dug into my scalp, scratching as I sucked her bottom lip. Moaning, she pushed against me. She flipped me and straddled my waist.

When we were done, I inhaled her citrus scent, content to stay tangled with her forever. She whispered as she rode the wave of her orgasm.

"Cassian, I'm falling for you."

I know.

It wasn't puppy love. What Rain felt was the real deal. Every day, I watched her starry-eyed affection grow.

She brought light to my endless night.

And I was destined to destroy everything that made her shine.

~

Rain

My worst fear came true. I fell in love.

After moving in, it hit me. I never wanted to leave. I was crazy about Cassian, so desperately in love, I'd already named our future children—Melody and Byron. We'd be a family of bizarre names.

How cute would that be?

Most of the time, I didn't fantasize. I fretted over his safety. When local news reported a Walnut Creek bank was robbed at gunpoint, I panicked before remembering

Cassian worked at a jeweler. The best part of my day arrived when he walked through the door.

No one ever said falling in love was painful.

Cassian turned off the engine as he parked at the Oracle Arena, an oval building shining in the darkness. "You've been quiet."

I love you. Do you feel the same?

I inhaled deeply and tried to form the words. "What are we doing here?"

"Guess."

"Football game?"

"I wish." Cassian unbuckled his seat and left the car.

I followed him, curiosity biting my thoughts.

Cassian led me past the line to an event. He took me through security that guarded tour buses. Suspicion crept into my mind.

"Wait." He fished something from his jacket pocket. "Put this on."

He untangled a square piece of plastic attached to the fabric. Brushing my hair over my shoulders, he wrapped it around my head. I read the label and gasped.

"My God, Cassian!"

"Backstage passes. Includes a meet and greet with Gorillaz."

"Oh, babe." A lump swelled in my throat. "This is awesome. Thank you so, so much."

"You're wel—"

I launched into his arms, squeezing him hard. He laughed and kissed the shell of my ear.

"I'm sorry I was such a jerk. Even then, I was afraid of losing you."

"I'm yours." Always.

I didn't say it, but Cassian's bittersweet smile hinted that he knew what was written on my heart.

Chapter Twenty-Two

Rain

I believed in second chances. People didn't always put their best foot forward at the start. Sometimes it took a third or *fourth* try, which was why I gave in when Dad left a long voicemail begging for forgiveness, and an impassioned plea to call him back.

He apologized for denigrating my relationship and committed to right every wrong. He said he couldn't handle losing me. His voice shook until he broke down, *crying*. I spent the next twenty minutes consoling him. It was a strange departure from his normal behavior. I should've known he had an agenda. By the end, I promised I'd attend his fundraiser.

The dinner was a glitzy affair that hosted San Francisco's high-society members. Five thousand dollars purchased a seat at the senator's table. Ten grand bought them a retreat in Napa and a private supper. When the day of the event came, my nerves got the better of me.

"Come," I begged Cassian, who sulked on the couch. "Pretty please with a blowjob on top."

A smirk flashed through his melancholy. "Still no."

He'd flatly refused when I brought up the fundraiser days ago. He said nothing more, but it was obvious he didn't approve of me going. Why else would he scowl as I ran around the house?

I growled my disappointment, heading toward the bathroom to double-check my eyeliner. "This will be so awkward. I could use your company. It's not like you'll have to talk to him."

Cassian silently watched TV, a red flag because Cassian rarely sat for more than a few seconds. He did push-ups to pass the time and tolerated my Netflix binges, but I never once saw him plunk down on the sofa and binge shows, aside from his weekly *Ice Road Truckers*.

His grumpiness hung in the apartment like a suffocating cloud. After a few moments, he shut off the program and raked his hair. He stared through his clasped fingers at the ground, as though hoping it'd swallow him whole.

I rejoined him in the living room, fiddling with my jewelry. "Are you disappointed with me?"

"What? *No.*"

"Then why are you crabby?"

"I don't want to say anything shitty about your old man." Cassian sank into the cushions and closed his eyes. "But I think you'll be sad when you come back."

He was probably right.

"I'd appreciate it if you came with me."

"Sweetheart, I'm not made to mingle with rich folk. Besides, he'd flip his shit if I went."

"Why?"

Cassian clammed up, his frown darkening.

"I told you, he apologized. He doesn't have a problem with us dating."

"Oh, Sunshine. You are so innocent." Cassian laughed, a hopeless sound that filled my stomach with needles. "He said that to make you go."

A second blow winded my gut. I studied my mom's heels, which were pinching my toes.

"I'm sorry. This is why I keep my mouth shut when it comes to your father. I'm not a fan, and that's putting it mildly."

"Seeking my father's approval is pathetic."

"It's not," he snapped. "You want a relationship with your dad. Hell, sometimes I want one with mine. That's nothing to be ashamed about."

I sat on the couch, my thigh brushing his. I grazed his arm, but his gritty tone stopped me from taking his hand.

Usually, his growl sent pleasure ricocheting off my nerves.

Now he sounded dead.

"Is there something you're not telling me?"

His body tensed. "No."

A cold front drifted from him like rolling fog. His touch-me-and-I'll-kill-you expression scared most people, but it was a farce. He was fiercest when he needed comfort the most.

I slid across his lap and fell against his chest. Glowering, Cassian cradled me with a gentleness entirely at odds with his thin-lipped rage. As I stroked his hair, his frown softened, and his muscles relaxed.

"I know I'm not perfect. I'm asking you to be patient with me." My heart squeezed when he pressed his lips to my forehead. "You've been such a wonderful boyfriend. The best I could've asked for. I'm crazy about you. I love you."

A thrill of adrenaline shot up my spine. I hadn't meant to blurt it right before I was supposed to leave.

What would he say?

Why wasn't he saying *anything*?

Cassian froze, locking me in his arms. A fierce blush consumed my neck and face. Shock widened his eyes, which seemed bluer than a moment earlier.

A fist battered the door.

The intrusion hurtled us into an awkward position.

Either Cassian would ignore the sound, or he'd seize the distraction to escape.

He swept the strands from my cheek. Tipped me backward. I hoped he'd kiss me and tell me he felt the same. His lips brushed mine.

"Open up!" called Quentin. "It's me!"

Cassian pulled away, releasing me. "The fuck is he doing here?"

I licked my throbbing mouth. "I guess he's—he's my security."

Worst timing ever.

Cassian stalked toward the entrance. He almost ripped the door off his hinges. An impeccably dressed Quentin stood, waving at me. He looked like he'd spent the summer on the beach.

"Q!" I pushed Cassian aside. "You look great. How are you?"

"Thanks." Quentin grinned. "Damn, girl. You clean up nice."

I hugged him. "What an awesome surprise! I had no idea you were coming."

"Rich called." Quentin disengaged from me, facing Cassian. "You letting me in, or what?"

Cassian backed into the apartment, looking like Quentin shot his puppy. Quentin squeezed through, and I smiled, silently apologizing for Cassian's rudeness.

I nudged his foot. "Would it kill you to smile?"

His scowl darkened as Quentin strolled around our home, pointing out band posters.

"Can't believe he lets you put those up. Cass, don't you hate pop music?"

I flinched, but Cassian didn't bat an eye.

"Yes, but in relationships, you *compromise*."

Smiling, Quentin stuffed his hands into his pockets. "Why aren't you wearing a suit?"

"I'm not going," Cassian muttered.

"*What?*" Quentin turned to me for confirmation. "He has to go."

"It's all right. He doesn't want to."

"Dude, you have to come." Quentin took on an oily manner. "Aren't you her boyfriend?"

"*Yes.*"

"Then you should be there, supporting her father." Quentin cocked his head, his eyes slanted with malice. "Unless you have a good reason not to."

"Shut up."

I faced Cassian, bewildered by his attitude. "Jesus, tone it down. It hasn't been five minutes, and you're already at his throat."

Quentin tore his gaze from Cassian, softening. "Sorry. I didn't mean to upset you."

"That's okay—"

"He's not sorry," belted Cassian. "He's fucking with me."

Both of us jumped from Cassian's roar.

"Whoa. I was teasing. My mistake. " Quentin's mocking smile flashed across the room. "You haven't changed. Easy to taunt."

"And you're still an annoying ass." Cassian vanished into the bedroom. "I'm coming. Give me a few."

The door slammed. I winced.

Embarrassing. "I'm sorry. I don't know what his problem is. He's in a weird mood today."

"You guys are living together?"

"I'm as surprised as you are. I resigned to a life with Mom and her carousel of boyfriends, but then Cassian offered to let me stay at his place."

"What happened to your father?"

"Got kicked out for dating the help." I rolled my eyes hard. "Can you believe that?"

"Huh."

"But he called and apologized. He's trying not to be a jerk, but his instincts are horrible. Who cares what job someone has?"

"He told you that's why he was pissed?"

"Well, not exactly." I frowned. "He never said why. He just wanted me to dump him."

Quentin glowered at the door Cassian disappeared behind, like a dog eager to pounce. Cassian emerged in a navy suit and a white shirt. I grabbed the tie looped around his neck and tied it for him. A smile staggered across his face.

"I guess you're getting what you wanted. As usual."

Cassian chucked me under the chin and kissed me. His lips seared mine. They were gone in an instant, but it left me dazed.

"We need to leave." Quentin sauntered out of the apartment, giving Cassian the stink-eye.

"Quit looking at me like that, asshole. I gave you good reviews."

"What makes you think I'm mad?" Quentin tossed over his shoulder, heading into the elevator.

"You're not being subtle, Q." I entered the cramped space, my stomach knotting as Cassian joined us. "Can we please make it through the evening without a pissing match?"

It was strange, witnessing my easygoing bodyguard transform into a dick that rivaled Cassian at his worst.

"Sure," he murmured, dropping the tone. "We should catch up."

Cassian's fingers bit into my waist as the doors widened. I released his hand, walking with Quentin.

"What happened after you left us?"

"Packed my shit and went to LA, where I worked a job with twelve-hour shifts. That's why I haven't responded to your texts."

"It hasn't been the same."

"I heard," he clipped, flashing a smirk in Cassian's direction. "You gotta give me the details about the hospital thing."

"Oh *that*," I muttered. "It was wild."

I launched into the photo op disaster as Quentin brought me to the Lexus. He opened the door, shaking his head when I described the paint balloon.

"The *senator* didn't want to increase security," argued Cassian. "I was clear about what might happen."

Quentin raised his hands. "I'm not blaming you."

But he clearly got a kick out of provoking Cassian, who should've known better. When he joined me in the backseat, I kissed the shell of his ear.

"Babe, stop being such an easy target."

He pulled back, and I started at the fury boiling in his eyes.

What put Cassian in such a *mood*?

Tension strangled the air inside the car as we drove to San Francisco. Quentin and Cassian's sniping strained my already frazzled nerves. When the vehicle parked at a hotel in Union Square, I jumped out, glad to leave their suffocating presence.

My heart pounded as Quentin escorted us through security and into the venue where my father's face beamed from every direction. I spotted my dad's real silvery-blond hair and headed forward. Cassian scowled at the banquet hall teeming with people as though it was on fire.

"Cassian, what is it?"

"Nothing."

He gripped my hand tight enough to cut my circulation. I winced as we strolled past radio shock jocks, athletes, and other well-heeled guests schmoozing my father. The crowd surrounding his table drifted away, revealing two empty chairs meant for Cassian and me.

I stepped toward them, but Cassian refused to budge.

"Cassian?"

"I'll buy drinks," he said hoarsely. "Meet you there."

He remembered I was nineteen, right?

A ball lodged in my throat as he shifted from my side. He slipped into a cluster of tweed-wearing hipsters without a backward glance.

"What the heck is *wrong* with him?" I asked.

"Don't get me started."

I hated that he'd left me alone because I didn't want to join my father. Awkwardly, I hung back until Dad waved me over. It was as if I was the only non-mourner at a funeral. My half-brothers, Baron and Oliver, barely glanced from their phones. Karen stared into her goblet as though she wanted to drown. Dad's chief of staff glowered at my father's glass as though he could make it explode with sheer will. Dad shook him off, annoyed.

Then he pressed a hand into my shoulder, his voice dipping as he leaned over. "My advisors tell me it's a terrible idea to bring you up to speed, but you're better off knowing why I needed you here. There's an article dropping soon accusing me of multiple things."

That would explain the heavy drinking and his staff's pointed glares.

"Like what?"

A crimson drop slid down his chin. He seized a napkin and dotted his skin. "Insider trading, among other things. I have full confidence that I'll be cleared, but do you think that'll satisfy the lynch mob? They ruin lives and ask questions later. Social justice feels more like vigilante justice every day. Harming people for the sake of harming people."

Dad's drink wobbled as he returned it to the table. He scratched a patch of stubble. I'd never met this disheveled version of my father and didn't know what to make of him.

"How much did you drink?"

"It's the end of my career. I'm allowed to drink."

"We're at your fundraising dinner, and it's packed. What do you *mean*?"

"You'll see." Dad rubbed his face, sighing.

"Are you being blackmailed?"

"I wish. Then at least I could file charges against the reporter. The destruction of my career is inevitable, like a red giant collapsing in on itself before it exhausts its fuel. Nothing can stop it from imploding."

He wasn't making any damned sense. Dad had probably lost a poll and took it too hard.

"Dad, talk to me."

He focused his watery gaze on me. His campaign manager showed signs of wanting to interrupt, but Dad ignored him.

Slowly, he smiled. "You might be the only person here who cares."

"What about your boys—and er—Karen?"

"The woman snarling after my trust funds? Oh, yeah, she cares. As for my sons, well, they're like me. Nannies raised them. They don't give a damn what happens, as long as the checks keep arriving. You've been around me enough to realize how empty my life is."

I thought it was full. His daily schedule had a longer list than my year, and constituents lined up for hours to hear him speak. Then I considered the facts. He spent his evenings alone, in front of the television. His wife couldn't stomach his presence. Baron and Oliver played along for handouts. The people surrounding him were a mishmash of hired help, aides looking to network, and interns seeking college credit, which made him more isolated than even Cassian.

It was sad. He deserved happiness.

"Why are you telling me this?"

"Because I owe my daughter the truth. Rain, I assumed you were like them. I was wrong."

"Wrong?" I repeated, stunned.

A stream of waiters floated among the tables to serve the first course. Dad ignored the poached salmon and arugula salad, seizing my palms under the table. He was firm despite his brittle appearance.

"You have a good heart. You care about me, even though I've done nothing to deserve your warmth."

The sudden admission caught me off guard, slicing through the armor I'd erected after being disappointed so many times. I bit my lip to stop from tearing up.

He drew me into a stiff embrace, his arms tight against me. Dad wasn't in the habit of hugging, but at least he tried. It was all I wanted.

"I'm sorry," he whispered. "I've been distant to you. There's no excuse for it, but I need you to understand why. Everyone told me to keep you at arm's length. They suspected you were after my money, and I believed them when I should've given you the benefit of the doubt. I'm sorry, Rain. I'm sorry I didn't believe in your kindness. Please forgive me."

"Don't." Emotion thickened my throat. "You—you'll make me cry."

Too late.

Happy tears wrenched with sadness flooded my gaze. I dug into his back, smiling through the mist. God, I was headed for a full-on ugly cry in the middle of his fundraiser.

"You needed me, and I wasn't there. If I'm proud of anything, it's how well you turned out despite my absence."

"I forgive you, Dad."

He pulled away, looking wretched. "I don't deserve it. I've done terrible things."

"What things? Dad, you're crying."

Dad suddenly stood, excusing himself from the table. I followed him out of the banquet hall, past the stage, and through the crowd of people queued at the bathroom. We stopped at the end of an empty corridor. His guards slipped through and pushed everybody aside, allowing my father and me privacy.

Dad broke the second we were alone.

My God.

He wiped his shining, wrinkled skin. "I made a mistake, and it's coming to haunt me."

"What did you do?"

"I called in a favor to the governor and asked him to pardon two convicted felons." He winced as though revolted by the memory. "They destroyed a family shortly after their release."

"Oh my God." The air vanished from my chest. I couldn't imagine having that on my conscience for five minutes. "That's horrible, but you're not responsible for their actions."

"A reporter put the pieces together. Interviewed the former governor, the surviving family members, everyone. He's been working on this article for months and I've just found out. It'll publish soon, and it doesn't matter how many at-risk youth organizations I've funded. They don't care about the dollars I've spent on that. It'll be what I did *sixteen* years ago."

He was caught in a terrible position.

I didn't envy him. "What will happen?"

"I'll resign when the uproar reaches its zenith, and hire more security."

"Can I help?"

"No." Dad shook his head, a smile shining out of his grief. "But thank you."

I couldn't stand him so broken and helpless. "There's got to be something that'll ease the damage. Are you sure nothing can be done?"

Dad started to decline and then froze. "Actually, *yes*."

"What?"

"No, I can't ask you to do it. Not worth the cost."

I prodded him, curious. "Tell me."

"It's a bad idea."

"For God's sake, Dad. S*pill*."

A deep frown wrinkled his forehead. He opened his mouth and hesitated. "I'm not asking you to do this, Rain. I don't want you to do anything you're unprepared for, but if you could find it in your heart to—to help me—"

"Dad, out with it."

"Marry the bodyguard. A senator's daughter eloping with her security guard is a huge scandal. Coverage of the news would drown the exposé. I just have to figure out when it publishes."

He wanted me to *marry* Cassian. Jesus, that wasn't a small favor. Dad looked like he regretted bringing it up.

"That's insane." Shock rippled up and down my spine. "What should I say—hey Cassian, want to get hitched to save my dad's career? He'll never go for it."

"He might if you phrased it differently."

I laughed. "You don't know him that well."

"He has strong feelings for you, or he wouldn't have confronted me."

Marrying Cassian wasn't the issue. I couldn't imagine a bigger thrill than wearing his ring and calling him mine. I pictured him at an altar wreathed with wildflowers, clasping his hands as we pledged our lives to one another. I'd dreamed of our wedding, but if my dad had his way it'd be at a courthouse. There wouldn't be flowers, guests, or a dress.

"I have no right to ask, so don't feel pressured." Dad's tearful plea tugged at my heartstrings. "No matter what you decide, I love you."

Three little words. They shouldn't have held so much

power over my happiness. Love was dangerous, but there wasn't anything I wanted more in the world. I craved it from my father and Cassian.

Dad hugged me. I returned the embrace, confused by the warmth that burst through, unbidden.

"I'll talk to him, Dad. Right now."

"Now?" Dad squawked, alarmed. "He's here?"

"He'll understand." I kissed Dad's cold cheek. "Don't worry."

∼

A MAN STOOD at the bar, leaning over a black marble counter. His giant stature diminished the stools by his side. Cassian turned as though he'd sensed me lurking. He didn't beam when I approached.

"Cassian, you okay?"

A tempered storm brewed in his eyes, but it calmed for me. I loved that he was only gentle with me.

"More or less," he muttered.

"I want to suggest something. Promise me you won't freak."

His eyebrow arched. "Do I look like I scare easy?"

"This might make you run." I met his unsmiling gaze, shaking. "Do you think you could—would you marry me?"

"*What?*"

Cassian's utter bewilderment sent a torch through me.

"Would you ever marry me?"

"Are you proposing? Because I always saw *myself* on a knee, not the woman."

I slapped my forehead. "No, I'm not, but that's—I mean—it's just—"

I stopped babbling when he cupped my face, smiling.

"You're worried, but you don't have to be. I'm staying put. I'm also not ignoring what you told me. Give me time to figure shit out. I'm not sure what love is, but you make me feel things I haven't felt in years."

My heart sank at that lukewarm response. It wasn't the answer I'd hoped for. "I see."

"It's too soon. Let's talk about it later, okay?"

A lump lodged in my throat. "We have to discuss it now."

"You're nineteen. What's the rush?"

"Because—because Dad needs me."

His lips sagged into a frown. His touch fell away. The light seemed to fade, casting him in darker shadows. "What?"

"Dad's convinced his career is over because of something that'll be published soon. He thinks if we get married, everybody will be focused on the news and not on other bad press."

Cassian's features contorted with rage. "What else did he say?"

"That he made a terrible mistake, and he'd atoned for it."

"Did he? *What else?*"

I flinched at the snap in his words. "That he loved me."

"And you believe him?"

"Why wouldn't I? He was sobbing. His arms wrapped around me, and he said—he said a bunch of stuff. Like he wished he'd been there for me, and he apologized for misjudging me."

Cassian's brows pinched together. "Montgomery is using you. He's not sorry for how he treated you, any more than he was sorry for the *mistake*. He's a liar."

My stomach clenched. "You weren't there, Cassian."

"I don't need to be. He's full of shit."

Why did he always think the worst of my father? "He wasn't lying. His grief was *real*. Don't look at me like that. I'm not stupid."

"Babe, I never called you that. I admire how trusting you are, but it also makes you vulnerable to people like your dad. He's a politician. He's good at deceiving. I'm sure he gave a performance that'd beat Meryl Streep."

"Why would he lie?"

"He wants you to save his ass," he growled, losing some of his patience. "He knows what you want. A father's love. So he gives it to you the minute he's in trouble, and then he manipulates you."

It made too much sense. Cassian's instincts stirred a horrible unease in my gut. Dad's sudden change of heart *was* too convenient, but I wouldn't accept Cassian's accusations.

"You don't love me, so nobody else can?"

Cassian flinched. "Jesus. That's not what I meant."

"How am I supposed to take it? You don't feel the same, and that's fine, but stop being cruel."

"I'm not trying to be. I *swear*."

"But you are! Why would you say that?"

"Rain, listen. I've given you my opinion of your dad before. You never accepted it because it's painful. No one likes to be told their father doesn't care. It is not a reflection on you." Cassian wore a tender expression that almost did me in. "You are amazing. He's incapable of love."

"Like you?"

"No." Cassian pulled me into his arms. "I don't believe that anymore."

A confused whirlwind mingled the hurt with heartsick desire as Cassian held me. It wasn't enough. I wanted more, and if Cassian couldn't give me what I sought, I'd never be happy.

My spirits sank even further. Dad's regret was a lie—a performance. How could he love me? He barely knew me. He acted fatherly when it suited him, but had never made sacrifices.

I was so desperate for his approval, I believed him.

"You're right," I whispered. "You're always right."

"I wish I weren't. Seeing you like this tears me up."

I clung to Cassian as nausea pitted my stomach. Dad had conned me thoroughly, and the sickening pain sapped the warmth from my skin.

"Let's go."

"Are you sure?" Cassian stroked my hair. "We don't have to."

"I don't want to be anywhere near him." I blinked away mist. "Ever again."

Cassian kissed my temple. "I'll find your security and we'll leave."

"I'm here," boomed another man's voice. "And I'm done being a silent observer."

Cassian's brows knitted as he disengaged from me, facing Quentin. The younger bodyguard wore an ugly expression that jolted my adrenaline.

"Quentin? What's wrong?"

He ignored me, his contempt focused on Cassian. "You're a piece of fucking work, man. This has gone on long enough."

A tic jumped in Cassian's jaw. "Jealousy isn't a good look for you."

"I'm not jealous. I'm concerned." Quentin softened as he turned toward me. "Rain, he's been lying to you."

"About what?"

Cassian clenched his fists, and a slow red flame seemed to burn under his skin. His body language screamed *guilty*.

"That's right, asshole," Quentin spat. "*I know*."

"You don't understand."

"Spare me the bullshit, bro. You are fucked in the brain and need to see a shrink." Quentin drew back his venom as he addressed me. "Cassian's using you. He has a history with Montgomery. He wanted revenge."

My pulse slammed anxiety into my blood, my heart contracting so hard that a relentless pounding filled my ears. I waited for Cassian to deny it, but he didn't. He stood, fixing me with a hopeless stare that confirmed my deepest insecurity—that Cassian had never been truly interested in me.

I pictured all the moments he'd slandered my father, and despair crashed over me. "Is it true?"

"Yes." Cassian dropped his gaze, as though he could not bear to look at me. "I've known your father for years, but I'm not using you. I swear to God, I—"

"He took the job because he hated Montgomery," added Quentin.

Another blow winded my stomach. "You did?"

Cassian's eyes were filled with utter misery. "Yes."

Holy shit.

A deep crater split my being, and from it burst an agonizing pain. It coursed through my veins like poison, surged up my throat, and wrenched from my chest.

"Rain, please." Cassian held me, but his touch sickened me. "Hear me out."

"*Get the hell away.*" I knocked his hand from me. "Is that why you chased me? You wanted to embarrass him."

"Yes, but my feelings changed!" Cassian grabbed my bicep, his lips white and shaking. "I care about you. You know that."

"I know nothing of the sort. Fuck off."

"*Sunshine.*"

That name shattered my calm. Rage swelled like a wave, as well as a horrible impulse to be violent. I whirled my arm. My palm cracked across his cheek, and a vibrant red color rose on his skin.

I'd never hit anyone in my life.

Regret stung my gaze as a shell-shocked Cassian disappeared into a pearly glow. "You are the worst thing that's ever happened to me."

He flinched, his gaze dropping as though I'd really hurt him.

Good.

"Rain, you need to listen to me."

"I don't." I needed somewhere private to wail. "Take me home, Q."

"Rain, wait!" Cassian jogged beside us as Quentin led me through an exit barred to guests. "Stop!"

Quentin ushered me through security and shoved Cassian. "Dude, it's over."

"Rain!" Cassian bellowed, pushing against the guards. "Come back!"

Blinded by agony, I followed Quentin to the car. The moment I slid inside, I closed the partition. My chest wracked with terrible sobs. The betrayal and the humiliation heaved like a tide of vomit. It was too much. I took my feelings—all of them—and crammed them in a vault. Then I locked the door.

I would never love again.

Chapter Twenty-Three

Cassian

I couldn't stop hurting.

I wasn't unaware of losing Rain for a second, because every good feeling vanished. It was like the sun winked out, bathing the world in ice.

She moved out, leaving nothing behind but a pair of socks. That was all I had besides the joy she'd brought into my life. Fucking *socks*.

I'd been an idiot.

I loved her.

I *desperately* loved her.

Nothing could cause me this much pain except a soul-deep connection. It took losing her to bring that realization home.

I *needed* to win her back.

I sent dozens of flowers to her mother's apartment—they were returned to my place. My long, rambling voicemails went unanswered. Rain ignored my many *I'm sorry* texts, but I didn't blame her.

I couldn't explain myself in a message bubble.

No, we had to talk. But when I knocked on their door, Marie turned me away.

It made me crazy, knowing she was there. I couldn't reach her. Travis might return. It worried me as I drove by the triplex, scanning for a flash of purple. Eventually, a "notice of construction" sign appeared on the lawn.

Marie and Rain had *moved out*.

I had no idea *where*.

I wanted to rage, throw shit at the walls, and scream. What I refused to do was work, practice shooting, or anything that used to help me cope. Love would not be tamed. It rejected distractions, but after a week of fruitless searching, hopelessness crept in.

~

ALL EVENING, people gave me curious looks. Twelve roses wrapped in paper sat next to my stout. The world-weary bartender asked zero questions when I slammed the bouquet on the counter. He poured a shot, and when I'd consumed enough alcohol to put down a horse, he switched me to beer. I even ate bar peanuts. If that wasn't rock bottom, I didn't know what was.

He wiped a glass. "Who are the flowers for?"

"It doesn't matter." I'd bought them out of desperation and knocked on the boarded-up door, like a psycho. "Take them."

The bartender's hand clapped my shoulder. "She'll come around."

No, she won't.

Not without the full story, at least. Rain wasn't in the mood to listen. She'd been through too much drama with her dad.

I might never see her again.

A fresh wave of despair socked my gut as the world swam in complex shapes and colors. I'd had a chance, and I fucking blew it. All I had to do was say three little words. If I had, maybe she would've listened. I opened my phone in a drunken haze, squinting at the blurred names. My thumb slid down. I stabbed a number at random.

"Hello?"

Richard.

"Hey. It's Cassian. Cassian Grant."

"Yeah, no shit. How many Cassians do you think I know? What's up?"

"I'm at a bar, drinking myself to death."

He fell into silence. "Are you being dramatic or is that what you're doing?"

"*Both.*"

"I'll bite. Why?"

"I lost her." It was so hard to focus on anything but Rain. "I lost her, Richard."

"Wow, you're smashed. I can barely understand you." Movement echoed from the speaker. "Hold on, buddy."

"What are you doing?"

"Getting my keys. I'm coming to pick you up."

Richard didn't need to see me in this pathetic state.

"No, I'm fine. I'll call an Uber."

The groan of a garage door almost drowned his voice. "Give me the name of the damned bar."

"I couldn't even tell you." I laughed. "I'm too fucked up."

"Do you see any coasters?"

I grasped the counter for a cardboard disk. "*Guinness.* Nope, that's the brand. Anchor Steam. Pale ale."

"Jesus. Ask the bartender."

Good idea.

I flagged the bartender, and he whisked to my side. "Where am I?"

"O'Shea's Sports Grill."

"Did you hear that?" I grumbled.

"Yep," Richard replied. "All right, we're on our way."

We? "Forget me. I'll be okay."

I blathered into the cell for an embarrassing amount of time before the lifeless screen made me feel even more like an idiot. My attention swung to my beer, which sucked ass, but I drained it because I deserved punishment. The more I drank, the more I hated myself. This must've been how my dad started. Drinking himself stupid at bars. Numbing the pain with poison.

God, I needed to sober up.

I did a double take when I glanced at his head. A plaid newsboy hat tucked in his gray hair.

"What the fuck are you wearing?"

Richard shrugged. "What?"

I pointed. "What is *that*?"

"It's called a hat, dumbass."

"Makes you look old. I've never seen anyone younger than sixty wear one of those."

He slipped it off, frowning. "My girlfriend likes it."

"Seeing someone already? Tell me about her."

"She's amazing. *Amazing.*"

I wasn't jealous. "How'd you meet?"

"You're so wasted."

"Don't care."

"You don't care," he echoed. "Cass, you couldn't be more full of crap than a Christmas goose. You're in a bar with a bouquet of roses, giving off a vibe of despair so strong at least three people asked me if you were okay, but you were too drunk to notice. By the way, I can smell you five feet away. But forget that, because *you* don't care."

"I don't."

"Much as I'd like to hear you insist on how not-sad you are, I'm here to drive you home." He grabbed my arm and squeezed. "Up."

I resisted his pull. "No."

My apartment was the loneliest place in the world because her absence stabbed my gut whenever I looked at the bare walls. She'd taken everything. My boring décor was all that remained—and a dead succulent plant. Losing her threw my empty life into sharp relief.

"Cassian, you got to leave," he barked. "You're wasted."

The rude tone wasn't like him. "Rich, you mad at me?"

"No, I'm not. Let's go."

I stared at him. The parts of Richard I made out looked angry. "Just tell me."

"Now's not the time."

"*What is it?*"

Giving up, Richard slumped in the chair. His grizzled face loomed closer. "For starters, you never mentioned you had a beef with Montgomery. I heard it from Q."

"Quentin needs to shut up about things that don't concern him."

"I'm glad he told me. I think the girl's better off without you. The senator could've sued the fuck out of my company."

"He'll have his hands full in two days."

"With what?"

"There's an exposé about Senator Montgomery

publishing soon. A reporter contacted me months ago. He wrote my story along with everyone else's."

"What happened between you?"

Pain swam among the murky images my mind refused to bury. "He killed my sister. He wasn't there when she was murdered, but it doesn't matter. She would be alive if it weren't for his greed."

"I'm not following," Richard whispered. "Your sister was *murdered*?"

"Yes." I rubbed my forehead, groaning. "I took the job because I needed him to fucking pay."

"Cassian, that's sick."

Yes, it was.

Time to leave. Richard probably hated me, and I didn't blame him. I could've destroyed his livelihood.

I stood.

Richard forced me down. "What were you going to do to *Rain*?"

Shame engulfed my cheeks in heat. "At first, I wanted to fool around with her and rub it in his face. When I met her, everything changed. She was too sweet to be his daughter. Kind to a fault. Beautiful. Not what I expected. Montgomery didn't take her security seriously. I couldn't leave her. I was way too attached. Richard, she was the best thing in my life."

Richard watched silently as the cloud of disappointment hanging over me seemed to disappear. He clasped my shoulder and squeezed.

"How did it go wrong?"

"She found out I took the job out of vengeance. I didn't get to explain. She doesn't know how much I love her."

Richard stared at me like I sprouted antlers before flagging the bartender. He ordered a drink, brows knitting as he seemed to absorb what I'd said. After taking a long draft of his Dark and Stormy, Richard faced me.

"I need to confess something. My girlfriend is your—I mean she's Rain's mother."

"*What?*"

"I've been dating Marie on and off, the last couple of weeks."

I'd been mad with grief, searching for Rain, and he'd had her address the entire time. "Are you kidding me?"

"No, I'm not." Richard smiled, and it wasn't the sarcastic smirk I remembered. The dude couldn't stop grinning. "When I hung out at her place, she invited me inside, and we hit it off. She was nice. I knew I shouldn't have—but I gave her my number. She called me the second I got home."

Hope infused me with energy, chasing away my drowsy buzz. "Where do they live? Jesus Christ, Richard, tell me. *Please*. I can't find her. I love her!"

"No."

"Fuck you—tell me where she is!" I grabbed his collar and tugged him close. "I have to know!"

"No," he whispered, gently removing my hands. "You want to know. There's a difference."

"*Fine.* You're right. Do me this one favor, and I'll do *whatever*. Need me to work for free? *Done.* Want me to pick up your in-laws from the airport? *No problem.* Anything."

"I'm not giving you their address. You have to clean your shit up."

"Clean?"

"Yeah, you're a mess. Let's get out of here."

He dragged me from the bar. I stumbled through, crashing into people before we burst outside. I blinked from the harsh sunlight.

"Heavy motherfucker." Richard hauled me to a car, where a man sat in the driver's seat.

I collapsed into the backseat, hauling myself upright as the blond guy turned.

"Hi, Cassian," Quentin drawled, fingers drumming the wheel. "Heard the nineteen-year-old dumped you. That blows."

"Screw you." I pounded his chair.

"Hey," Richard shouted. "Don't be nasty."

"What is *he* doing here?"

"We were hanging out, and he wanted to come!" Richard yanked on his seatbelt. "Let's go."

Wasn't he supposed to be hitting on Rain, or at the very least, taunting me?

When we parked at my complex, Quentin climbed out.

"You'll throw out your back again. *Stay.*" Quentin opened my door. "Today, princess."

"I'll be fine."

The world tipped as I stood.

Quentin wrapped his arm around my waist, yanking me straight. "You need to relax. I'm teasing."

Too drunk to argue, I leaned onto him as we began the dangerous journey toward the elevator. "Why are you helping me?"

He shrugged. "I guess I feel bad. The reporter who contacted me didn't give the whole story until I sat down for an interview. Then I—ah—I Googled your sister's name and read what happened." His voice got quieter until I strained to hear him. "Sorry, man. I didn't know what you went through. I was deployed in Iraq for a six-month tour. It's not the same as losing a family member, but I saw shit I wished I could forget. I've done things that haunt me, and I've watched my friends die."

I gripped the railing when we reached my floor, the shock slowly drawing from my veins.

"I apologize for everything I said. You've been through hell." Quentin shoved his hands deep into his pockets, chewing his lip. Sympathy blazed through his eyes. "You're not alone."

I nodded, my skin needling as I returned his gaze. I wasn't used to this. "Sorry for being a prick. You're a great bodyguard—a much better one than I'll ever be."

He grinned and headed for the stairwell. "See you, Cass."

Chapter Twenty-Four

Rain

To get over a bad breakup, all a girl needed was butter and sugar, and I possessed an army's worth. It gave me something to do besides cry about Cassian. Nothing mattered except getting this Swiss meringue frosting right.

A chime echoed from the timer, distracting me from icing the last batch. I grabbed the mitts and opened the oven, blasted by heat. I took the tray, but cupcakes covered the kitchen island, the table, and every other counter. I set them on top of the refrigerator and slid the raw batter onto the racks.

I turned my attention to the mound waiting to be iced and slathered on the peppermint-flavored meringue. The cake was too hot, and it slipped off.

"Damn!"

Mom's flip-flops smacked the linoleum as she wandered in, wearing a pink robe. "What are you doing?"

"Baking."

"I see that." Mom frowned at the sea of desserts, taking her mug to the sink. "Are you feeling okay?"

"Yeah, sure. I've run out of space. Do you think we could empty the fridge?"

Mom's thin-lipped smile faltered as she palmed my shoulder. "That's enough cupcakes."

"No, it's not." I shrugged from her touch and reapplied the frosting. "I'll need hundreds."

"Er—why?"

"Because I'm doing a bake sale for Kensington."

"Who's that?" she asked.

"Dad's opponent."

"Again, *why*?"

Because I hate my dad. "I need to be more involved in my community."

"Where are you doing the bake sale?"

"At the July Fourth fair. *What?* It's not about the money. A senator's daughter supporting her father's rival will make national news. It'll be devastating for his campaign."

I was on a mission for revenge.

Dad had called twice when I disappeared from the

fundraiser. One voicemail asked where I was, and the other begged me to consider his proposal. After I ignored both, he vanished as though he'd forgotten I existed. Thinking of him gathered a vortex of rage.

Mom's frown deepened. "I don't think it's a good idea."

"I'm doing it."

"Rain, you have to eat. Use the bathroom. Shower. *Something* other than plot revenge." A plaintive tone crept into her voice. "Let's see a movie. Or visit the mall. You've got to get your mind off Cass—"

"No." If I stopped for a second and felt the full weight of what happened, I'd fall apart. "This has nothing to do with Cassian. Montgomery deserves to be taken down like the fraud he is."

"This isn't you. You're upset and hurt. I understand, but pouring all this energy into hurting someone? I don't want you to do anything you'll regret."

My spatula trembled over the mixing bowl. "The only thing I'll regret is not making a lattice pie that spells out *Fuck Montgomery*. He's a liar who needs to be held accountable."

"What about Cassian?"

"Screw him."

"*Rain.*"

I shut off the oven and left the kitchen as tears filled my eyes.

God, I sucked at compartmentalizing.

I still loved him. Baking was a pitiful distraction from my hurt feelings. At night, I scrolled through paparazzi photos of us, and my heart broke all over again. I cherished every moment of our short-lived relationship, which was pathetic because Cassian had hoodwinked me into falling for him.

Part of me wanted to run into his arms, but I couldn't let that weakness triumph. He'd used me. He'd chased me to hurt my father. Nobody would ever do that to me again. Trusting Cassian had been the biggest mistake of my life.

"Rain, we're having company."

I grunted a response as Mom jumped into the bathroom. It was probably her new boyfriend. I changed into a tank top and jeans, raking my fingers through my tangled strands to look presentable.

I liked Richard. He helped us when we moved out—Mom scored a great office administrator job five miles away. She had finally picked a good man, and I was happy for her, but he reminded me of Cassian.

A chime echoed through the apartment. Mom fluttered to the entry, smoothing her ebony mane before opening the door. Richard stood in the sunshine, carrying bags. His broad frame squeezed through. Like Cassian, he was a big guy. A salt-and-pepper beard lined his chiseled jaw. Richard was also painfully sweet in a way that echoed

Cassian. He lavished compliments on my mother and treated her like a queen.

"I brought you girls lunch."

"Oh, that's so generous." Mom cupped his face and pecked his lips. "Thank you."

Richard grinned like a fool lost in love. Mom took the food, giggling when he hugged her from behind. She turned in his arms, and they kissed.

A knife twisted in my heart.

I missed Cassian.

They drifted apart when I joined them in the kitchen but still clung to each other's hands like teenagers. It was nauseatingly cute.

He smiled, looking for a place to set down the bags. "You guys having a party or something?"

Mom glanced at me. "Rain's passionate about baking."

"Not really. It's a hobby."

He nodded as though covering every surface in the house with cupcakes was a normal thing. "Can I have one?"

"No."

"Yes," Mom ground out, glaring at me. "What is *with* you?"

She wasn't used to me being rude, but the new me didn't give a shit about pretending to be nice. I tried killing Cassian with kindness, and what did it get me?

Heartbreak. Humiliation. Betrayal.

Mom whispered excuses for my behavior. I wouldn't force my presence on them. I clenched my jaw and slipped onto the deck. Heat baked the wood, burning my naked feet. The harsh summer stripped the landscape of color. The hills never looked so ugly as they did in July when everything was dead.

I struggled to see beauty in the world. Rumors filled the news of a federal indictment, and I couldn't surf the web without reading my father's name. Worse, the media hounded us with requests for interviews. My phone buzzed with the voicemails of journalists from all over the globe. Book deals. Statements. The circus wouldn't stop.

What would I tell them, anyway?

I settled into the plastic lawn chaise and stretched out my legs. Heat blasted my hair, which had turned brassy with all the sun, but I couldn't summon the energy to care. After a few moments with my eyes shut, the door opened. A gust of air-conditioning hit my toes as heavy footsteps creaked the planks.

"It's me," Richard murmured. "Your mom has a headache and is laying down."

Probably a lie. "Fine."

He moved into sight and tested a chair, which groaned alarmingly. He abandoned it, standing.

"Rain, are you okay?"

"Sure."

Richard sat on the floor and fixed me with a probing stare. "Your mother told me what you're up to."

"Here to talk me out of it?"

He shook his head. "But I think you're more upset about Cassian than your father."

"I hate him, too." Fury worked its way up my throat, building into a white-hot ball. "I *trusted* him. I thought he liked me."

"He does! Rain, he's hurting, too. I've never seen him so...lifeless. Give him another chance. Listen to what he has to say."

"Absolutely not."

"Why?"

"I'm not in the mood to get my spirit broken twice. I loved him, and he betrayed me." I wiped my cheek, annoyed he brought it up. "I will not be my mother. You don't know how many assholes she dated until she found you."

"Cassian's not a bad guy. He has flaws like any other man, but he protected you from the beginning. You have no idea."

"It was his *job*."

"Not just that." Richard softened, gazing at his linked hands. "Have you looked at the article about your father?"

"Which article? There are dozens."

"A new one published in the *Washington Times*."

I chewed my lip. "I'm sick of the news."

"You should read it. Cassian's quoted a lot."

What was Cassian doing in an article about my father? "How come?"

"I'll send you the link." Richard pulled a phone from his pocket, his face sagging into a deep frown. "It's—it's very intense. Read it in private."

Richard sent me a message and disappeared into the house. When the sliding door shut, I peeked at the text. I shuddered at the headline.

Workplace Harassment to Homicide Cover-Ups – S. Montgomery Accusers Reveal All

Nausea shot into my stomach as the accusations detailed a string of crimes committed by my father, but when I finished Cassian's story, agony pierced my heart. I dropped the phone and burst into tears. I gasped through my sobs, gulping air.

It was horrible. He hadn't lied about his sister's death, but he'd allowed me to believe a *much* kinder version.

Why?

Did he think I couldn't handle his darkness, or was he sheltering me from the truth? I opened my contacts, thumb hovering over *Cassian*.

He *was* protecting me.

Since the beginning, he'd kept me safe. He'd never let me out of his sight. Cassian came to the fundraiser for my dad, even though he destroyed Cassian's family. He tried to tell me, but I didn't listen.

Flames leapt under my skin.

I couldn't go back to him without making things right. I scrolled up on my phone. My finger pressed *Dad*.

Chapter Twenty-Five

Cassian

Rain needed me.

Half the country screamed for Montgomery's head on a spike. Cheap asshole invested in *his* security, but his daughter was defenseless against the raving lunatics online. The dickhead hadn't reinstated her bodyguards.

When the story dropped, people I hadn't heard from in years reached out. Ex-girlfriends, former bosses, colleagues, and college roommates sent supportive emails, but she never called.

I missed her. Every day, I felt a little more empty.

My victory over Montgomery was like ashes in my mouth. There was no joy in revenge.

I hoped she'd read the article and return to me, but I

pushed my ache aside and focused on her safety. I scanned the exposé's comments, amused at everyone's fury and the irony that I wished they'd dial it back.

The mob was vicious. They wanted him dead, but the threats didn't stop at Montgomery. The vitriol spilled to his family, too. His staff. His fucking nutritionist. Anyone associated with Montgomery.

Paparazzi photographed his wife packing her Prius with an overnight bag. She whisked to SFO and jetted to an unknown location. Days later, she appeared in front of a judge to file for separation. The FBI indictment came after and public outrage grew from sparks to a raging forest fire.

Senator Montgomery should've been lying low, but the idiot was scheduled to appear at a campaign rally in San Francisco the same weekend as a half-marathon. Security would be a nightmare. Richard informed me Rain planned on attending, so I made it my job to protect her.

Traffic crawled to a snail's pace as my taxi approached Fort Mason, a former army port in the Marina and the site of Montgomery's rally. It sat on a narrow strip of beach. If the senator had any sense, he'd close the walking path from Embarcadero, set up a riot police barricade, and keep a tight perimeter.

"Forget it," I told the driver. "Let me out. I'll walk."

I strolled Embarcadero, a palm-lined waterfront packed with a mishmash of sightseeing tourists, Montgomery protestors, and joggers. The event began in an hour, and it might take that long to get there.

Shit. I needed to hurry.

I joined the chanting crowd armed with provocative signs as they marched the northern coast of San Francisco, heading toward the maritime park. Images of Montgomery graffitied with devil horns and obscene language flashed everywhere. They screamed a rousing battle cry that grew in excitement as a distorted voice egged them on with a bullhorn. I gave up on the sidewalk and sprinted through the streets. My sister's eight-year-old toothy smile beamed against cardboard. Her face followed me as I ran through grass.

The protesters had already reached Fort Mason. White and red placards speared the air as a hostile chant built up gusto. I headed toward the Mission-style building flanked by overwhelmed police. Security left their posts to help cops with the metal barricades. The place was exposed. There would be no quiet VIP exit to use to slip away unnoticed, and the swarm demanded blood.

Fucking disaster.

Where was Rain?

Rain

Dad raised a fist as he concluded his speech, a gesture which his supporters seemed to love. I had listened to his ninety-minute rant against the article making waves across news networks. He attacked everyone from the reporter who wrote it to former colleagues who spoke against him, but not once did he mention Cassian or his sister.

Of course he wouldn't. He was a *coward*, and I barely contained my loathing of him. When I called him, I lied my ass off to get into his good graces, but I didn't give a damn about a relationship with my psychopath father.

That *thing* wasn't my dad.

When the senator reappeared backstage, the fiery glow captured by the televised screens still raged in his being. The rallies always infused him with almost manic energy. Dad ripped the tie from around his neck and exploded at the first person to glance his way, an aide.

"Where the hell is my Perrier?"

"Sorry, Senator."

The twenty-year-old rushed to fetch a bottle, and the senator seized it. He guzzled the sparkling water and wiped his mouth.

He was without conscience. A soulless husk of a

human being who had ruined an untold number of lives and felt zero remorse for an eight-year-old's death.

I wanted to know why.

Dad finished the bottle and tossed it in the trash, his limbs shaking. He'd explained that it was adrenaline from speaking in front of thousands.

"Great speech, Dad."

His pale eyes cut into me. "Just tell me what you want."

I couldn't stand another minute in his presence, anyway. "I read the article."

"And?"

"Tell me *why*. Don't lie. I don't care if you lie to the world, but you owe me the truth. You never said you and Cassian had a history."

"I owe you nothing, and I have no idea what you're talking about."

"You lost Karen. If you're not careful, you'll lose me, too."

The senator didn't seem troubled by that prospect, but he waved at the aide to leave the room. When the door's echo faded, he faced me with a rock-hard expression.

"A tech mogul promised me stock tips if I helped his sons who were serving a six-year sentence for robbery. I called the governor, who owed me a favor. He pardoned them. They made a terrible decision, and they'll spend the rest of their lives paying for."

He was a filthy cheat on top of a liar.

"What about Claire?"

"She was an unfortunate accident."

"An accident? Dad, she was murdered by two men who owed you their freedom. The same guys who invaded the home of Cassian's father, who wanted to publish a career-ending article about *you*."

"Coincidence!"

"You expect me to believe that?"

"I don't give a damn," he spat. "You've clearly swallowed that cock-and-bull story."

"It was well-researched with dozens of sources corroborating the same facts. You are lucky there's nothing hard linking you to the crime, but everyone knows you got away with it."

"I bribe paparazzi to keep them from publishing photos." Dad paced the room, his voice growing in volume. "What's the difference between that and using my influence to stop a story from being run? *Zero*. Politicians do it all the time, Rain, and I don't see them complaining about it."

"Because you sent thugs to the journalist's house, and a young girl was killed!"

Dad stopped. Remorse flashed over his gaze, and he seemed to deflate. His shoulders hunched. His mouth parted.

"I-I never meant—" Dad broke off, his whisper almost disappearing. "I didn't—"

The door opened, cutting off my father mid-sentence.

A bodyguard popped in. "Sir, the crowd is getting unruly. We should leave."

The senator wiped all trace of guilt from his expression. I reached inside my jacket and paused my phone's recording.

Fuck!

Montgomery sighed. "All right. Rain, let's go."

"Not yet."

"What is it?"

This was my last chance to come clean, and I wouldn't waste it.

"I used to think I was a stain. I was the spot on your legacy. You never made me feel like anything else. But you know what? You're the stain. I'm ashamed you share half of my DNA. You're the sick, twisted bastard who destroyed that family."

Dad said nothing, but fixed me with a glacial stare before his bodyguards exited the building. My heart pounded as I followed, hating him, and disappointed that I'd failed Cassian.

As I stepped outside, a roar blasted my ears. Sunlight bleached my vision until the square shapes of signs bled through the white. Protesters boxed us in from all sides. People threw empty water bottles at my feet. A wall of enraged protestors surged against metal barricades. Police struggled to hold them back. A cop shouted into a radio for help, his hand trembling when he replaced the speaker.

Jesus.

Guards surrounded my father, but access to the SUV was blocked. Dad screamed at his security as the crowd converged, overwhelming officers who shoved them, and then several broke through. A bottle smashed on cement. Rocks bounced off car hoods, and more men joined the violent protesters jockeying for the front.

Dad separated from his security, running toward the SUV. The bodyguards sprinted after him. If I didn't join him, I'd be at the mercy of the mob. I shot forward, a scream bubbling in my throat as I chased the bodyguards, who forced a narrow passage through the cluster.

I squeezed through, disoriented by the screaming. I caught up, heart seizing at the violence hurled at us from all directions, and then a man reached into a jacket. He swung at the senator.

A body collided into me as a blast cracked the air. Screams pierced my ears as I crashed into the concrete. Agony slashed my limbs as a heavy weight pinned me to the ground. Gravel dug into my skin as I fought to inhale. People stampeded the pavement.

What the hell happened?

The guy rolled off me, and I bolted upright. His hand clung to my waist. I followed his thick bicep to his rock-hard shoulder, and up to his chiseled jaw, settling on his pained grimace.

"Oh my God, Cassian!" I cupped his face as he groaned. "What—what's wrong? Are you hurt?"

Of course he was. Nothing would knock a man of Cassian's size on his back except a mighty blow.

A gunshot.

"Cassian. You'll be okay."

His lips moved, but all he did was groan. Was he going into shock?

"Cassian, don't you dare leave me!"

"I can't. I'm in love with you."

Chapter Twenty-Six

Rain

Blinded by fear, I searched for the wound. I groped his chest and back, my fingers slipping across his wet shirt.

Oh, please, God. Don't let him bleed out.

Heaving, it took all I had to flip him. Sweat drenched his shirt, and silver glinted from a tiny, black hole. I fingered the fabric, touching metal. The body armor had caught the bullet.

He's fine.

Tears caught in my throat and squeezed their way up to my eyes, while relief flooded my knotted stomach as he turned over.

"You have a bullet in your back." I threw my arms

around his neck and sobbed, kissing his cheek. "I can't believe you—how did you know what'd happen?"

"I was watching."

I whirled around for help, surrounded by panicked protesters fleeing the scene and cops who'd arrested the shooter. "Help us! Someone!" I waved at the black SUV that contained my father, but it drove past us, tires screeching.

Fucking dick.

Finally, I flagged down an officer, who called an ambulance.

"Cassian, you'll be okay. Help is on its way." I laced my fingers with Cassian's hand, trying not to sound freaked. "You're all right."

"Broken ribs," Cassian hissed, flattened on the ground. "Fuck me."

"What can I do?"

He shook his head. "Just stay with me."

"Of course."

I propped his head on my lap and stroked his hair.

Cassian took deep, steadying breaths. "I have to tell you something."

"Babe, it can wait." Inhaling seemed to pain him. I couldn't imagine what talking did to his injury. "You need to rest."

"No. *Please.*"

"Okay, okay."

Sirens screamed in the distance as Cassian's deep-blue eyes locked with mine.

"I've known about Montgomery since I was thirteen. The fire wasn't an accident." Mist gathered in his gaze, and I couldn't say if it was from physical or emotional pain. "My sister was killed."

My heart collapsed. "Cassian, I read the article."

"I want you to hear it from me." He shut his eyes, as though gearing up for the next part. "It was a home invasion. They broke into the house. Beat my dad with a baseball bat. He was sleeping—didn't see it coming. I woke up with a hand over my mouth and a knife at my throat. They tied up everyone.

"I got a sense that they were there to intimidate my father but went overboard. They didn't know how to deal with three panicked people, especially an eight-year-old beside herself with fear. They put a bag over my sister's head because she wouldn't stop screaming. She suffocated. When—when they realized what they'd done, they lost it. Tried to get rid of the evidence."

Warmth vanished from the air and leeched from my bones. "They burned your home."

"Yes." Cassian swallowed hard. "My dad escaped and went to the neighbors, and I attempted to save Claire, only—she was already gone. The men jumped into their car, were pursued by police, and crashed a few blocks away."

Tears rolled down my cheeks. "I'm so sorry."

"Dad was an investigative journalist. He was working on a big article about your dad. It took him six months to research and follow up on all the sources, but anyway. He reached out to Montgomery, asking for comments. Montgomery needed the story buried. It would've stopped his career in its tracks, so the senator or someone in his pocket contacted two guys who owed him a huge favor."

"Why didn't you tell me?"

"Because I love you. Because he's your father, and I didn't want to destroy your relationship. I lied. I'm sorry. I never wanted to hurt you. Please believe me, Rain. I couldn't help but fall for you when you knocked on my door with scones." He smiled at the memory, squeezing my hand. "You changed my world. You make me see it differently. I'm kinder because of you. I can't return to the way I was, even if you'd rather we went our separate ways, but I hope you don't. You're the best person I've ever met, and I love you. I'll always love you."

I hid my face in his neck, succumbing to the pressure building in my chest. "I love you, too."

He was all that mattered. I couldn't live without him.

Not a second more.

∼

Cassian was discharged from the hospital after an

MRI showed bruising on his kidneys. The doctor sent him home with strict orders for bed rest. He obeyed for two hours.

I pestered Cassian about blood in his urine, who shot me *you're-cute-but-I'm-getting-annoyed* looks as he hobbled around the house. I'd moved back in and we slowly mended our wounds. Things were almost back to normal. The shooting and Cassian's broken ribs drove everything from my mind.

Cassian brooded on the couch. His lack of mobility bothered him, and I caught him testing his injury constantly. He eyed me warily as I sank into the cushion next to him.

I faced him. "I need to come clean."

"Uh-oh." Cassian smiled grimly, crossing his arms.

"It's nothing *terrible*. I just didn't want to pile on more stress."

Cassian's brows knitted. He dragged me onto his lap, and I sighed with relief when his arms wrapped around me. I forgot how safe he made me feel. His breath skated my head as he kissed my temple. "What did you do?"

"I recorded my dad. That's why I was at the rally," I blurted. "I wanted to trick him into admitting something about your sister, and it kind of worked. Let me play it for you."

Cassian listened, his face impassive as the conversation

blared from my phone's speaker. When it ended, his jaw tensed.

"Thought I'd never hear him acknowledge it."

"I wanted him to go further," I whispered.

"Don't take it too hard, Rain. If you succeeded and this tape got out, he would've ruined you. Once he found out you recorded him without his consent? You would be sued. He'd drag your name through the mud and wrangle you in legal fees until you went bankrupt."

"Cassian," I croaked. "He *almost* admitted it."

"That doesn't matter to a court. A judge would toss that out as inadmissible evidence. Besides, they already convicted two men for the murder."

"But—but he can't get away with it."

"Babe, he's going to jail. It might not be for her death, but he won't stand up against the indictment. Claire will never have justice. I've made peace with that. I can't do this anymore. All my life, I've been angry. I have to move on."

"I wish I could've helped you."

"You did." He pressed his lips into my cheek. "You brought me closure."

"I am so ashamed. He's my father. That's why I didn't call. I had no idea what to say. I'm sorry for everything."

"Hush. You don't have to answer for anything."

"Someone has to."

Cassian kissed me, cutting my cry as his fingers dug into my scalp. He pressed me against him in a feverish embrace. "I love your selfless heart. Don't ever leave me."

"*Never.*"

Chapter Twenty-Seven

Rain

3 Years Later

My flip-flops smacked the pavement as Mom paraded me like a show horse. She wrapped her arm around mine and marched to her neighbor, a sweet as pie seventy-year-old retiree.

"Janice, look at my daughter's ring!" Mom seized my hand and showed her the princess cut jade stone in a gold setting. "Isn't it *beautiful*?"

I grinned as Janice gasped at the unusual ring. "Cassian picked it with you, didn't he?"

"Yes, he did. He knew exactly what to get, but wanted

to make sure he was right. He said you weren't a diamond-ring kind of girl."

"He was right." It shouldn't have astonished me that he knew me so well. "Cassian's the best fiancé a girl could ask for."

They both *awwed* at that.

We celebrated our engagement at Richard's house, which had the bigger backyard and a pool. After I excused myself, I wandered the party and waved at Quentin, who was engaged in conversation with Cassian's father. Cassian stood at the barbecue in a light-blue shirt that mimicked the cloudless sky. Steaks sizzled as he shot the shit with Richard, my new stepdad, a role he took seriously. Mom and Richard married last spring in Vegas. We spent so much time together that I caught myself wanting to call him Dad.

I hadn't thought of my real father in months. When the FBI completed their investigation, the senator was charged with insider trading, tax fraud, and misuse of campaign funds. A grand jury convicted him on all three counts. He was sentenced to five and a half years in prison. After that, I pushed him from my mind. I'd wasted enough of my life on him.

Richard shocked us by announcing his retirement as CEO from the security firm and selling the company to Cassian. My fiancé was transitioning from bodyguard to businessman. The new position meant he wouldn't have to travel anymore, and I wouldn't spend our time apart biting my nails until he returned. Plus, we wanted a family in the next few years.

I wrapped my arm around Cassian's waist and kissed the back of his neck. Cassian put down his spatula and pulled me into his chest.

"Did you try my beer?" I asked.

Cassian lifted a bottle from the grill, showing me its empty contents. "Amazing hef."

I punched his shoulder. "It's a Belgian white!"

"You know they all taste the same to me, babe." He grinned as I growled deep in my throat. "Just kidding. You made a wise choice by dropping the books and picking up the apron."

"Thanks."

When I turned twenty-one, I hit up all the local businesses with applications and was hired by a small-batch place as assistant brewer.

I loved my job.

"Can you believe this is your life?"

I gestured to the guests spilling over the backyard, picking through our snacks, and drinking. The best part of these past few years had been watching Cassian come *alive*. He changed. He smiled and joked so often, he barely resembled the emotionally unavailable man I met in my father's living room.

Cassian surveyed the scene with me, beaming. "This is *our* life, Sunshine."

And from here on out, it would be beautiful.

No more darkness.

Blue skies forever.

ACKNOWLEDGMENTS

I owe so many people for this book! They say it takes a village to raise a child. Well, the same applies to books.

Thank you, Nick, for kindly offering your invaluable expertise in many email exchanges and phone calls. You have opened my eyes to this vastly underpaid, unappreciated job, and I am so glad I emailed you! (If you'd like to learn more about bodyguards, pick up Nick Spill's *Way of the Bodyguard*)

Thank you, Kelley Harvey, for your unflinching honesty. It helped immensely. Thank you, Christine LaPorte, for your top-notch editing.

Muchas gracias to Sarah Hansen of Okay Creations for the amazing cover! Thank you Jenn and Terri, for your fantastic beta reading notes!

Lastly, thank *you* for making it this far! Without

readers like yourself, I wouldn't be able to do this for a living. From the bottom of my heart, thank you!

Love,

Blair

ABOUT THE AUTHOR

Blair LeBlanc is an author of Contemporary Romance and lives in Seattle with her two ill-behaved cats.

Before she settled in Seattle, she lived in Northern California where she studied English Literature at San Jose State University. She pursued a career in medicine before making an about-face to write full-time. She also pens psychological thrillers as Rachel Hargrove.

She enjoys beer tasting, live music venues, and singing her heart out at horrified bar patrons.

Email: admin@blairleblanc.com